IN A HANDFUL OF DUST

Also by Mindy McGinnis

Not a Drop to Drink

Handwritten inscription:

Sherwood Branch –
Find Your Place!
Mindy McGinnis

IN A HANDFUL OF DUST

Mindy McGinnis

KATHERINE TEGEN BOOKS
An Imprint of HarperCollins Publishers

Katherine Tegen Books is an imprint of HarperCollins Publishers.

In a Handful of Dust
Copyright © 2014 by Mindy McGinnis
All rights reserved. Printed in the United States of America.
No part of this book may be used or reproduced in any manner whatsoever
without written permission except in the case of brief quotations embodied in critical
articles and reviews. For information address HarperCollins Children's Books, a
division of HarperCollins Publishers, 195 Broadway, New York, NY 10007.
www.epicreads.com

Library of Congress Cataloging-in-Publication Data
McGinnis, Mindy.
     In a handful of dust / Mindy McGinnis. — First edition.
          pages   cm
     Summary: "In a barren land, teenage Lucy is taken away from the
community she has grown up in and searches the vast countryside for a new
home"— Provided by publisher.
     ISBN 978-0-06-219853-2 (hardback)
     [1. Survival—Fiction.   2. Water supply—Fiction.   3. Self-reliance—
Fiction.]   I. Title.
PZ7.M4784747In   2014   2014009661
[Fic]—dc23   CIP
                                                                         AC

Typography by Erin Fitzsimmons
14 15 16 17 18 LP/RRDH 10 9 8 7 6 5 4 3 2 1
❖
First Edition

For M&M—I will always read to you.

IN A HANDFUL OF DUST

Part One

POND

One

Maddy died hard.

The polio that had hobbled her hours before swept through her torso and stilled her movements. Only her pupils could convey the panic as her lungs collapsed. Her chest stopped rising and falling, but Maddy's eyes rolled from Lucy's face to the ceiling and back again for a few minutes after, clouding with confusion. Finally they were still. A rattle chased Maddy's last breath out of her throat as Lucy held her friend's hand.

Vera leaned across the bed to loosen her granddaughter's grip. "She's gone, sweetheart. You can let go now."

"Are you sure?"

Vera's capable fingers closed around Maddy's wrist, but she nodded before checking for a pulse. "You need to go wash up."

"Use the boiled water," Lynn said. She was standing at the foot of the bed, her arms crossed in front of her.

"I know," Lucy said tightly, her throat still slick with tears. Lynn's eyes flicked away from Maddy to touch on Lucy, and they softened slightly.

"Knowing and doing are two different things. Use the boiled water, then come back here." Her eyes returned to the corpse, and her brow furrowed. "We need to talk."

Lucy walked out of the stifling cabin and then down to the creek, grateful for the blast of fresh night air. She knelt by the flowing water and splashed her face free of tear tracks. A strong hand pulled her away from the water and she yelped, landing on her backside on the muddy bank.

"What'd Lynn say to you?" A stern voice came out of the darkness. "She told you to use the boiled water and first thing you do is come down here and stick your face in the crick."

"Scaring me onto my ass is a hell of a way to remind me," Lucy said, drying her hands on her pants. "You were outside?"

"Don't have much else of a place to go. When your grandma's tending the sick, I like to be nearby to help, what little I can do." Stebbs put his hand out, helping her from the ground. "I didn't mean to be so rough with you. Not an easy night for the living."

Lucy leaned into him, inhaling his comforting smell, familiar all these years. Clean air and fresh dirt lingered around him, and she felt stray tears slip down her cheeks.

"Not easy for the dead either," she said. "She was looking at me, those big eyes of hers full of fear like nothing I've ever seen before, and all I could do was sit there, Stebbs, and . . ." The spreading stillness that had clamped onto Maddy's body seemed to have found Lucy's tongue. "I heard the rattle, like Lynn always says you do. Then she passed, and everything was quiet."

Stebbs tucked her head into his chest, and they walked back toward the cabin he shared with Vera. "True enough, there's those that go that way. But in the silence you know they've gone. Something is missing."

Lucy nodded her understanding. Though she'd asked Vera if she was sure, the wrongness of Maddy's eyes had already answered the question. "I imagine you'll be needing another mattress," Lucy said, wiping her nose.

Vera's reputation as a healer had spread beyond the boundaries of the small community; people traveled hundreds of miles to bring their sick to her door. Too often they died inside her walls, in her bed. Then anything the dead touched was condemned to flame.

The door to the cabin opened and Lynn stepped out, Maddy's body shrouded in a sheet and curled in her strong arms. She spotted Lucy and Stebbs. "You want me to wait for you?"

Lucy nodded, and Stebbs gave her a quick squeeze on the shoulder before releasing her. "Don't let her know I used the stream," she whispered into his ear. "I'll never hear the end of it."

"I'll keep quiet on that count," he said. "But from now on out, you mind her."

A breeze kicked through the tree branches above them, heavy with budding leaves. Lucy crossed her arms against the chill, grateful when Stebbs took off his jacket and handed it to her.

"You go on," he said. "She'll be in a hurry to get rid of the body."

Vera came to the door of the cabin, her silhouette backlit from the candles within. "Stebbs," she called into the darkness, "I'm going to need you in here."

"Other people have come here to die. We've burned and buried plenty," Lucy said as he zipped the coat up for her, flipping up the collar against her neck. "But this is bad, isn't it?"

"Yeah, little one," he sighed. "I'm afraid this one will be different."

Maddy had never been a large girl, but the deep blackness of the pit Lynn tossed her in made a mockery of the white sheet, reducing it to a pale smudge in the lingering light.

"Sorry about that," Lynn said, after the body hit the ground. "There's no nice way to get her down in there."

Lucy shrugged. "'S okay," she said, but the awkward angle of the body, dead or not, hurt her heart. Lynn's hand, crusted with dirt, rested on Lucy's shoulder and she reached up to take it.

As a child Lucy had believed Lynn could protect her from

everything, call down the rain, and keep the coyotes at bay. Lynn had done all these things, but her face was grim at the thought of a threat she couldn't fight with her gun.

"So it was polio?"

"Your grandma thinks so," Lynn answered. "Seems there's different types, some worse than others. She wants to talk to us about it, when we're through here."

Lucy looked back at the crumpled white bundle. "Right," she said. "When we're through here."

"You gonna be okay with this? It's different when it's one of your own."

"Sounds like maybe it's something I need to get used to," Lucy said.

Lynn reached for the gas can at her side, dousing the body from the edge of the pit before tossing the match, her mouth a thin line. "No getting used to it."

The black pillar of smoke rose behind them as they walked to Vera's cabin to find Maddy's mother cringing on a stool in the corner.

"I need to know when she first got sick," Vera was saying. "Think hard about anything she said to you about feeling poorly."

Monica had stayed away from Maddy's bed as she died, unable to handle the sight of her only daughter smothering to death. Now her gaze was stuck to a spot on the floor, as if she might find answers in the pine knots there. When she finally spoke, her wisp of a voice was nearly lost in the creaking of the branches outside. "Sometime yesterday, maybe."

Maddy and her brother, Carter, made no secret of their mother's fearfulness. Carter had told Lucy once that even during good times, Monica looked for the bad to come, and during the bad she was more likely to hide than face it. Now Monica's shoulders seemed to slump under the weight of blame.

Lucy approached her friend's mother cautiously, as if she were a half-wild kitten discovered in the grass. "You don't have to feel bad about not knowing she was sick. Even if you'd brought her sooner, it wouldn't have helped."

"That's true," Vera said. "There's no cure for polio, and this strain moved quickly. That's why I need to know when things first went wrong. If the incubation period is as fast as I fear, we don't have much time."

Behind her, Lucy heard Stebbs mutter to Lynn, "If it's as fast as Vera thinks it is, time's already run out."

Lucy moved closer to Monica, took the woman's trembling hand. "How bad off was she when you brought her?"

"Pretty bad." Monica sniffled, and a runner of snot was sucked into her nostril. "When she came back from swimming with you and Carter, she said she had a headache. But it's the first real hot times of the spring, and her diving into the cold water, I didn't think much of it."

"What was the first indication it was more?" Vera asked.

"She woke up in the night, crying something awful. Carter and me, we came running." Monica used Lucy's sleeve to wipe away the fresh tears coursing out of her eyes. "She was having spasms, and she thought it was a charley horse, you know? So she got out of bed to walk it off, and she—she—"

"She what?" Lynn broke in, patience expired.

Stebbs put a hand on Lynn's shoulder. "She couldn't walk?" he asked.

"When she tried she just fell over, said her legs weren't working right. So her brother picked her up and ran her over here."

"Carter brought her about two or three in the morning," Vera said. "What time did you go swimming?"

"It was after we planted the seedlings," Lucy said.

"About two o'clock, by the sun," Lynn added.

"Twelve hours," Vera said softly. "Twelve hours to beginning paralysis and twenty-four to death."

"Is that fast?" Stebbs asked.

"Too fast to do anything about. Whatever source Maddy picked it up from, anybody who came into contact with it is already infected."

The pale hand holding Lucy's clenched in fear, and her own heart constricted at the words. "What about Carter?" Monica asked. "What about my son?"

"If he's not symptomatic by now, he should be okay," Vera said. "Which means you're all right too, little one."

Lucy let out the breath she'd been holding along with the woman next to her and nodded, any worries she had for herself only small drops on the wave of worry that had crashed over her at the thought of Carter being sick.

"You feelin' all right?" Lynn asked. "No headaches or anything funny with your legs?"

"I'm all right, Lynn. Really." Lucy waved Lynn off, but Lynn still looked her up and down, as if she expected to see the virus surface in the form of fleas or ticks. "Even if I wasn't, it's not something you can just pull outta me, you know?"

Monica's sweaty hand pulsed inside Lucy's own. "No, there's nothing you can do," she said, as if reassuring herself.

"So if the girl got sick after swimming in the pond, but her brother and our little one is all right, what does that mean?" Stebbs asked.

"It means the pond probably isn't the source," Vera answered.

"Damn right it's not," Lynn said. "I've been drinking that water my whole life."

"You've been drinking water from the pond after you'd *purified* it," Vera corrected. "I wouldn't rule it out."

"It can't be the pond," Lucy argued. "Why wouldn't I be sick then, or Carter?"

"It's hard to say," Vera said. "Polio is usually contracted person-to-person, but it can be waterborne."

"So she got it from somebody else? But who else is sick?" Lucy asked.

And the first knock on the door came.

Two

The knocks continued through the night and into the morning; the healthy came carrying the sick, and the sick carrying the virus. Lynn and Lucy dragged blankets to the grass downwind of the cabin for the invalids to be laid on. Most were dying even as Lucy settled them onto the ground, the eerie rattle that she had first heard from Maddy now filling her ears like the sound of cicadas. Vera talked with those who could still speak, desperate to find out where they had been before confessing there was nothing she could do for them.

"There's really no cure?" Lucy asked, as she dumped a bucket of stream water into the kettle Lynn had set up near the bank. "There's nothing Grandma can do?"

Lynn shook her head. "Way I understand it, it kills some, cripples some. Some only get a bit of a fever from it. Vera said it usually hits the kids, but it can get adults too. There was some president that had it."

"It kill him?"

"No, your grandma said it crippled him, though. So I guess there's no telling who's gonna get it, and what it's gonna do to them."

Lucy snapped a branch over her knee. "That sucks."

"Maybe," Lynn said as she took the kindling from Lucy. "Maybe those that get sick are just happy to have it done, no matter how it ends. Like when Poe said,

> *"The sickness—the nausea—*
> *The pitiless pain—*
> *Have ceased, with the fever*
> *That maddened my brain—*
> *With the fever called 'Living'*
> *That burned in my brain."*

Lucy sighed and cracked another stick in half. "Couldn't your mother have taught you any happy poetry?"

Lynn smiled, but it was the one, slow and sad, that always came with talk of Mother. "She taught me what she knew. So has Stebbs. He told me once that people like me and him are badly built for times like this, when there's nothing we can do."

"You need an enemy," Lucy said, understanding immediately.

"I do. And when it's a sickness, I guess the best weapon I've got is the fire for the bodies."

"That and the fact you're not likely to be kissing anybody," Lucy said, poking Lynn in the ribs with the end of a stick.

"That's more of a precaution than a weapon," Lynn said, easily grabbing the end and pulling Lucy onto her knees with one swift jerk. "And don't worry yourself about whether I'm kissing anybody or not."

"Touchy." Lucy rose, brushing the dirt off her knees.

"But you've got a point." Lynn smacked her flint together, trying to coax a spark into the branches.

"What's that?"

"I've seen the way you and Carter have been looking at each other lately, and you shouldn't be doing any kissing either." A small spiral of smoke rose from the kindling, and Lynn rocked back on her heels. "Now's not the time to be figuring out if you're more than friends."

Lucy tried to ignore the flush that spread up her neck and to the roots of her tightly cropped blond hair. "I'm not stupid."

"Stupid doesn't factor in when a boy's mourning his sister and looking for comfort."

"I'm not—"

The older woman held up her hand. "That's all I'm saying about it. I'm not asking any questions, just telling you whatever's going on needs stowed until we know more about this sickness. Understood?"

"Understood."

Lynn held her eyes for a moment, then crouched low to breathe life into the fire she'd started. "I know we've not talked about . . . uh, some things."

"Stebbs already explained to me about sex, if that's what you're getting at," Lucy said, and the flush that had begun to recede reclaimed some ground.

"That poor man." Lynn's fire flared, and she studied it.

"What's this about, Lynn? Why you talking to me about love when we're burning the dead?"

"'Cause we're about to hit some hard times, and I need you to listen to me. I tell you to go to the basement and not come back up, you go. I tell you to climb a tree, you head for the highest one, you hear?"

"You're worried."

"This whole conversation is me being worried."

Even though the sun burned brightly, Lucy could feel a chill from the little graveyard nearby where her mother and stillborn brother lay, her uncle Eli with them. Lynn's eyes shifted there too, as if following Lucy's thoughts, and the chill settled into Lucy's bones. If Lynn was worried, there was real danger.

Lucy reached for Lynn's hair, long and unbound, tangled by the wind. "Sit down," she coaxed. "Let me work on this rat's nest."

"Sitting down doesn't do anybody any good," Lynn argued, but sat nonetheless.

Lucy watched Lynn's shoulders relax as she worked the knots

free, then bound her thick hair into one large braid. "You need to learn how to do this yourself."

"Can't see the back of my own head." Lynn said. "I should hack it all off, like yours."

"No, I like it." Lucy gave the braid in her hand a yank.

Lynn yelped good-naturedly. "All right, let go of me. We got work to do."

Lucy kept her hand on Lynn's braid a moment longer, delaying the trips from the line of sick to the pit where the fires burned. "It's hard, watching the small ones go."

"I know it. You were terribly sick when you were small. It was more than I could stand."

"And the medicine from back then, it won't help these kids?"

"No. Your grandma said it's only good against sicknesses caused by bacteria, and polio's a virus. She said even before the Shortage, there was nothing anyone could do for polio once you had it."

"So she's trying to figure out where it came from?"

Lynn rose to her feet. "That's the plan, it seems. Figure out who or what Maddy got it from. In the meantime, we're not to let anybody near our pond."

"That should come naturally enough to you," Lucy said, and Lynn gave her a swat on the behind.

They walked up the bank, away from the shade trees and into the heat of the spring sun. Around the bend in the stream they could see

Stebbs and Vera's cabin. Beyond were the rows of sick, waiting to die or recover. A few had blankets tossed over their faces. Lucy stopped in her tracks, unable to go farther. "I can't stand lifting the edges to see who we lost."

"Won't make 'em any less dead." Lynn took Lucy by the hand, her touch more gentle than her words. "Don't forget your handkerchief," she added, pulling hers up to cover her nose and mouth.

Lucy followed suit, and they made their way through the lines. Vera spotted them and wound her way through the maze of the ill. "Lynn, I'm sorry, but I need you to—"

"I've got it." Lynn headed for the nearest bundle.

"Who was it?" Lucy asked.

Vera spoke softly. "There were quite a few, here in the early morning. Myrtle lost her two youngest."

"Hank and little Frannie?" A sound followed their names up through her throat, a wordless mourning that Lucy couldn't keep in. "How'd she take it?"

"She's sleeping right now, was up all night caring for them. I don't have the heart to wake her just yet."

Vera motioned Lucy away from the line of blankets, and they walked into the tall grass, the only privacy there was. "I haven't told anyone else yet, but Alex Hale died too, and Caroline Bowl."

"But they're Lynn's age, at least. I thought it only killed babies."

Vera motioned for Lucy to lower her voice. "Usually, yes. From

17

what I know of polio it mostly killed children, the old, or the weak. But Stebbs and I were the last generation to be vaccinated. You remember what *vaccination* means?"

"It means you can't get sick."

"That's right." Vera sighed and raised her heavy black hair, shot with silver, off her neck. "For now all we can do is separate the sick from the well, find the source, and hope for the best. I moved the adults over to the other side of the road, by the bridge. There's no sense in the children seeing their parents ill. It'll scare them more than anything. They need to be told everything is going to be all right."

"And what do you want me to do?"

Vera closed her eyes against the sun that was helping the contagion bloom and grow in her patients. "Can you tell *me* everything is going to be all right?"

Lucy spotted Carter in the mid morning, moving among the sick with a canteen. Her usual surge of happiness at seeing him— somewhat boosted of late by the feeling of her heart jumping into her throat—faded when she thought of Maddy.

Looking at Carter now caused the tears to spring into Lucy's eyes, and she turned her back on him. The child at her feet glanced up at her. "You okay?"

She dropped to her knees beside his blanket and put her hand on his forehead. "Adam, you're making me look bad. I'm supposed to be the one asking after you."

He shrugged. "Seems like you're laughing most of the time. Just not today."

"Not today. How *you* feeling?"

"Better, I think," he said cautiously, as if voicing the possibility would make it a lie. "Thirsty."

"Water over here," Lucy called out, and Carter was beside them in seconds.

"Hey, little man, you're looking strong," Carter said, and Lucy had to crush her eyes shut to prevent tears from leaking at the sound of his voice.

A smile tweaked the corners of Adam's mouth. "Maybe."

"Better let me hold it," Carter said, then looked at Lucy. "Vera said not to let it touch their mouths, so it's more like pouring it down their throats." Lucy saw he had two canteens, one with an *X* made out of electrical tape on the lid.

"What's that?"

"One's for the sick. The other's mine, and for the people that got nothing to do but wait."

Lucy nodded quietly, breaking away from his gaze. His eyes were dry, but she knew Carter well enough to see the pain in them. She slid her arms under Adam's shoulders and pulled him into a sitting position. His eyes closed in relief as he swallowed, and Lucy laid him back gently.

"Rest," she whispered to him, brushing some hair off his

forehead. "I think you're one of the lucky ones."

"One of the few," Carter said, and her hand found his.

"I'm so sorry," she tried to say, but her voice broke and the tears she'd been fighting swelled out of her in a rush, coursing down her cheeks and spattering Adam's shirt along with the wasted water that had seeped from around his weak lips.

Carter's arm went across her shoulder and pulled her into him, squeezing strength into her body. "I know it, I know," he said, his own voice thick. "But not here, not in front of the small ones."

She nodded and pulled away, but he kept his hand on her shoulder. She'd not given much thought to his hands until the past few months, when the calluses and the strength of his fingers had taken on new meaning as she'd wondered how they'd feel against her skin. He brushed this thumb against her cheek, moving the tears back into her hair.

He cleared his throat and stepped back from her. "I need to refill this," he said, picking up a canteen. "Wanna come with?"

They headed toward the stream, the midday sun baking the backs of their necks.

"Adam seems to be getting better," Lucy said cautiously.

"I think so, yeah. Might take some time though. I've noticed the adults who went down are bouncing back quicker than the kids."

"And their legs?"

"Not good," Carter shook his head. "Jeb Calkins is getting better, sure enough, but he can't move either of his."

Jeb was a single man, with a young son. "Who's going to take care of Little Jeb?" Lucy asked.

"Shit, who's going to take care of Big Jeb?" Carter dipped the canteen in the creek. "What's going on here, Lucy . . . it's bad. It's going to change things. We'll be a community where half the adults are cripples, most of the children invalids."

"Stebbs is crippled, always has been. Doesn't slow him down none."

"Stebbs has a twisted foot, broken in a trap and never healed right. That's different from losing the use of your whole leg."

Lucy sat on the bank, quiet. Carter's reasoning explained why Lynn had been scared. As usual, she'd realized what something meant in the long run, like how this year's garden would affect the next, and why a sickness moving through the deer meant she should avoid killing the young ones, so they could repopulate. It wasn't only people who were being crippled, but their entire way of life. Without healthy adults, they could not defend themselves. Even though outside threats were not nearly as common as they had been a decade earlier, there were still passing bands of people who wanted what they had—water.

And now it would be easier to take it from them.

Three

The next day a fresh wave of patients came in. Siblings lay on blankets their brothers and sisters had vacated, either by going home or to the pits Lynn kept burning.

"I don't understand it," Vera muttered, her head resting in her hands while her blank eyes coursed over her notes: jumbled, mismatched scraps of paper torn from whatever had been handy as she questioned the sick. So far, nothing had led her back to the beginning, to Maddy.

"You need to rest, Grandma," Lucy said from her seat on the floor. Her own body was worn out from long hours tending the patients, her emotions worn so flat she no longer flinched when even the smallest bundles headed for the fires. Lynn looked no better, her hair covered with a fine powdering of soot from the dead.

"I can't rest," Vera said. "Not until we know where this came from. All we're doing is treating the symptoms, not stopping the sickness."

"Maybe so." Stebbs moved behind her, his strong hands working to ease the tension in her shoulders. "But you're not going to make any sense out of those scribbles in the state you're in. You've not slept longer than a few hours since this started."

"I wouldn't even call it sleeping, what you do," Lynn agreed. "You just kinda sit real still and doze."

"It's an old doctor's habit, and good to know I've still got the knack."

"Knack or not, you're going to bed, Doc," Stebbs said sternly, and Lynn motioned to Lucy to follow her outside.

"She might be immune to polio, but that don't mean this epidemic won't kill her," Lynn said as they walked down to the stream. "Vera says polio thrives when it gets hot. This outbreak is just a taste of what could be coming, if we don't figure out the source. She won't sleep sound 'til that happens."

Lucy found a spot in the tall grass that was well beaten down and took a seat. Heat lightning flickered across dark thunderheads that had formed on the evening horizon. "Not a good sign," she said, gesturing toward the pink bolts.

Lynn glanced up. "Nope. No rain, no cool air." A moan rose from the rows of the sick, out of sight beyond the tall grass, but not out of hearing range.

"You doing okay?"

"Mostly," Lucy said. "It's just all the harder because I thought it was through." The sight of Adam, one leg dangling limp and useless at his father's side as he was carried away, had been bittersweet. He had lived, but what kind of life he would have in their world was yet to be seen.

"I thought it was done too. I even thought about putting out the fires."

"That was downright hopeful of you."

Lynn grunted, as she always did when Lucy teased her, but the hard lines of her mouth softened. "Stupid too."

"You sleeping here again tonight?"

Lynn glanced at the chimney of their shared home, barely visible in the distance in the dying light. She sighed. "We're needed here." She stomped her own area of grass and lay down. "Get some sleep," she said brusquely, and rolled over, her braid dark with grime.

Lucy tossed a clod of dirt at her back. "You need a bath."

"You need to go the hell to sleep," Lynn shot back, but even in the dark, Lucy could hear the smile.

Adam's father never got up the hill to their home. A rider found Devon, collapsed and weakened, when he heard Adam yelling for help, his voice hoarse from calling. Adam rode back to Vera's in front of the stranger, his father crumpled against the man's back. Stebbs pulled Devon off the horse as Lucy helped Adam from the saddle on the other side.

"What happened?"

Adam's lower lip quivered, but he kept the tears from falling. "Daddy got real tired, carrying me up the hill—said he needed to stop and rest a bit. I got sleepy, and when I woke up he was sitting all funny, and he couldn't get himself up. I yelled and yelled, but no one came."

"I found 'em," the stranger in the saddle said. "Heard the boy calling. Sounded more like an injured animal than anything else. I was awful surprised when I came upon the two of them."

"We thank you for it," Stebbs said. "There's plenty that woulda left 'em."

"Left 'em or done worse," the rider admitted.

"Can we give you something for your trouble? A drink?"

Lucy stiffened at the words. Water was like gold, and never offered freely to strangers. The man looked from Stebbs to Devon. "Don't believe I'll be drinking any of your water, no offense."

"None taken." Stebbs nodded curtly, and the stranger rode off, anxious to put miles between himself and them.

"Can you put him somewhere?" Stebbs nodded to Adam, who was still in Lucy's arms. "I'll take Devon."

"What do you think, mister?" Lucy said to Adam, forcing fake cheer into her voice. "Want to camp out tonight?"

"Can I go to the healer lady's house?"

"My grandma, you mean?" Lucy headed for the cabin, Adam's body light in her arms. "Why you wanna go there for?"

"She fixed me before. I thought maybe she could finish it up now and make my leg better."

Lucy swallowed hard before speaking. "Sweetie, didn't anybody tell you that you won't ever be using that leg again? It's ruined."

Adam shrugged. "Dad says it never hurts to ask. Worst anybody can say is no."

Vera glanced up when Lucy walked through the door with her burden.

"Devon fell ill taking him home," Lucy said as she laid Adam on the bed.

"Where's Devon?" Vera had been at the table, poring over her notes again. A fresh patient meant new information, and she was on her feet in a second.

"Stebbs has him down with the sick."

"How'd he get back here on foot with Adam?"

Lucy began tucking pillows under Adam's shoulders to prop him up. "A man on a horse found them, brought them back here."

"And where is this man?"

"Took off when he saw what we were dealing with."

"Stebbs let him *leave*?"

The shock in her grandma's voice got Lucy's attention. She looked

26

up to see that Vera had gone white, her fists clenched.

"Yeah, why?"

"If he picked it up from Devon, he'll infect everyone he meets. Or die alone in the wilderness."

Lucy glanced back at the little boy in the bed, his frightened eyes bouncing between the two women. "Let's hope he didn't catch it then."

"Quick as this is moving, it's a better bet to hope he dies alone."

It fell to Carter and Lucy to deliver the news to Devon's wife. The family lived on a remote hill, because Abigail's mistrust of people ran deep, even more so than Lynn's. She preferred to take her chances on the hillside, somewhere her family had a good view of everything around them, their own well, and no other houses in sight.

Lucy trudged up the incline, her calf muscles burning. "I don't know how Devon could've made this climb carrying Adam even if he were healthy," she said.

Carter wiped the sweat off his forehead. "I know she's got her reasons, but damn, this is inconvenient for the rest of us."

"Lynn says she's got a right to live up here, if that's what she wants."

"And what do you say?"

Lucy tripped on a branch and muttered a curse. "I say she can't expect help to come running if we can't hear her yelling for it." Her breath hitched in her chest, and she slid to the ground. "Sorry, I gotta stop." Days of tending the ill had stripped her of strength.

Carter rested next to her, their backs against a huge oak. "I'm not in a hurry to get up there, anyway. You and I aren't exactly her favorite people."

One of Lucy's more ill-advised pranks had involved swapping out Abigail's prized newborn calf with a stuffed animal of a cow. The punishment had been steep—Lynn had made her haul water from the pond for a month—but the fun had been worth it.

Lucy rolled her eyes. "I think being one of Abigail's favorite people requires blood relation. So I'll pass. Besides, there was no harm done."

"You're still a rabble-rouser." Carter knocked his knee against hers.

"And you're trouble." She knocked it back.

"Remember you and me and Maddy slept up in her haymow so we could see her face when she came down to the barn in the morning?" Carter went on, laughing. "And Maddy didn't know there was a bunch of kittens up there, 'til one of them jumped on her? Turned out that herbal soap your grandma gave Maddy for her birthday had catnip in it."

"I swear I didn't know that." Lucy giggled.

"Maybe not, but you knew full well it was just a kitten in her hair, and you started screaming about bats anyway, and she went through the roof. You and me was trying to shush her up, but she woke up baby Adam all the way in the house."

"Yeah." Lucy's smile faded. "Yeah, I remember."

And now Maddy was dead, and the baby whose cries they'd wished away that night was a crippled little boy whose father might not live through the day.

Carter quieted as well, his own thoughts turning toward the present. He rose to his feet, holding out a hand for her. "C'mon then," he said. "Let's get this over with."

Abigail didn't answer Carter's knock. He tried again, but they heard no movement in the house. He pulled his fist back to try another time, then froze mid motion. "You don't suppose she caught it and died up here, do you?"

Lucy backed off the porch, glancing around the overgrown yard to the outbuildings. "Doubt it. The garden's recently watered and the cows aren't kicking up a fuss, wanting to be milked. She's in there. She just doesn't want to talk to us."

"Better make my point then," Carter said, and redoubled his efforts, pounding on the door.

Lucy stepped farther out into the yard and glanced up into the second story of the old farmhouse. A curtain hastily slipped back into place. "She's up there," she said to Carter. Then, more loudly,

"Abigail, it's Lucy from down by the pond. I need you to come out here and talk to us."

Carter joined Lucy in the yard and called up at the window. "Abigail—it's about your son. Get down here or we'll walk off and you won't know what's happened."

A thin voice crept through the open window. "If he's dead, I don't want to know."

Carter sighed. "He ain't dead. Now come down."

They heard shuffling as she walked away from the open window, then nothing for several minutes until the front door creaked open. A small woman with ratted blond hair peered around the corner.

Lucy tried her best smile, one that could melt even Lynn at times. "We need to talk to you about Devon."

"Thought you said this was about Adam?"

"Him too," Carter said, stepping toward the porch.

"You stay back there," Abigail said sharply, her thin voice suddenly strong. "I can hear you fine from the yard."

"All right then." He slowly backpedaled to stand next to Lucy. "I think she's got a gun," he said to her softly.

"Who doesn't?" Lucy sighed, then raised her voice toward Abigail. "We came to tell you what's going on with your man and boy. You can put the rifle down."

Abigail stepped out onto the porch, rifle pointed at the ground.

"Tell me what you like, makes no difference what I'm holding at the time."

"It's slightly rude," Lucy said. Carter shot her a dark look, and she clamped her mouth shut.

"Rude ain't nothing that I've done. Rude is breaking into people's barns and pulling tricks on them."

"Lots of people are sick, Abigail," Carter said quickly. "Devon's one of 'em."

A line appeared between Abigail's eyes as she studied the two teens. "Adam's the one who's sick. Devon took him down to your healer to make him well."

"And she tried, Abigail, she did," Lucy said, emotion making her voice thick. "But this sickness—it's not like a normal fever. It's polio, and Adam . . . he's okay, but . . . he's . . ."

"He's crippled," Carter said. "No way around it."

Abigail's mouth tightened. "What about Devon? What's wrong with him?"

"Same thing," Carter answered. "It's not good, Abigail. You should come down, be with your husband."

"You think, do you?" Abigail said, her mouth twisting. "So everyone can get a good look at the woman who won't come down off the hill?"

Lucy glanced at Carter. He grasped her wrist, urging silence.

"You come up here, to tell me my man—who don't get sick—is

sick, and my boy—who was fine yesterday—is a cripple today. I wouldn't believe either one of you if you told me it was raining and my head was wet with the drops." She cocked the gun and strode toward them to the edge of the porch.

Carter stepped in front of Lucy. "We came up here to deliver a message," he said, "and we've done it. We'll be leaving now."

"You came up here to make a fool of me," Abigail hissed at them. "Devon ain't sick with nothing but lust, looking at that woman who calls herself your mother, little girl. You wanna make a laughing-stock of me, drag me down the hill so I see what's *really* keeping him down there?"

Carter stepped backward, pushing Lucy behind him. "Nobody's laughing down there, Abigail. I promise you that."

"Go on then." She jerked the rifle toward them. "Get on back down there and tell my man to come back to me, and bring my son. I know he's whole, and I know he's well, and I know you two are full of *shit*."

Her voice cracked on the last word and she retreated back into the house, slamming the door behind her. Carter and Lucy stumbled down the decline of the hill as they headed for the woods, Abigail's rising sobs breaking on their ears.

"Does she really think we'd make up a story to bring her down the hill for kicks?" Lucy asked.

"Hard to say." Carter held a tree branch for her to pass by before letting it snap back. She smiled to herself; a year ago he would've let it hit her in the face. "But don't let what some crackpot thinks of you ruin your day."

"It's more likely the dead bodies'll do that," Lucy said.

Carter laughed and grabbed her hand suddenly. "Remind me never to come to you for comfort."

She opened her mouth to apologize, but he waved her off and they walked on, fingers intertwined. They followed the stream downhill toward Vera's, neither of them commenting on the fact that they were holding hands, or how very normal it felt.

Lucy dropped his hand as they came into the clearing near Vera's cabin. She could hear Lynn clearly as they approached. "You'd better be damn sure about this," she was saying. "Once it's said, there's no taking it back."

"Something's up," Carter said.

The door was propped open, and through it Lucy could see Vera bent over her notes, exhaustion dimming the usual brightness of her eyes. "I'm sure," Vera said quietly.

Lucy knocked hesitantly on the open door. "Uh . . . are we interrupting?"

Stebbs shook his head. "No. You need to come in here. Both of you. And shut the door behind you."

Lucy's trembling hand struggled with the simple hook-and-eye lock. Stebbs was only serious with her when things were dire.

The three adults looked at one another for a moment, the weight of their silence resting on Lucy's heart more heavily than any words. "What? What is it?"

"Who's gonna tell him?" Lynn asked, looking to Vera and Stebbs.

"Tell me what?" Carter asked, his hand finding Lucy's despite the adults seeing.

Vera cleared her throat. "I've been looking at my notes, trying to figure out the source of the outbreak. You remember there was a lull, and then we got slammed by more sick than we had in the first wave."

"Like the brothers and sisters of people who were first sick," Lucy said slowly. "They were passing it to each other."

"Except they weren't," Vera said. "I thought so too, but then I realized the incubation period was wrong. If the second wave of patients were catching it from their siblings, they would've been symptomatic sooner. Instead they weren't showing up here until their brothers and sisters were better."

"Or dead," Lynn added.

"Incubation period?" Carter looked from Vera to Stebbs. "What's that mean?"

"It's the time period from when you're exposed to the virus to when it actually makes you sick. This second wave was getting sick *after* they came here."

"So they caught it here," Lucy said. "No big surprise, this

place was crawling with sick."

Vera shook her head. "No, sweetheart. We made sure there was no contact between the well and the ill. The first rule of keeping a contagion in hand is quarantine."

"People break rules, Grandma."

"If it were an isolated case or two, I would agree," Vera said. "But *every* person in the second wave had been here. So it had to have been someone carrying it between the two groups."

"Oh, Jesus," Carter said, color draining from his face. "It was me, wasn't it? I must've mixed up which canteen I was using for the sick and for the well."

Lucy felt his fingers go cold in her own. "You wouldn't do that," she said, voice hard. "You wouldn't make a mistake like that."

Stebbs walked over from his place beside Vera and put a hand on Carter's shoulder. "It's best you sit down, son. There's more to tell." Stebbs steered him away from Lucy to the empty chair opposite Vera.

"Lucy," Lynn said. "You come on over here with me now."

Her body tensed in rebellion, every muscle wanting to follow Carter, but Lynn's tone left no room for argument, and Lucy joined her against the wall.

"He wouldn't have done that," she said vehemently to Lynn. "He's smarter than that."

"It wasn't the water," said Vera. "Do you remember me telling everyone about the different kinds of polio, and how they affect people?"

"Yeah. Some people are paralyzed, like Adam. Some people only get a fever, and then feel fine. Some die, like my sister," said Carter.

"And some don't even know they have it," Vera said.

Realization dawned on Lucy, her heart collapsing under the weight of what Vera was saying. "No," she said, the word barely squeezing past her lips. "He is not sick." Carter's gaze jumped from Vera to Lucy, his confusion evident.

Vera reached across the table, clasping his hands in her own. "I'm so sorry. I tried to find another answer, but it fits. Your sister was the first, the people who came in after had all interacted with you at some point. The second wave was so perfectly timed, it had to be someone here. You were the one moving between the sick and the well, carrying messages and sharing your water."

"Can you . . . Is there any way to tell, to be sure?" Carter asked, his voice stronger than his shaking hands.

"Without a way to look at cells in your blood, no. All I've got to go on is timelines and crossed paths," Vera said.

"So you could be wrong," Lucy said.

"It's possible," Vera admitted, still looking at Carter. "But that would put me back at square one, searching for a source. So I need you to tell me—had you not felt well at any point before Maddy got sick?"

Carter shook his head, his throat too constricted for speech. Stebbs stepped behind him, put his hands on the boy's shoulders. "This is important, son. So think hard, and be honest."

"No fever? No muscle spasms?" Vera continued.

"No, nothing," Carter said.

"What about headaches?"

Carter stopped shaking his head and closed his eyes. "Shit," he said, slowly and quietly, the one syllable damning him. "Yeah. The day we went swimming. I had a blinder, but I went anyway." He opened his eyes and looked at Lucy. "'Cause I wanted to see you."

A breath slipped from her hitching chest, and a sob followed it. She tried to go to him, but Lynn's grip on her arm was like an iron band. She couldn't offer him comfort when he put his head on the table and sobbed for the death he had brought upon his sister, the racking breaths shaking his frame, his tears soaking Vera's notes. Vera and Stebbs did what they could, the inoculated surrounding the infected, the innocent watching from the shadows.

Four

"Y ou can't see him again, Lucy. I'm sorry," Lynn said.

Lucy sat on her bed in the home she shared with Lynn, her heartbeat a dim echo inside her body. Light flickered across the walls from the oil lamp on Lucy's nightstand, the flame burning low on the wick. Lynn sat at the foot of the bed.

"I mean it. It's not games now. I know you've snuck out of here once or twice in the past, but you can't go to him. I won't let you."

Lucy nodded absently, her mind still wrapped around the image of Carter sobbing, and Lynn pulling her away from his infected tears.

"What's going to happen to him?" Lucy asked, her voice thick with hours of crying.

"Can't say," Lynn answered. "Your grandma and Stebbs said they'd be by after a while. You can ask your questions then."

"It's not fair."

A wry smile twisted Lynn's mouth, and she shrugged. "What is?"

Lucy teared up again, fresh salt water burrowing new tracks over her swollen cheeks. Lynn took her hand and squeezed it. "No, it's not fair, little one. Carter did nothing to deserve getting sick. Knowing that he killed his sister, and brought death and twisted limbs on so many, is a weight to bear."

"I don't know if he can take it," Lucy said, her fear welling into a panic. "What if he—he—"

The specter of suicide, the death her own mother had chosen, wasn't a stranger in their bleak world.

Lynn shook her head. "I don't think he's the type, and I'm not just saying it."

A heavy knock on the front door reverberated through the house, up to the second floor where they sat. Lynn's hand shot to her side, and Lucy realized she was wearing her pistol.

"It's probably your grandma," Lynn said, her voice tense with other possibilities. "Sit tight."

Lynn left the room, and Lucy wiped her face on the comforter, scrubbing away the dried salt and fresh tears that had gathered. She heard muffled voices below, recognized Stebbs' low drone, along with Vera's comforting tones. Three pairs of footsteps came up the stairs, and Lucy lengthened the wick on the oil lamp. The flame flared and lit Vera's face as she walked into Lucy's room, her wrinkles etched more deeply than before, eyes sunk with exhaustion.

"How you doing, honey?" she asked Lucy, gathering her into a hug.

"Okay," Lucy croaked. "How's Carter?"

"We had a good long talk," Stebbs said, leaning against the wall. "He's sleeping now, back at our place."

Lynn propped herself against Lucy's dresser. "Poor bastard. You talk to his mom?"

"Yeah," Stebbs said uneasily, his gaze shooting to Vera. "Yeah, we did."

Vera took Lucy's hand and looked at Lynn. "Girls . . . we need to talk."

"Why? What's going to happen to Carter?" Lucy pulled her hand away from Vera. "What's going on?"

"Carter is a sick boy," Stebbs said. "He can't be around other people."

"For how long?"

"That's where it gets tricky," he said. "Your grandma can't say for sure."

Vera reached for Lucy's hand again, but she yanked it back. "What do you mean?"

Vera sighed. "Sweetheart, you've got to understand. When I was in medical school, polio was nearly eradicated—that means it hardly existed anymore. It wasn't something we spent a lot of time learning about."

"One of the things you didn't learn was how long somebody carries it. That what you're saying?" Lynn asked.

"Yes," Vera said. "He could be a carrier for a week, a month, or forever. I simply don't know."

"I fetched his mother," Stebbs said, "brought her back to our place, and explained the situation. Told her that her son would have to leave."

Lucy clutched a pillow to her chest, denial tearing a hot path down her insides. "No, you can't do that. You can't make him go just because your stupid college didn't teach you something forty years ago. That's not fair and you know it."

"What's fair then, little one?" Stebbs asked. "Letting him stay? Not telling people he's sick and having him infect others?"

"Stebbs is right, Lucy," Vera said. "It's the only thing I can think to do."

"But what if it's only for a week, or a month, like you said? What then? He's gone and he never comes back because you were *wrong*."

"That's true," Vera said. "But what if we take the chance, let him come back, and more fall sick? What do we tell them?"

"And then what?" Stebbs continued. "Try again later and tell the next round of sick it's their bad luck and we were wrong again?" He shook his head. "I know you got feelings for the boy, but we talked it and talked it and this is the only way we can think is best for everyone."

"Except Carter," Lucy said stiffly.

"What's best for Carter is if it hadn't ever happened," Stebbs said. "But we're past that."

"Easy for you to say," Lucy said, anger clipping her words. "You can't get sick."

Stebbs' face went cold, and his tone matched it. "Kid, there ain't been nothing easy about this. You don't know the half of it."

Lynn perked up at his words. "What's that mean?" Stebbs looked away from her, and she rounded on Vera. "What aren't you saying?"

"There is one other possibility I didn't mention in front of Carter," Vera said.

Lucy's heart leapt. Possibilities meant options, and hope. "What is it?"

Vera claimed her hand and wouldn't give it up. She smiled sadly at her granddaughter before speaking. "It could be you."

"Me?" she said softly, touching her chest as if the continued beating of her heart stood in denial. "It could be me?"

"It's not you," Lynn said through her teeth, and moved toward Vera. "And damn you for saying such a thing to her."

Stebbs yanked her back by the shoulder. "Easy now. Getting angry ain't helping."

"Neither is saying a bunch of bullshit," Lynn spat.

"I wouldn't think it, much less say it, if there weren't a chance it was true," Vera said. "She was with the sick and the well as much as Carter. She was with Maddy. I can't condemn him without questioning her."

Lynn struggled out of Stebbs' grip and kicked the wall, but held her silence. Vera turned to Lucy.

"Sweetheart, has there been anything, any headache, fever, back pain? Anything at all out of the ordinary you can think of, before Maddy died?"

Lucy shook her head slowly, her mind poring over the hours and days before her friend's death. "No . . . I . . . I don't think so."

Images of Maddy flickered through her brain—her friend in a painful coil under the bedspread, her dead body lying at the bottom of the pit. She took a ragged breath, and Adam's tiny smile flooded her thoughts along with Carter's slumped body at Vera's table as he wept for his fate.

"Say it's not me, Grandma," she begged, clutching Vera's hand so tightly her nails left crescent cuts that filled with blood. "Say I didn't do it to them."

Vera's soft, cool hand trailed over her hair. "I can't tell you for sure. I'm sorry."

Lucy fell forward onto Vera, burying her head in her lap and sobbing as Carter had, with no hope and nothing left but pain. Vera clasped her arms around her granddaughter and cried as well.

"So what's it mean?" Lynn asked Stebbs, her mouth a hard line.

"That's what we're here to talk about, kiddo."

Lucy touched her throat as the shot of whiskey Lynn had given her burned down. She imagined it drowning out the virus that might be living in her veins, purifying her blood in a surge of alcohol. But it wasn't that easy.

They had moved to the kitchen at Vera's insistence. Her grandmother had washed Lucy's face and put a cold rag across her swollen eyes, while Lynn and Stebbs had shared a glance and uncorked a bottle of whiskey for everyone. It was Lucy's first taste of alcohol and she had sputtered, spraying droplets across the table that Vera wouldn't allow Lynn to clean up.

"I won't believe it's her," Lynn said again. "The boy admitted to having a headache the day before his sister got sick. It has to be him. I've been with Lucy as much as anyone, and I'm not sick."

"It's likely you're right," Vera conceded. "But there are other factors to consider."

"Like what?" Lucy asked.

"When I brought Carter's mom over to the cabin to break the news to her," Stebbs said, "she went biblical—fell to the floor, gnashed her teeth. . . . It was all Vera could do to keep her from harming her own self, which wasn't exactly helpful."

"Monica's never been one for helpful," Lynn said.

Stebbs shook his head. "Once we got her calmed down, we told her the boy would have to go. He took the news better than she did, I'll say that. She broke down all over again, said she'd lost her daughter and now we was taking her son away. So Vera told her she could always go with him."

"What'd she say?" Lucy asked.

"Exactly what you'd expect her to say," Vera answered. "No."

"She cut him loose?" Lynn asked.

"She's not made of strong stuff," Stebbs said. "Even if she had gone with him, she'd be more of a hindrance than a help to the boy."

Lucy imagined poor Carter standing in a corner of Vera's house, his mother rejecting him in favor of her own comfort. "Maybe she would've been," Lucy agreed, "but now he'll be alone."

"What's this got to do with us?" Lynn asked.

"When I explained to Monica why I suspected it was her son infecting the second wave of victims, she came to the same conclusion I had," Vera said. "She knew you and Carter had been working together during the epidemic."

"So she knows it could be Lucy," Lynn said, guessing the end before Vera could come to it, "and she's not likely to keep her mouth shut about it, with you two kicking her son out."

Stebbs nodded. "Monica's a coward, but not stupid."

The warm spot the whiskey had formed in Lucy's stomach had managed to calm her a little, and the exhaustion from hours of crying had lulled her into a stupor while the adults talked. But Lynn's words brought a spike of cold fear bursting through the warmth.

"Is she telling people I'm sick too? Are you going to make us leave?"

"We don't know what to do, honey," Vera admitted. "But yes, it's likely Monica will tell people you could have been the source. Which means a few things: people will expect us to treat you the same way as Carter, and if we don't . . ."

"If we don't, it'd stir up an already pissed-off hornet's nest," Stebbs finished. "Lots of people are mourning right now, and once that's done, they'll turn to wanting to know why their people died. They'll need somebody to blame."

"Even if we let you stay, you'd be in danger," Vera said.

"They'd hurt me?"

"They would," Lynn said. "Much as I don't like agreeing. They would turn on you, if they thought it'd protect them from falling sick themselves, or losing more of their own. People are harsh animals. You've not had to see that firsthand in a long while."

"Lynn's right," Stebbs said. "And Monica's an injured animal, ready to bite at any threat. Right now, that's us."

Lynn's hand went to her gun. "She can't bite if I shut her mouth for her."

"I won't allow that, Lynn," Vera said. "Killing her would only solve half your problem anyway."

"What's the other half?"

Stebbs gave Lynn a shrewd glance. "You're not going to like what I have to say next, but don't hit me, okay, kiddo?"

Lynn's eyes narrowed, and Lucy noticed she made no promises.

"Abigail came down the hill today," Stebbs said carefully,

keeping an eye on Lynn.

"Oh crap," Lucy said. "I forgot to tell you."

Lynn's eyebrows drew together. "Forgot to tell me what?"

Vera put a hand on Lynn's taut shoulder. "It seems she believes you and Devon have, um . . .'"

"Christ," Stebbs broke in. "She thinks you're sparking him."

Lynn flushed a deep red. "She thinks I'm . . . with . . ." She trailed off, eyes wide. "Well, I'm not."

"Much of a relief as that is to hear," Stebbs said, "I don't think she's going to believe you."

"Why not?"

"Lynn," Vera said softly. "Sometimes when people are—"

"What she's saying is that Abigail is cracked in the head," Stebbs finished. "She's convinced herself you're sleeping with her man, and no amount of truth is going to sway her otherwise."

"Have Devon set her straight," Lucy said, seeing Lynn was beyond words. "She thinks the world of him. If he says it as well as Lynn, she's bound to believe it."

"Devon passed away this morning," Vera said quietly.

"And with him dead, there's no one to do the denying but the one she's accusing, and Abigail half out of her head with grief—"

"And the other half of her head not being all that stable to begin with," Lucy finished.

"She'll be gunning for you," Stebbs warned Lynn.

She shrugged. "I got a gun too."

"And I bet Lynn's a better shot," Lucy said.

"Good shot or not, is that your plan?" Stebbs asked Lynn. "Climb up on the roof again and shoot anybody comes near? That the kind of life you want for Lucy? What you had? Skulking in the basement and sniping from the roof? Scared to talk to anybody for fear they're gonna take something from you?"

Lynn swallowed hard, and Lucy could see the struggle tearing her in two. Lynn's own mother had protected the pond against any who would take a drink from it, animal or human. The pond, and their home, had been the only world Lynn knew until she was Lucy's age. Only her mother's death and an injury had forced her to reach out to Stebbs for help; otherwise Lynn would've been content to remain as she had been. Alive, but alone.

"No," Lynn said slowly. "I wouldn't have that for you, Lucy. It's no kind of life, and you're not suited to it, anyway."

"I can do it," Lucy said, even though the thought of living in isolation made her skin grow cold. "You tell me and it's done. I don't want you to give up everything on account of me."

"Little one," Lynn said sadly, "that's what a real mother does."

The numbing effect of the alcohol had spread to her brain; it was the only way to explain the cool, calm way Lucy packed only the most essential things in a backpack. Her hand hovered over Red Dog, a

48

stuffed animal Lynn had given her as the first indication her heart was softening toward the little girl she'd taken into her home.

"Probably shouldn't," a gruff voice came from her bedroom doorway, and Lucy turned to find Stebbs leaning there.

She clutched Red Dog to her chest. "He was Lynn's when she was a kid too. Leaving him behind feels wrong."

Stebbs shuffled into her room, gently taking Red Dog from her hands. He peered into the black button eyes, seeing something other than a stuffed animal there. He cleared his throat. "Why don't you leave him with me? I'll keep him safe for you."

Lucy nodded dumbly, knowing it was a false promise meant to console a child. "Yeah, okay," she said, swiping at the tears leaking from the corners of her eyes.

"C'mere, girl," Stebbs said, and folded her into his arms.

She could only cry and inhale the strong smell of him, the woods and the water, the dirt and the air, one last time.

Lucy found Lynn pondering the racks of purified water they kept in the basement, a grim expression on her face. She glanced up when she heard Lucy's step.

"You ready?"

"I'm packed, yeah."

"That's not the same thing as ready." Lynn looked back at the bottles of water. "The thing about water," she said, almost to herself, "is that it's so damn heavy."

Years of hauling water from the pond to the holding tanks in the barn had taught that lesson to both of them. "Yeah," Lucy agreed. "It is."

"We can't carry enough to get us far. And we can't trust water we find along the way to be clean. And that's assuming we can even get to any that hasn't already been claimed." Lynn's voice drifted off, their problem evident.

"Want me to bring my witching stick?"

With her forked ash stick Lucy had found water for many of the families in their community, always in private, and always attributing the find to Stebbs. The ability to witch water was a blessing and a curse—it could save lives, or ensure the bearer was marked for life as a person of high value in a world where money no longer mattered. Those who could find water worked in secret for fear their ability would earn them a pair of chains, with a stern master on the end.

"Bring it," Lynn decided. "I haven't lived this long to die of thirst on the road."

"We'd be stupid not to," Lucy said.

"It'd be stupid to use it. That's a last resort, and you remember it."

Lucy nodded and sat down on the steps to watch Lynn, who couldn't tear herself away from the water. She ran her fingers over the bottles and heaved a sigh.

"Saying your good-byes?" Lucy teased.

"Beyond Stebbs and Vera, who else have I got to say it to?" Lynn asked, a self-deprecating smile on her face.

"There's others that like you, if you'd let 'em."

Lynn hefted her own backpack onto her shoulders. "Now's a poor time to start liking people," she said gruffly. "You say yours?"

"Yeah," Lucy said, pushing the single syllable past the lump in her throat.

Lynn gave her a searching look. "If you didn't do it good and thorough, you go do it again, understand?"

"You don't think we're ever coming back, do you?"

"Coming back or not, don't matter. We're leaving behind an old woman and a cripple in the wake of an epidemic. They're stuck with a bunch of helpless children, and half the adults here got one arm or leg that don't work. You say good-bye and you say it right, 'cause either we're gonna die or they are."

Lucy nodded, emotion choking off her voice when she tried to speak. The pond and her family had been her world for years, slowly sprinkled with new faces as more people found safety among them. Always her life had been planned—a man, a home, a well, and eventually children. Now it was all skewed, thrown off-balance by an invisible enemy she couldn't fight. "What if . . . what if it *is* me, Lynn? What if all those dead children and ruined people are my fault?"

Lynn was on her knees on the step below Lucy in a second, gripping her face so tightly Lucy could feel her skin stretching.

"You listen to me now—I know you, understand? I know you right past your skin, through your bones, and down into your blood, and there is nothing inside of you that could hurt anyone. I know it for a fact, I know it the way I know the sun's going to come up tomorrow the same place it did today. You hear me?"

"I hear you," Lucy said. If Lynn, who was faithless, had faith in her, it was all the validation she needed.

Lynn let go of her cheeks, smoothed the short strands of blond hair from her forehead. "If you want to go and say a bit to Carter, he's still over at Vera and Stebbs' place."

Lucy couldn't control her surprise. "Really?"

"I shouldn't let you," Lynn said. "But I know what not getting to say good-bye feels like. Stay a good piece away from him while you're talking, no matter how hard it is."

"I will." Lucy nodded emphatically, an odd mixture of elation and fear coursing through her body. She wanted to see Carter, needed to see him so badly that the possibility had her stomach dipping to her knees and her heart jumping into her throat. But the excitement was tinged with sadness, the knowledge that no matter what they said to each other, it would be their last words.

"You go on now," Lynn said, turning back to the bottles of water. "Be back in an hour. We're leaving as soon as there's morning light."

Five

The long grass was wet with night dew, soaking Lucy's jeans as she crept quietly to Vera's house by the creek. The sick were still lined up in rows, their blankets tucked around their hunched shoulders as they slept under the trees along the bank; the healthy made similar lines on the other side of the cabin, at a safe distance from their stricken loved ones.

There was a candle burning inside the cabin, and she saw Vera's shadow pass by a window. She tapped lightly on the glass, and Vera motioned her around to the door, smiling as she opened it.

"Are you packed, sweetheart?"

"More or less."

"I think 'less' would probably be best," Vera said.

"Lynn said I should say my good-byes."

Vera stepped outside and took Lucy's hand, leading her down to the creek bed. "I want to talk to you, before you go."

Lucy nodded, felt the warm rush of tears returning to her eyes. She'd been so wrapped up in wondering what she would say to Carter, she hadn't realized this would be the last time she saw her grandmother.

Vera pointed toward the bend in the creek, where a small break in the trees allowed them to see the cemetery crosses in the moonlight. "Do you remember your mother?"

"Not much," Lucy admitted. "I remember how sad she was, and how—" She broke off, not wanting to say anything that could be misunderstood. "How different from Lynn," she finished.

"I think 'delicate' is what you're trying to say."

"Yeah, that's definitely it."

"She was delicate, very much so. Your mother wasn't made for this kind of life, and while I know that, it still kills me every day to think what she chose instead."

Lucy felt her grandma's hand shaking in her own, and she squeezed it. "I'm sorry, Grandma. I'm sorry you had to lose her like that."

"And now I'm losing you." Vera turned to her, eyes wet. "Don't think for a second we didn't try to find a way for you to stay."

"I know it," Lucy said, her own voice growing thick. "Could you come?"

Vera shook her head, and the little flame of hope that had sparked in Lucy's chest died. "No, little one. I'm an old woman, and my man is a cripple. We'd slow you down, and more than likely die along the way."

"Lynn thinks you'll die if you stay," Lucy said.

"We may. But you two won't have to stop to bury us, and I can lie here with my daughter and her little son." Vera wrapped her arms around Lucy, who sank into her like a child.

"I'm going to miss you," Lucy said. "And I love you a whole lot."

"I love you a whole lot too, little girl," Vera said, then pulled back to give Lucy a stern look. "I'll let you see Carter, but you don't go past this line." She made a mark in the dirt with her foot. "Promise me."

"Why not?" Lucy asked, the tears she'd been shedding all day erupting again, along with her frustration. "If you think I'm infected too, what does it matter?"

"Sweetheart"—Vera's hand rested on her arm, her touch as light as always—"I don't think it's you. But I can't back that up in any way other than the feeling in my heart."

"Lynn said the same thing."

"She's got a mother's instincts without ever having borne a child, and for once she and I agree on something. You're not the carrier, little one. But like Stebbs said, Monica isn't stupid, she's figured out it could be you just as well as Carter, and we can't very well exile one of you and not the other."

"Then I'll leave with him," Lucy said, the words tumbling out of her as the idea occurred. "Lynn won't have to leave her pond and he won't have to be alone."

"And that leaves Lynn behind to deal with Abigail gunning for her with all the bitterness in her heart. And more than likely you'll be dead from Carter's love in less than a week," Vera said sternly.

Lucy was about to say that was fine, but the words were stuck.

Vera watched her closely. "That's not what you're meant for. Life's got more in store for you than dying to prove a point. This conversation is one I've been meaning to have with you, but I never thought it'd take the deaths of so many for me to talk to you about life."

"What do you mean?"

"I mean maybe this is your chance to break free, to get out and see the world beyond this little place. I know there's good out there; I've seen it. It's not all hardship and strangers the way Lynn thinks. There's more to life than a water source, and I've prayed you'd get to see that before you settled here."

"A water source is pretty damn important," Lucy said.

"It is," Vera conceded, "but it's not the only thing there is. Take this chance for what it is, Lucy. Get out of here. Don't live Lynn's way, or Stebbs' way, or even my way. Live, and go find something new."

Underneath the weight of fear in her stomach, Lucy felt a quiver of excitement, something that had long lain dormant. It reminded her of days in Entargo, her tiny fingers pulling back the curtains even as Neva protested, so that she could see the streets below, teeming with people she had yet to meet and the endless possibilities of what could happen that day.

"So you promise me you'll keep your distance from Carter when you're talking, and you keep that promise," Vera said, bringing Lucy back into the present.

"I promise," Lucy said, her voice stronger than she felt.

Vera disappeared into the trees and Lucy stood alone in the dark, her shoulders trembling. A stick snapped and she jerked at the sound, her pulse racing.

"Lucy?" Carter's voice sounded thin and unsure. "You there?"

"Carter?" she called out, and heard the rustle of dead leaves underfoot as he came near. "Over here."

He emerged out of the dark, so changed from the boy she knew that she had to resist the urge to run to him. His eyes were sunken and red-rimmed, his shoulders slumped, and his hands shook as he leaned against a tree for support.

"Your grandma said I can't come closer than this maple," he said.

"I've got a line in the dirt over here telling me what to do," she answered, and he smiled a little.

"That's just like you, to have a line."

She laughed. "We really did it this time, didn't we?"

"And here I always thought Devon was teasing when he said I'd be the end of him."

Her face fell. "It's not your fault, Carter. You didn't know."

Carter slid to the ground by the maple, his feet dangling over the bank. "What's Lynn always say? 'It is what it is'?"

"It is what it is," Lucy agreed. "And it sucks."

"That's two different ways of saying the same thing," Carter said, and a silence fell between the two of them while they both waited for the other to say the inevitable.

Lucy cleared her throat. "Lynn told me about your mom, that she . . . she . . ."

"Sold out on me?" Carter tossed a stick into the stream, and they heard the splash without seeing it. "Big surprise there."

"I'm sorry about it."

Carter shrugged. "Vera said you and Lynn are leaving."

"Yeah, she thinks . . ." She paused, measuring her words. "Did she tell you it might be me?"

"She said so, but I don't believe it."

"Why not?"

Carter looked at her across the space dividing them, his gaze so intense she felt her pulse jump. "I can feel it in me, Lucy," he said, his voice barely audible over the swaying tree branches. "Sick or not, I feel it. And I feel the weight of all those dead little kids on me."

Lucy thought of Lynn, who had held her and sworn she had

nothing to feel guilty about, her own conviction burning bright enough for the two of them. Carter had no one, and she was forbidden from comforting him. The silence between them had grown thick, and she didn't know how to break it.

"So what are you going to do?" Carter asked. "Where are you going? South?"

Lucy shook her head. "Lynn said the only thing we'd get away from in the south is the winters, and we'd be giving up more than that by leaving the pond. I guess a long time ago my uncle Eli told her California is still, you know . . . normal."

"Normal, huh?" Carter smiled and threw another stick into the creek. "What's that mean?"

"Eli told her they'd built a bunch of desalinization plants to make ocean water drinkable, so they weren't hurt bad by the Shortage."

"A drinkable ocean? That's a lot of water."

"And no winters, from what Stebbs and Grandma say."

"Sounds like heaven."

"It could be," Lucy said. "But getting there'll be hell. There's a lot between me and it."

"And I've never known you to back down," Carter said. "The only thing bigger than the world is fear, Lucy. Don't let it get the best of you."

"What about *you*? What are you going to do?"

Carter stood up and stretched, his long arm muscles gleaming in the white moonlight. "Oh, I figured I'd find some old ugly hermit somewhere, spit in his mouth, and see if he gets sick."

"That's a great plan, buddy," Lucy said.

"I had real plans once, you know?" Carter said. "I was starting to think maybe you and me, we could have a little place of our own someday."

"Yeah. I was starting to think that too," Lucy said, tears catching in her throat.

They looked at each other across the void they could not bridge, their silent, saltwater good-byes streaming down their faces.

"You should go," Carter said abruptly, turning away from her. "Stay safe, stay with Lynn. Name a baby after me."

"Shit," Lucy choked. "I'll name two."

"Now that's just stupid."

Lucy laughed through her tears, and he turned around. "Go on now, Lucy. It's not going to get any easier."

She turned and ran through the woods, crashing through the underbrush and into the wet grass that whipped at her legs. The cold night air felt like it would burst her lungs but she kept running, sprinting past the still bodies of the sick.

The four of them stood in an awkward circle as the sun came up. Stebbs and Vera with their arms around each other, Lucy and Lynn weighed down by their packs.

"You've got everything now? You double-checked your bullets?" Stebbs asked Lynn. She had her rifle strapped to her back, a handgun at her side.

"You gave me enough ammunition to kill every stranger between here and the West Coast," Lynn said, hunching her shoulders against the weight of her pack.

"Good Lord, don't shoot everyone you meet," Vera said.

"Not right away, anyway," Stebbs added.

Lynn looked over at Lucy. "You ready?"

"I am," Lucy said. She almost wished Stebbs and Vera had not come. Good-bye had been hard enough once.

"Well," Lynn said, and kicked at a clump of grass, "I guess that's it then." She looked up at Stebbs, and Lucy realized Lynn had not said good-bye to anyone.

"Maybe I'll see you again someday, asshole," Lynn said, and shook Stebbs' hand. He pulled her into a hug and clapped her on the back, careful not to hit her rifle.

"Maybe, kiddo," he said, his voice shaky. "Maybe."

Lynn pulled away from him, swiping at her tears. "Don't let anybody move into my house," she said sternly, and reached for Lucy's hand.

They walked to the edge of the grass together and stepped out onto the road.

Part Two

THE ROAD

Six

L ucy had a blister.

The back of her boot had rubbed a raw spot on her heel within the first two days of walking, a water-filled blister forming shortly after. Every step felt like a tiny needle was driving into her foot, but she gritted her teeth against the pain and waited for it to break. She'd have to say something to Lynn once the water filled her sock, but she'd keep her mouth shut until then.

Lynn had been quiet too; lips still, eyes always moving. It reminded Lucy of the way she'd been when they first met. The tense way she now held herself, the calculated steps, all echoed the girl who had been constantly watching for anyone who would make her their prey.

When Lucy woke at sunup on the third day, Lynn was already

awake. She sat hunched by her pack, the map Stebbs had given her overflowing across her legs, her long hair dragging across the farthest edges when the wind toyed with it.

"What're you thinking?" Lucy asked, propping herself up on her elbows.

"I was just wondering when you were going to tell me your foot was in such a shape," Lynn said, without looking up.

"Didn't want to bother you," Lucy answered, pulling her naked foot back under the blanket. "It's not a big deal."

"It will be if it gets infected. I don't like the idea of cutting your foot off and then having to haul your ass to the West Coast."

"I don't think I'd like the cutting-my-foot-off part," Lucy said. "But anytime you want to carry me is fine."

Lynn smiled but still didn't look up from the map. "We'll rest a bit today. Let me look at your foot. No arguing," she added, when Lucy opened her mouth to object.

Lucy rolled onto her back to watch the sky slowly fading from darkness to a light blue. "What's the story with the map?"

"Trying to figure out the best way to do this," Lynn said. "Other than head west and cross our fingers."

"Can we really do much more?"

"We can look for water along the way and adjust our route to pass close by. Small places, like our pond back home, will be well protected. But there's a big lake coming up here, Lake Wellesley, and

66

there's no way every inch of it is covered. We'll get in, fill our bottles, and get out."

Lucy plucked a blade of grass, pinching it between her fingers and blowing on it to make it sing.

"That's not annoying or anything," Lynn said, still bent over the map.

Lucy tossed a handful of grass, which caught in the breeze and landed in Lynn's hair.

Lynn sighed and folded up the map. "All right, what is it?"

"This Lake Wellesley sounds familiar."

"It's not far from Entargo."

Entargo. Lucy let the remaining grass in her palms slide away on the breeze at the name of the city where she had been born. Despite the few happy tendrils of remembrance that Vera had called to mind, Entargo was a faint memory, darkly steeped in her father's blood. Her parents had been exiled from the city for an illegal second pregnancy.

"Are we going to see it?"

"Do you want to?"

Lucy thought hard before answering. True, there were horrible things tied to the city in her mind, but she wondered how much of the negativity was because of Neva's influence. Her mother had been frightened for her life in the last months they'd lived there, right when Lucy's toddler mind had grown sharp enough to notice.

Even now, Entargo posed a threat. Stebbs had raised the idea of taking Lucy there, but Vera had quickly vetoed it. Anyone going into the city would have their blood checked first, and if a contagion was found, they were quickly eliminated in an effort to stop the spread. Despite her convictions that Lucy was clean, Vera wasn't willing to take the chance that Lucy's body would fall on the same stones as her father's.

Lucy bit her lip as the few positive memories of the city swirled with the bad. "Is it out of the way?"

"A bit," Lynn said. "But I've heard about that place my whole life and never once seen it."

"I didn't know you were interested," Lucy said.

"You're from there," Lynn said curtly, but Lucy knew she wasn't the only reason. The ghost of her uncle had kept other men at bay for a decade. She wasn't surprised that the thought of seeing the city he'd come from mattered to Lynn.

"I think I'd like to see it again," she said, doubt clouding her words.

"You don't sound so sure."

"I know there were good things there, along with the bad. If we're heading west as far as we can walk, I'd like to see it again while I can."

Lynn pulled the map from where it lay in the long grass, unfolding it again to stare as if simply looking at their route would shorten it. "Yup. West as far as we can walk."

"Why not east?"

"A few reasons. One, we don't know for sure of any places set up with these desal plants on the East Coast. Your uncle said before he died that people in Entargo had word that the West Coast had pockets of stability, real electricity even. No one's ever heard a peep about the east. Two, Stebbs says even before the Shortage the east was packed full of people, the west more sparsely populated. Even though it'll be easier to find water in the east, there's also more people wanting it. Desperate people do stupid things."

"Like walk across the country?"

Lynn ignored Lucy's barb as she folded the map again, its creases already fraying into illegibility by her constant handling. "We'll be coming up on Entargo by the end of tomorrow. Now let's see that foot."

Lucy reluctantly brought her foot out from under the blanket and put it on Lynn's knee for inspection. Lynn's mouth went back to a flat line when she got a good look at the blister.

"Lord, child, I wish you'd worn a better pair of shoes."

"This was the pair I always wore back home for gardening. I thought they'd be the best bet. But by the look on your face, I shouldn't ever take up gambling."

"I think traveling agrees with your humor, if not your feet," Lynn said, pushing Lucy's foot off her lap. "First house I come up on that's for sure empty, I'm going to look for a new pair of shoes for you. Boots, even better."

"And in the meantime?" Lucy wiggled her toes.

"In the meantime, you stay put. And barefoot."

"Stay put? You're leaving me?" Lucy jumped to her feet, the tiny bubble of excitement that had begun to bloom in her belly suddenly popping at the thought of being left alone.

"Just for this morning," Lynn said, glancing at the sun. "Maybe the afternoon," she admitted. "As long as it takes to get you some better shoes. You'll be fine. No one can see you up on this hill. There's no fire, no smoke, nothing to make anyone come up here to look unless you draw attention to yourself."

Lucy noticed that even though her words were meant to be reassuring, Lynn made sure Lucy's rifle was loaded. She strapped her own across her back and hesitated before putting the handgun in her belt.

"You take it." Lucy waved her hand. "You'll be going into close quarters."

Lynn nodded. "You're sure you're okay?"

"I've been exiled from my home. I have a blister before we're out of the state. Yes, Lynn, I'm okay."

"Seriously, now." Lynn frowned. "If you don't want me to go, if you don't want to be alone—"

"I'm not scared of being alone," Lucy said quickly.

Lynn turned and loped down the hill to the gravel road they'd been following the day before. Farmhouses dotted the hills and overgrown fields that surrounded them. With luck, Lynn would find serviceable shoes in one that was close and be back before midday. Lucy tried to reassure herself that it wouldn't be long, and that the empty sky above her hadn't grown larger the second Lynn disappeared.

Seven

"Lucy . . . Lucy, wake up!"

Rough hands were shaking her, and Lucy kicked out instinctively, sending the man reeling back. She flipped onto her belly and was crawling for the rifle before she recognized the voice saying her name. "Carter?" she said in disbelief, pulling herself off the ground.

He nodded from the shade of the tree, his hand covering a bloody nose. "Good to see you again, I think," he added, pulling his hand back from where she'd kicked him in the face.

"Shit, I'm sorry." She moved toward him, but he held up a bloody hand to stop her.

"Don't want to take any chances," he said, backing away from her.

She stopped, but it wasn't easy. Her heart told her to go to him, but caution kept her rooted in place. "You still think it's in you?"

"I don't know. I've been picking apart every little feeling I get now. Wondering if I'm tired from walking or just plain sick like Vera thinks. I can't say for sure if it's in me, but I've figured out what ain't."

"What do you mean?"

"Whatever it takes to live. I don't have it, Lucy."

The denial she'd been about to voice died on her lips when she took a good look at him. Carter's hands were filthy, his wrists starting to thin out already due to hunger. The delicate skin around his mouth was bruised, fading to yellow at the corners. And he had no weapon, no backpack, no food.

"Where's your gun?" Lucy asked. "Where's your stuff?"

"Somebody bigger than me took it." Carter sighed, his tongue poking at the bruise by his lip. "Along with some of my teeth."

"You were robbed?"

"Didn't take long," he said. "I started out same day you guys did, going the other direction. I hear footsteps behind me about noon, I turn to see who it is, and next thing I know, my face is on the road. I woke up awhile after, my face damn near boiling from the heat of it against me for so long."

Lucy cautiously knelt down beside him, and he turned his head to show her. Gravel pocked his cheek in spots, melted into the skin. She brushed at it without thinking, and he recoiled from her touch as much as from the pain.

"You shouldn't be near me."

She took his hand in her own even though she knew he was right. "If you believe that, why'd you come find me in the first place?"

"To say good-bye, again, I guess." He shrugged. "Which is plain stupid. We said it good and solid already. I'm just not ready to let you go yet."

"You're not going to," Lucy decided. "Follow us. Lynn doesn't have to know. If you can reach Entargo, there's people there that can test your blood, and if you're clean, there's no reason you can't come with us to California."

"And if I'm not, they shoot me dead."

"Take the chance," Lucy said. "What else is there?"

"Nothing," Carter agreed. "There's nothing for me. I don't have people like you do, Lucy. Vera and Stebbs, they're positive it's not in you, and Lynn's leaving her whole life behind just to be at your side. My mom, she heard it might be me and she wouldn't even look in my face anymore for fear of catching it herself. With Maddy gone and me on my own, I just can't . . ."

Lucy tightened her grip on him. "You can't what?"

"I can't see anything for me."

She tossed his hand away. "So what then, you give up? You're done? You going to find a nice place to curl up in a ball like a sick possum and just die? Even with me offering you a way out? Follow me, Carter. I'll leave food out. Lynn's leading us straight to water every day. You can make it."

"I can't keep up, Lucy," he said, looking away from her. "I can't keep your pace, and you can't give me half your food without hurting yourself. I won't let you do that."

"I don't usually eat much," she said stubbornly.

"You're not usually walking across the country either," Carter said.

"I'm leaving it out anyway," she said, sticking to her plan. "So you can either follow and make it matter, or the critters can have it and I'm weaker for no good reason."

"Lucy, don't do this—"

"It's done. Now you get out of here before Lynn comes back and shoots you."

He placed one hand on either side of her face with a sad smile, and her thoughts raced for a string of words that would make the feelings in her heart and the harsh nature of their world work hand in hand.

But there was nothing.

Deceiving Lynn wasn't an entirely new experience for Lucy. She'd snuck out of their house more than a few times, told small fibs about broken windows, even bailed out of chores once or twice on a whim. But failing to tell her Carter was trailing them outdid all her white lies, and the guilt didn't sit well. But she could bear the burden, knowing the alternative was to leave Carter to die.

Lucy ignored her conscience pangs as Lynn wrapped her foot in some bandages she'd found, padding the heel well before sliding the new boots over Lucy's feet.

"How they feel?" Lynn asked.

"Pretty good, might be a little loose."

"Loose can give you a blister just as bad as tight can," Lynn said, her forehead creasing.

"Yeah, but I need the room for the bandage," Lucy said quickly, not wanting Lynn to leave the camp again. "And who knows how long it will take us to get to California. . . . I might grow into them."

"Hopefully not that long," Lynn said as she lay down on her blanket, eyes sliding to the horizon and the dark clouds piling up above the sunset. "Might rain."

"Feels weird not running for buckets."

"We should set out our bottles. They'll catch something at least."

They piled their backpacks and blankets underneath the spreading canopy of the pine as the clouds neared, flickering lightning licking the edges of the storm front.

"Think it'll be bad?" Lucy asked.

Lynn watched the clouds for a moment. "Not very," she decided. "It'll be one of those that gives us a soaking and then moves on. I should've noticed it sooner. We could've been in one of them houses below."

Lucy slid under the lowest branches of the pine, the needles tickling her back as she lay on her stomach. "There's good cover here. We'll be fine."

Lynn scooted over to lie next to Lucy, her face propped in her hands. "Something's not right," she said, her eyes darting over the horizon. "I don't know if it's bothering me I didn't see that storm coming sooner, or . . ."

"Or what?"

"Or if it's like I feel somebody is watching."

"Nobody is watching us," Lucy said quickly. "There's nobody out here but you and me."

"Maybe. But keep your gun close," Lynn said, her nerves still clearly on edge. "I guess I'll lay here in the dirt and watch the first rainfall I've ever not been running around willy-nilly to collect."

The next day dawned clear. As Lucy dragged herself out from under the pine, she saw Lynn critically inspecting the water bottles they'd left out the night before.

"Catch much?"

"Not too bad, but I think a critter got curious in the night, knocked this one over." She held up an empty bottle. "Not a drop in it."

"Critters, what can you do?" Lucy shrugged, forcing the image of Carter chugging the water, his bruised and broken lips cracked with thirst, out of her mind.

"Shoot 'em," Lynn said, and shoved the empty into her pack along with the rest. They made good time once Lucy had convinced Lynn her new boots weren't bothering her. She regretted putting on such a convincing show; if Carter couldn't keep up with them, he was a goner. They ate a sparing lunch of Stebbs' venison jerky along with some dried peas, their rations so meager Lucy knew the small amounts she could spare for Carter would only keep him alive for so long.

"Do you think we should hunt while we're still in an area we know?"

"Maybe," Lynn said, "but we've got plenty of food to keep us going at least out of Ohio. Once we're low, we can start thinking about hunting smaller animals, something we can eat in one or two meals. We can hit some empty houses up, see if there's anything left in the way of cans."

Lucy looked past the words Lynn was saying and into her tone. "But not yet?"

"Not yet," Lynn said, looking up at the midday sun. "Mostly I want to get moving. The faster we get to California, the sooner we don't have to worry about things like food and water."

"Right," Lucy agreed, knowing full well Carter wouldn't be able to do "fast" for long.

The gravel road they were on switched into a patchy pavement, then intersected with a wide highway with a straight yellow line painted down the middle. Lucy walked to the edge where the grass had begun to reclaim its territory, shooting up through the blacktop and reaching for the sun.

"Which way?"

"If you still want to see Entargo, we go left," Lynn said. "Up to you."

"Let's go left then," Lucy said, and walked onto the road, her new boots clunking against the tarred surface.

Lynn followed, her hand resting lightly on the butt of the gun jammed in her jeans. "I don't like traveling the bigger roads," she said. "Could mean more people."

"More than what? Zero? 'Cause that's how many we've seen."

"Doesn't mean we haven't been seen," Lynn argued, but fell silent as they walked.

The highway cut through fields once sown with corn, now choked with waist-high grass and clumps of maples that had seeded themselves over the years. Houses that had been neglected for decades stood like skeletons, their siding peeling off like flaps of skin to show the framework. Around three in the afternoon, Lynn stopped Lucy.

"We're gonna want to steer clear of that one." She nodded into the distance at a house that looked no more imposing than the others they'd passed.

"Why that one?"

"See the sun glinting off all the windows? None of them are broken. Somebody's living there. No point giving them the willies by walking past."

They veered off the road and into the abandoned fields, going slowly over the uneven ground and decades of brush growing unchecked. They cleared a rise to find the remnants of a town nestled in the valley, the road they had been following cutting straight through it and marching into the distance, where a new sight broke the horizon.

Lynn frowned. "What's that?"

"The city," Lucy said, her heart skipping a beat. "It's Entargo."

"Yeah, but what . . ." Lynn trailed off, her confusion evident. "How come I can see it so far away? What am I looking at?"

"That's what we called a skyscraper. It's a really, really tall building."

"Taller than them cell phone towers we've got out our way?"

"Oh yeah. Much taller."

"Huh." Lynn put one hand on her hip, brows still furrowed.

Lucy tried not to smile. It was so odd to see Lynn perplexed. "What were you expecting?"

"Don't know." Lynn shrugged. "Something more like that, I suppose." She gestured toward the village below them. "Just more spread out."

"There's places that look like that," Lucy said, surprised the memory was still there. "It's where the people mostly lived, the housing areas. But the big buildings like that were mostly for the government, and the hospital where Grandma worked is one of them."

Lynn nodded, eyes distrustfully riveted on the gray towers. "Isn't it scary to be up that high?"

"Not really. We lived in one something like that, called an apartment building. Lots of people live in one, you have your own rooms, but you're all stacked up on top of each other."

Lynn sat down, unscrewed the cap of her water bottle. "You didn't have your own house?"

Lucy took advantage of the break to rustle in her pack and slip a few pieces of jerky to the ground while Lynn wasn't watching. "Having your own place might sound better than living in one of the towers," she explained, "but it wasn't. Mostly the people that lived in the outlying areas were on their own. If you lived in the city in one of the towers, you were safer. They were guarded, always. Our water was cleaner. We even had bathrooms."

"Didn't know you remembered much about it."

"It's hard to forget having a bathroom."

"I have a bathroom," Lynn said defensively.

"Sure you do. Remember what happened when I tried to use it?"

"Lord, that was a mess I did not enjoy cleaning up." Lynn stored her water bottle and shouldered her pack. Lucy took her time doing the same, aware that every second she delayed could make a difference to Carter.

"Still wanna see it?" Lynn asked.

"Sure."

"All right. We'll see how close we get. Somebody takes a shot at us, I don't care how much you miss your bathroom. We'll give it a wide berth."

"Somebody takes a shot at me, a bathroom might come in handy."

Eight

Lucy stood on the overpass, stunned.

Entargo was dead.

"Cover your nose, little one." Lynn slipped her handkerchief over the lower half of her face. "There's no knowing what's on the wind here."

She did as she was told, hands numb. The outer belt they stood on ran above and outside the perimeter of the city, giving them a good view of the streets, empty except for the trash blowing through them.

"Whatever happened here, it wasn't long ago," Lynn said, her voice muffled. "Breathe through your mouth. There's no stench that way."

The rows of dead back home had been burned quickly to ward

off contagion, so Lucy had never smelled rotting people. The smell of death and decay was no stranger; wild animals ripped one another open all the time, leaving behind the bits they weren't interested in to fester in the sun.

But the smell of death rising up from the city was so strong that breathing through her mouth felt like inviting the thickness of the air to gag her. The wind shifted against her back and took the worst of it to the north, but she kept her handkerchief in place.

"What do you think happened?"

"Cholera, I'd say."

Lucy looked at the older woman. "How can you know?"

"I don't see any bodies outside the city; doesn't look like people tried to flee, or had the chance. Cholera will drop you in hours, once it gets ahold. Spreads like wildfire too, so once one person got sick, the people nearby were good as dead. I'm guessing nobody wanted to own up to being sick, for fear of being tossed out, so everybody kept their mouths shut, infected others, then died."

"Lots of things kill you quick," Lucy said. "Who's to say it wasn't polio here too?"

"'Cause underneath the rot, I can smell the shit."

"That's how cholera kills you?"

"Yup. Whether you got a bathroom or not." Lynn's eyes shifted to the rooftops, and Lucy saw some movement there.

"Buzzards," Lucy said. The scavengers of the dead perched along the roofs, lining every skyscraper and town house alike.

"Time to go," Lynn said abruptly.

They walked through dusk to reach Lake Wellesley, the organic smell of the water so strong it pulled them to it like a magnet. Lynn found a spot to camp under a clearing and they spread their blankets, eating without a word.

Exhaustion lay like a weight on Lucy. She had known their trip would wear her down, put blisters on her heels, and maybe even make her be quiet once in a while. But she hadn't been prepared for the deep ache that filled her limbs, the momentous effort it would take to move at all once she'd sat down for the night.

"You should sleep," Lynn said, glancing at Lucy in what remained of the light.

Her eyes snapped back open. Lucy hadn't even known she was dozing. "What about you?"

"Used to it." Lynn shrugged, without elaborating.

Sleep tugged at her, promising a release from her aches, but Lucy fought it. She needed to get some food to Carter. She was about to excuse herself to the woods when a flash of light on the opposite side of the lake caught her eye, and Lynn's head shot up.

"I'll be damned," Lynn said, watching the fire sprout, its flickering image mirrored on the surface of the water. "Somebody else is here."

"Few somebodies." Lucy nudged Lynn and pointed to the east bank, where another bright fleck of orange had shot up, as if encouraged by the appearance of the first. "Whoever it is, they feel comfortable enough to light a fire."

"Maybe that's 'cause they belong here. And we don't. Stay close."

Her hope sputtered out as quickly as the strangers' fires had come to life, but Lucy wasn't terribly worried for Carter's safety for the night. She'd found a few opportunities throughout the day to leave him food, cutting more deeply into her own rations than was probably smart. And now they were at a huge body of water, one other people were using with impunity. He wouldn't starve tonight, and he wouldn't die of thirst either. She would find him tomorrow, she thought, as her thankful body gave in to unconsciousness.

Lucy was surprised when Lynn said they would stay by the lake for another day.

"What's gotten into you? I thought we were hell-bent on California."

"We are," Lynn said. "But I'm curious about those other fires, and what the situation is here."

"You think we could stay here, don't you? We might not go all the way west?" Oddly, she didn't feel the elation she'd expected. The promise of California had seeped its way into her soul without her being aware of it, and the chance to live a different version of the same life—only with a bigger water source—didn't hold the allure she had expected.

"All I think is, this is a large body of water, there's plenty of wood, lots of game."

"So why don't you look happy?"

Lynn rolled up her blanket and jammed it in her pack before answering. "'Cause if things are so great here, how come nobody's guarding it?"

"It's too big to patrol? Or maybe the water is sick?"

"Both are possible. We're going to walk the perimeter, then go down to the bank. I'm going to take a drink."

"That's a crappy plan, Lynn."

"I'm drinking," Lynn said, with finality. "Then we'll sit for the day and see what happens."

Lucy rolled up her blanket, glancing around for any sign of Carter as she did, but there was nothing. She followed Lynn as they picked a path around the perimeter of the lake, her heart sinking.

She had no way of knowing if he was getting the food she'd left out, or if he was still following her. If he was, not leaving any out could kill him. If he wasn't, leaving food behind weakened her and made the road to California longer than it already was. Somehow the ocean had begun to pull on her, as real as the tide itself. Lucy wanted this phantom life that her dead uncle had spoken of, this vague promise that was California. But her past pulled on her conscience, as strong as Carter's body was weak. It only made sense for her to keep her stores for herself, strike west and not look back. But her heart wasn't worried about making sense when it skipped a beat at the thought of him searching for food she hadn't set out.

Lynn held back a branch and waited a tick for Lucy to pass,

but Lucy wasn't paying attention, and it snapped back in her face, knocking her to the ground.

Lynn turned at the sound. "What're you doing?"

"Sorry," Lucy said, embarrassed to have been caught daydreaming. "Wasn't paying attention."

"Might want to start."

Lynn gave Lucy a hand and pulled her to her feet, and they broke through the trees together to the edge of the lake. Lucy's breath caught in her chest at the sight. She could see the other bank but had to squint to make out details across the expanse of water, alive with ripples from fish teeming under the surface.

Lynn was fixated as well, so Lucy dropped to her knees and scooped a handful of water into her mouth before Lynn could stop her.

"I win," Lucy said, through a mouthful of water.

"Not if you get sick, you don't." Lynn regarded her coolly. "How's it taste?"

"Wet," Lucy answered, her tongue curling around the answer as she sucked up stray drops that ran from the side of her mouth. It was cooler than the water from their pond at home and left an aftertaste of wildness. Lucy watched as fish reappeared at the bank after having darted into the shadows at their approach.

"They don't seem bothered by it," she said. "The water can't be all that bad."

"Maybe not." Lynn watched her critically. She put a hand to her eyes to block the sun and regarded the far shore. "It'll be a trek, but I say we walk the whole perimeter, see if anyone has tried to set up permanent."

Lucy scooped another mouthful of lake water, fascinated by the taste. "You don't think we'll find anybody, do you?"

"Doubt it," Lynn said brusquely. "It's too perfect, too nice here for someone not to have set up already. Assuming you don't get sick from the water, I'd guess there's someone watching, somewhere, making sure nobody gets too comfortable."

They started off around the lake, retreating back into the cover of the woods to higher ground, where any permanent residents would have built their homes. Lynn kept a wary eye on Lucy, but she felt fine. The water sloshed pleasantly in her stomach, and she kept glancing through the trees at the glittering face of the lake, knowing something so valuable would not go unprotected in their world.

They found no one. The fires from the night before had been extinguished and stamped out, the burnt edges of the scattered sticks standing out in stark contrast to the green of the forest floor. Both camps looked as if they'd left in a hurry.

"They get tossed out, you think?" Lucy asked, when they stopped to rest opposite from the shore they started from.

"Looks that way. Their fires were kicked around. I'm guessing they outstayed their welcome. But there's no signs of a struggle.

They were told to leave, not made to."

"So what do you wanna do?"

Lynn was quiet for a minute as she watched some fish break the surface of the lake, hungry mouths grabbing for bugs. "I want to catch some fish, cook them over a fire, have a hot meal tonight. And then we'll move on."

"Fish sounds good," Lucy said.

"Slide on down to the bank with me then. We'll see what we can do."

They'd caught fish with their bare hands before. It was a skill that required stillness, something both of them had mastered with the rifle long before they'd applied it to fishing. Within an hour they were both wet to their shoulders and their bellies were coated with mud from lying on the bank, but there was a pile of fish between them.

Lucy lost track of herself while they fished side by side, their shoulders touching when one of them made a lunge for a fish. Her mind wandered away from Carter, the waste of Entargo, even the sick they had left behind them at home. The sun settled on the horizon, and Lynn pushed back onto her heels and wiped scales from her hands, pulling Lucy back to reality. She looked at the wriggling pile between them.

"We shouldn't have caught so many," she said. "We can't eat them all tonight."

"No," Lynn agreed. "But we can cook some and take the rest with us tomorrow. I'm not getting routed without taking something with me."

They made their first fire of the trip that night. Lucy wandered away from their camp searching for more sticks, with the sound of Lynn's flint smacking together echoing off the trees. Her eyes darted in between the trunks, searching for the flash of skin, the bright blue of Carter's eyes. But there was nothing.

Lynn was quiet as well, intent on cleaning her rifle. The fire flickered off the barrel, and Lucy allowed it to mesmerize her, finding solace in watching Lynn's familiar routine.

"Do you miss home?"

Lynn's hands didn't stop moving; her eyes didn't move from her gun. "Got too much to think about to miss anything," she said. "I'll miss it later, when I've got the time."

"I wish I could be more like you," Lucy said. "Not let stuff get to me so much."

Lynn snapped the barrel of her gun back together and looked at Lucy over the fire. "Don't ever wish to be like me, little one. It's not who you are. And it ain't easy."

"I didn't mean—"

"You being like me would be like the sun wishing it was the moon. That's not good for anybody."

Lucy looked away from Lynn, guilt flooding her even though she knew Lynn was right. Lucy had never had to kill, because Lynn kept her safe. She'd often wondered how much of the hardness around Lynn's heart was from her uncle Eli's death, and how much of it from self-inflicted scars. Lynn would do anything for her, leave behind the home she'd killed for in order to give Lucy a better type of life.

Even so, Lucy couldn't help but search the trees in the flickering firelight for any sign of Carter, as if her past were slipping, ghost-like, through the forest. The hope for something better had settled into her, firing desires Lucy didn't know she harbored. The peace of her childhood with Lynn, the warmth of the home, the sanctity of the pond, seemed restrictive now that she'd been out in the world, even for a short while.

So many times she'd snuck out her window into the night, the cold air filling her lungs and the drop to the ground rushing her blood along. Adventures had always called to her as a child, but she'd been hand in hand with Maddy and Carter then, life a waiting surprise and the promise of safety always taking the danger out of their pranks. Now Maddy was dead, Carter was missing, and the intense way Lynn checked and rechecked her rifle reminded Lucy that safety was not a given.

Nine

L ynn could usually move in perfect silence, so the rustle of her return woke Lucy from her sleep. She rolled over.

"S'wrong?" The coals of the fire gave enough light for her to see Lynn jump at the sound of her voice.

"Thought I heard a coyote out there, but it was nothing. Go back to sleep," Lynn said brusquely.

Lucy burrowed deeper into her blanket in search of the pocket of warmth she'd left behind. She was drifting back into sleep when a stranger's voice cut through the night, sending her blood coursing through her veins.

"Hello, the camp!" a woman's voice cried out, and Lynn shot to her feet, knife in her hands.

Lucy scrambled in the shadows for her gun. She found it nestled by her side, the barrel of the rifle warm from her body.

"I hear you," Lynn said into the dark, eyes darting through the night. "What d'you want?"

"Set by your fire is all," the woman said, her voice seeming to come from a different direction this time. Lucy shifted her gun.

"You alone?" Lynn called.

"Just a woman alone, same as you all," came the answer.

"Come on in then," Lynn said, hand still gripping the knife. "But come slow."

A few seconds passed. Lucy could feel sweat beading on her temples even in the cool of the night. She strained her ears for any noise but heard nothing. When she looked to Lynn with a raised eyebrow, the older woman only shook her head. She didn't know which direction to look either.

Lucy turned her head toward the lake and spotted the woman leaning nonchalantly against a tree.

"Lynn," Lucy said tightly, and nodded toward the woman, who uncrossed her arms and held her empty hands out in front of her once she knew she'd been seen.

"I see you there," Lynn said. "No need to play games."

The woman shrugged, hands still in the air. "You said come slow."

"I didn't say come silent," Lynn said, but motioned her on into the camp. Even watching her, Lucy was hard-pressed to hear her movements as the woman walked into the meager light of the coals, her face a calm mask.

The woman was older than her voice. Deep-set lines etched her brow and dug a furrow between her eyes. There were matching streaks of gray running from both temples in her brown hair. Lucy looked her over, fascinated by a new face from the older generation, someone who had known life before the Shortage. Unlike Vera, there were no laugh lines around her eyes.

The woman studied them back, in the moments they had to inspect one another as the fire flickered to life under Lynn's ministrations. Lucy felt the woman's eyes running over her. She dropped her own gaze and felt a flush spread over her cheeks at the close scrutiny. At home they had all known one another so well, no one was ever a particularly interesting sight.

"I'm Jossica," the woman said abruptly, breaking the silence that had fallen. "But my people called me Joss."

"Where's your people?" Lynn asked in a tone that made it clear she was hoping Joss would return to them somewhat quickly.

"They were run off," Joss said. "We made camp on the other shore, night before this. You probably saw the fire."

"We saw two fires last night," Lucy said. "We thought all the people had left."

"All but one."

"They leave you behind for a reason?" Lynn asked, and Joss glanced up at her.

"You can have a seat, and I wouldn't mind if you put that knife down either. You look like you know how to use it."

Lucy watched uneasily as Lynn lowered herself to the ground, still crouched, knife in hand. "What makes you say that?" Lynn asked.

"Just a way you have about you." Joss shrugged. "Wouldn't want to run into you in the woods alone at night." The fire flared, filling the crevices of her face with light and revealing a stunning pair of penetrating green eyes.

"My people were booted when I was out hunting. Came back and found their fire all kicked to hell, everybody gone. World being what it is, I'd rather not be on the road alone trying to catch up to them, and I thought you two wouldn't mind another pair of useful hands."

"What can you do we can't?" Lucy asked.

"I doubt there's anything I can do that either one of you can't," Joss answered. "But a woman traveling alone is done for, and two is only one better."

"And three only one better than two," Lynn said.

"Maybe. But there's safety in numbers, and three *is* bigger than two. I've been traveling awhile now, and I've seen some things." Her gaze shifted away from Lucy and back to Lynn.

Lynn return the glare without a flinch, but she sheathed the knife. "Having you along couldn't hurt, I suppose," she said, to Lucy's surprise. "'Til you find your own people?"

Joss nodded. "Assuming, of course, we're all headed the same direction?"

"We're going to—" Lucy began, but Lynn cut her off.

"We're headed west," she said, silencing Lucy with a glare. "Trying to get away from a sickness."

"Who says there isn't sickness in the west?"

"Who says there is?"

"Life's a gamble, isn't it?"

Lynn shifted away from the fire to move over next to Lucy, dragging her blanket with her. "We're going. And I'm sleeping for what's left of the night."

Lucy bundled her blanket around her and curled into a ball, her back pressed against Lynn's for warmth, their sleeping forms fit well from years of huddling together for heat. The familiar feeling of Lynn's breathing moving in time with her own pulled Lucy back to simpler days, when life was a string of sunrises and sunsets, with long afternoons in between spent with Maddy and Carter.

She snaked her arm out from under the blanket and curled a fist in Lynn's long hair, a habit from childhood. Lynn's hand covered her fingers and squeezed back in reassurance.

"Are we out of Ohio yet?" Lucy sat in the shade of a pin oak, grateful for the escape from the beating sun.

"Not yet," Lynn said testily, the map spread over her knees once again.

Joss sat near Lucy in the shade, her water bottle resting nearby.

She had filled her bottles at Lake Wellesley but had no food of her own. Joss had taken on all the duties she could to make up for her lack; she gathered kindling if Lynn felt safe enough for a fire, and always volunteered to take the first watch. She'd even ventured into the kitchen of an abandoned house and made a paste of vinegar and baking soda that had cured a nasty poison ivy rash on Lucy's arm. But none of Joss' good points seemed to have an effect on Lynn. She'd been quiet and guarded since the new addition.

"Let me know when we are," Lucy said, trying to get Lynn's attention.

"When we are what?"

"Out of Ohio."

Lynn glanced up from the map. "I will."

"Being out of Ohio will be interesting."

Lynn ignored her, immersed in planning their route.

"I've been out of Ohio," Joss offered.

"Really? Before or after the Shortage?"

"Before. I'm not from here, actually. I grew up in Florida."

"Florida . . ." Lucy let the word slide off her tongue. Lynn had forced something of an education upon her, mostly revolving around a musty set of encyclopedias her own mother had stored in the basement. She knew Florida existed, and that it was south, but anything more was new information.

"What's it like?"

"I can't tell you what it's like now, I haven't been back. But I'm sure it's still hot, and there were crocodiles thick as your coyotes."

Lucy shivered, relishing the little chill of fear that ran up her spine. "That would rattle me."

"No worse than packs of wild dogs, I guess," Joss said, watching Lucy from the corner of her eye, with a playful smile. "Crocs are just scaly wild dogs that'll drown you and eat you."

"All right." Lynn snapped the map shut. "Let's go."

"What now?" Lucy asked.

Lynn shouldered her pack and gave Lucy a blank look. "We walk."

"Walking. I love walking."

Lynn rolled her eyes as she shouldered her pack, but Lucy caught the smile spreading across her face before she turned away. Lucy allowed herself one glance around before they struck out onto the road, but there was no sign of Carter. Half of her breakfast lay wrapped in leaves beside a tree, regardless.

"So what did you do for a living, before the Shortage?" Lucy asked Joss, grateful for the distraction of a new person.

"I was a yoga instructor."

"You were a what now?"

"A yoga instructor," Joss said patiently. "Yoga is an ancient form of meditation that uses breathing exercises and holding certain postures to help you focus."

"So you taught people how to breathe and stand still?"

In front of them, Lynn barely concealed a snort.

"There's more to it than that. You could benefit from it," she said to Lynn's stiff back.

"I focus best on something when I'm actually doing it," Lynn said without turning around. "Not standing and breathing and thinking about it."

"I meant more of the relaxation it can offer," Joss said, but Lynn didn't respond.

"If you took the tension out of Lynn, she'd collapse from the shock," Lucy said to Joss, who laughed easily.

Teasing Lynn was something Lucy and Stebbs had excelled at, picking at her serious exterior until they got a smile, or sometimes, an explosion.

"I had a studio in Florida, but I left and came to Ohio right before the trouble started."

"Why'd you leave Florida?"

"Reasons."

As usual, someone's reluctance to share only made Lucy more curious. "Was it a man?"

"Lucy," Lynn reprimanded her from ten feet ahead.

"She's all right," Joss said. "No harm in curiosity."

"So what happened? How'd you make it this long?"

"At first, I was lucky enough to be in a city. When they turned water lines off in the outlying areas, we still had access. For a price."

"I grew up in Entargo," Lucy volunteered. "I didn't know water came from anywhere other than the sink. So why did you leave the city?"

Joss shrugged. "Circumstances beyond my control, mostly. What about you? Why did you leave?"

"Well, my mom—my real mom, not Lynn—was pregnant. Again." Lucy saw Lynn's head shaking at the level of sharing, but Joss didn't even blink.

"Ah, two kids?" she said. "Family regulations got you kicked out?"

"Yup. They made us leave, and my dad was killed." Lucy found the words from her past flowing, offering a distraction to which she gladly succumbed. Sharing an old hurt, long scarred over, was easier than the pains of the present. "I was lucky though. I found Lynn, and she's been with me ever since. So what about your people?" Lucy asked. "Family?"

"No . . ." Joss trailed off, watching her feet for a few seconds before answering. "Just a bunch of strangers trying to keep each other safe on the road. I've got no place to go. I'm waiting for it to find me. What about you two?"

"California," Lynn said, as if daring Joss to talk her out of it.

"Good thing you love walking."

They camped off the road behind a barn with a rotted-out roof, the bare slats home to hundreds of swallows. Joss and Lucy talked Lynn into allowing a fire, and Joss produced a can of soup. She also had a bottle of wine.

"No," Lynn waved her off with a word, but Joss kept the

proffered bottle pointing toward her.

"I wasn't kidding earlier when I said you might need to relax some."

"You two have some, and I'll take first watch," Lucy said, aware that Lynn hadn't slept well the night before. Lynn reluctantly accepted the bottle and took quiet sips while Lucy pumped Joss for more information.

"So people seriously paid you to teach them yoga?"

"What you have to understand is people then had things you don't."

"Like more than two pairs of underwear?"

"Well, yes," Joss said, "but I mean they had things like the promise of safety, the knowledge that food could be had cheaply and at any time, and water at the turn of a faucet. Having all that makes it possible to use your time in other pursuits. You could *want* things."

Lucy's heart skipped a beat at Joss's words. Wanting something more sounded wonderful, but it seemed like a distant possibility in the ruggedness of their world. "And some people wanted to learn yoga back then?"

"Definitely. But you could do other things too: take piano lessons, read a book, play a sport. There's a ton of things your generation knows nothing about."

"Yeah, sorry," Lynn said. "She's too busy gathering water and wood to practice her breathing."

"In some ways, it's a shame," Joss answered, and Lynn buried her response in the mouth of the wine bottle. "Most people these days, it takes all their time just to make sure they live. Before, we threw ourselves into actually *living*."

"Like having fun?"

"More than that. Sometimes it almost made me stark crazy, the pressure of having all those choices. I could've been a lawyer, doctor, bus driver, violinist—hell, even an astronaut. When I was a kid, we talked all the time about what we wanted to be when we grew up."

Lynn wiped her sleeve across her mouth. "I'm happy I grew up at all."

"That's exactly what I'm saying," Joss countered. "Used to be we were raised on dreams. Now we tell the kids they're lucky to be alive. In that way, I do miss the city. There were more options there. You were exposed to more things."

"The city, huh?" Lynn said, glancing up from the bottle of wine. "It exposed a lot of people to cholera."

"Sickness happens out in the country too. You're running from it, after all."

"Maybe," Lynn granted. "But people weren't meant to live that way, inside of boxes stacked on top of each other."

"What were you expecting Entargo to be like?" Lucy asked, curious as to what Lynn's vision had been.

Lynn shook her head, gaze lost in the dying embers of the fire. "I don't know. But when I saw it, all I could think of was the lump your grandma cut out of old Mr. Adams, you remember?"

Lucy nodded. It was hard to forget the cancerous mass one of their neighbors had reluctantly revealed to Vera, a black tumor that had bulged from the back of his knee.

"It was like that, for me," Lynn continued. "An unnatural growth cropping up somewhere it had no business, in the middle of fields and forest, with straight cement roots no amount of cutting will ever get out of the dirt." Her eyes lingered unfocused on the flames. When she spoke again, it was with the tone of voice Lucy knew meant she was using words not her own, quoting a poet long dead from a book of her mother's that lay mildewing miles behind them.

"And in these dark cells,
packed street after street,
souls live, hideous yet—
O disfigured, defaced,
with no trace of the beauty
men once held so light."

Lucy reached across the fire and plucked the bottle out of Lynn's hands. "No more wine for you."

Ten

The road was mesmerizing. Lucy put one foot in front of the other, kept her gaze on the horizon, and never stopped moving. The overgrown country roads slashed across the fields in unbending lines. The sky had been gray since morning, echoing back the colors of the road and just as endless. From rim to rim it was filled with clouds that gave no rain, only a teasing promise some might fall. Maybe.

Joss and Lynn were silent. The air was dense with humidity, stilling even the wildlife. For hours the only movement Lucy had seen was the swirl of gnats in front of her own face, drawn by the sweet smell of her sweat. She trudged on, picking a landmark in the distance and passing it, then picking a new one.

Her thoughts slid back to Carter and Lake Wellesley, wondering if he'd been ousted along with the other people squatting around its banks. There were plenty of empty houses nearby. If he could find a water supply and begin stockpiling wood for the winter, there was no reason why he wouldn't make it. But the hopelessness in his face when he'd last spoken to her hadn't given her much to hold on to. If he didn't want to live, he wouldn't.

The forked ash stick in her pack rubbed between her shoulder blades, reminding Lucy she could have found water for Carter, helped him in a priceless way no one else was capable of. If she'd had the presence of mind to share her secret as they stood saying good-bye in the moonlight, she might have been able to see if his trembling hands were capable of witching. At the least it would've bought her a few more hours with Carter, and possibly a source of life for him.

She slapped at the gnats in frustration, angry with herself for not being quick enough to think of sharing her secret in that moment. Water couldn't cure him of the virus in his blood, but it could keep him safe, and tied to a piece of land where she'd be able to find him again.

And she was going to. Joss' comments from the night before had planted a seed in Lucy's brain that sprouted during the night, giving life to a new goal. If people in California didn't have to dedicate their time to fighting off starvation, maybe someone like Vera had used their spare moments to learn more about the illnesses that cut down people like scythes through wheat. Someone, somewhere, could know how long Carter would be communicable.

And if it wasn't forever, she was going to find him again. If it was true that there were places where she could do more than gather water and find food every day, then Carter deserved to live that way too. Joss had said it was important to want something, and once Lucy had warmed up to the idea, she refused to make a choice. She could have California and Carter both. She wanted everything.

"There's a place coming up called Fort Recovery," Lynn said, using her handkerchief to wipe the sweat from her brow.

"I could go for some recovery," Joss said.

"Too bad, 'cause we'll be going 'round."

"Why are we avoiding it?"

"It's big," Lynn answered. "Too big to not have someone in it somewhere."

"Do you always think people are a bad thing?" Joss asked.

"Generally."

They wandered off the paved road Lynn had been following, veering onto one patched with potholes. Lucy's boots had conformed to her own feet fairly quickly, but the blister hadn't formed a callus yet, and the pink, raw skin still chafed at the end of every day. Picking over the holes in the road wasn't doing her any favors.

The grass grew higher than their heads on both sides of the road, arching inward and brushing against their faces as they made their way west. Trees towered overhead, forming a total canopy that cooled the black tar beneath their feet, drying their sweat. The setting sun burned in front of them, sending red rays into their faces.

Lucy fought a prickle of annoyance when Joss stepped on the back of her heel.

"Sorry," Joss muttered from behind her.

Lucy waved off the apology, too tired to speak. Even so, she couldn't help but notice that Joss always stayed closer to her if they were in an area that was wooded, or anywhere along the road where cover could hide an attacker.

She voiced this to Lynn when she was sure they were alone by the stream they found that evening, filling their water bottles.

"She's using you for cover," Lynn said. "Probably figures if anybody pops off a shot at one of us, they're going to aim for me first, as I'm the leader. You're smaller, less likely to be a target. And she knows it."

"Nice." Lucy capped her bottle tightly. "And here I kinda liked her."

Lynn shrugged. "She's doing what she's done her whole life to survive, that's all. And it could be she just would rather walk with you than me, has you figured for the kind one."

"Right. You're the brawn, I'm brain." She splashed some water over her face and looked down with distaste at her wet shirtfront. "I was holding out hope, but I think I may have to admit that you're the boobs of this outfit too."

Lynn laughed for the first time since the road. "For all the good it does."

Their sounds brought Joss down the creek, water bottles in hand. "What's so funny?"

Lucy glanced back down at her chest. "Oh, I wouldn't exactly call it funny," she said. Lynn laughed again, the sound bouncing back off the water and into the cold, clear night.

"I got some news for you," Lynn said to Lucy halfway through the next day.

"What's that?"

"We're out of Ohio. Have been since we passed Fort Recovery."

"Huh," Lucy said, surveying the land around her. "So we're in what, Indiana?"

"Yep," Lynn said as she readjusted her pack on her shoulders.

"Indiana is awful flat. So what's our route?" Lucy asked.

"Not much in our way. We head due west, and we'll get to Illinois."

"Is it flat?"

"Not sure."

"How's your water?"

Lynn reached over her shoulder and into her pack without breaking stride, pulling a half-empty bottle from it. Lucy was down to her last one as well, the water warm from being carried next to her body. She didn't know how much Joss had left, and their companion wasn't offering up the information.

"Will we stop soon?"

"Soon enough," Lynn said, shooting Lucy a look that told her not to worry.

Abandoned fields that had once been farmed for corn and beans were returning to prairie all around them. The greenness of the new grass matched Joss' eyes and was almost painful to look at as the sun beat down from the cloudless sky. The road was the only mark of past civilization, a streak of black that sliced its way forward, Lucy's feet doggedly eating up the miles it created.

Hours later, Lynn broke to the north, tapping Lucy soundlessly on the shoulder and striding off the black and into the green without a word. Lucy followed, and she felt rather than heard Joss move through the tall grass behind her. On the horizon, a streak of darker green broke the skyline.

"There's another stream up ahead," Lynn said. "Be pretty hard to guard every inch of moving water, and I haven't seen a house for miles."

"Can we stop for the night?" Lucy asked, even though the sun was hours away from the horizon. Supper from the night before was the last meal she could spare to set some aside for Carter. Her knees threatened to buckle underneath her, and her legs felt like lead. Being on the road was sapping her strength in ways she had never imagined. Life at the pond hadn't been easy, but there was always energy left over to spend as she pleased, running through overgrown fields with Maddy or chasing after Carter to see who dove into the pond first. Now only stubbornness put one foot in front of the other, and Carter was the one left behind.

"May as well, but we'll camp away from the banks, and make no fire."

They beat a path to the trees following the meandering route of the little stream, whose water was cold, clear, and unclaimed. The three of them sat in silence on the pebbly bank, Lucy soaking her aching feet.

"Might want to drink upstream from my feet," Lucy advised, when Joss cupped a handful of water. She pinched her nose to illustrate her point. "Just saying."

Joss smiled and moved upstream. Lynn ignored her as she passed, her eyes once again devouring the map spread across her knees. Lucy wiggled a rock with her toe, and a crawdad shot out from underneath, and then out of sight. The stream curved to the south, where she could see a flash of red clinging precariously to the rocky east bank.

"Wild strawberries, Lynn," Lucy said, her mouth watering around the word itself. "Can I go get them?"

Lynn glanced behind her, to where Joss was lying on her back in the shade, arms crossed behind her head, apparently sleeping. "Take this," she said, pulling the handgun from her belt. "And keep your head on."

"Always," Lucy said.

The pressure of Joss' constant shadow lifted as she put space between them. Lucy felt almost cheerful as she climbed the bank and dropped her pack off to the side, in the tall grass. She tied the corners of her handkerchief together, but the little pouch it made wouldn't hold even a third of the berries.

"Guess I'll have to eat some," Lucy said, resigned to her fate. She sat in the tall grass and plucked berries one by one, popping them into her mouth and enjoying the warm gush of juice between her teeth.

Lucy didn't hear the footsteps behind her, but the distinct sound of her pack being unzipped sent her whirling around to see Joss bent over it, forked ash stick in her hand.

Joss looked at her, eyes wide. "You're a dowser."

"Nope," Lucy said, crunching down on a berry and trying to appear casual despite the fear that bloomed in her belly. "I just really like that stick."

"Don't be smart with me," Joss said, eyes roving up and down the stick. "Teach me how."

"It's not something that can be taught," Lucy said, not moving to get up. "The man who explained it to me, Stebbs, he was around before the Shortage. He used to tell people where to dig their well in exchange for a case of beer."

"And how'd he explain it?"

"He says it's not so much about the stick as the person holding it. When the water's moving underground it makes energy, and if you're the kind of person that can feel that, the stick responds to it."

Despite her words, Joss was still holding the forked ash as if she could wield it herself. "I don't get it," she said.

Lucy shrugged. There was no way to explain the feeling when she came across a vein of water. If it was near the surface, she sometimes didn't even need her stick to feel the energy coursing through her body, her teeth ringing. "I guess it's not for you to get then. Why you going through my stuff, anyway?"

"I was going to fill your bottles for you."

"Funny you tossed them over there then, and kept digging in my stuff," Lucy said, pointing to the empties lying in the grass.

Joss ignored her, still transfixed on the witching stick. "No wonder she keeps you so close," she said.

Lucy felt her jaw tighten. "Lynn keeps me close 'cause she loves me."

Joss glanced up at her, through the fork of the ash. "You keep telling yourself that, honey."

Lucy snatched her stick from Joss' hands and gathered her pack. She walked hastily back to camp with the older woman's footsteps close behind. Clouds had slipped over the sky, bringing a scent of rain with them. Lynn had set up camp in a copse of maples that had seeded themselves so closely that their trunks had each woven into another, twisting their bodies together as they reached for the sun. The branches hung low, providing decent cover, and the locked trunks broke the wind that blew the misting rain.

Lucy's instincts screamed for her to tell Lynn that Joss knew she could dowse, but the other woman stayed by her side as they settled in together, all three of them huddled closely for warmth against the cold. Lucy tried to relax as the night wore on, her body drawing heat from both Lynn and Joss on either side of her. She bit her tongue in frustration against the weight of another decision to be made that couldn't be taken lightly.

Because once she told Lynn, Joss was dead.

Eleven

The bodies swayed in the breeze, the tattered remnants of their clothes slapping against their skin. Their faces weren't covered, and Lucy couldn't look away from the nooses. The heavy hanks of rope were buried so deeply in their necks that swollen skin enveloped them.

"Jesus." Joss had a handkerchief up to her nose, eyes watering.

"They do something wrong, you think?" Lucy asked.

"Doubt it," Lynn said, eyes running over the three for clues. "Whoever did for their lives took their shoes too. Must've wanted them pretty bad."

"They didn't have shoes." Joss' voice was muffled.

"What's that?"

"They didn't have shoes," she said, pulling the handkerchief away for the briefest instant before cramming it back against her face. "Those were my people."

"Them?" Lucy peered into what was left of the faces. "You were traveling with three men?"

Joss eyed her over the wadded fabric. "You do what you have to do."

"Don't know what happened here then," Lynn said. "But it didn't happen too terribly long ago. We need to be moving on."

"We're not going to cut them down? Bury them?" Lucy asked.

Lynn glanced at her. "Not today, little one."

They left the road they had been traveling for another that ran parallel to it, Lynn's rifle unstrapped from her back and resting lightly in the crook of her elbow. Lucy followed behind, resisting the urge to touch the butt of the pistol jammed in her waistline. Shaggy woods, dense with undergrowth, shadowed them to the left. The right side of the road was unbroken grass, waving in the breeze. The wind rustled through the trees, and Lucy noticed Joss shift positions to put Lucy between her and the changing shadows playing inside them.

It was at least ten degrees cooler in the shade of the forest, and Lucy felt goose bumps popping out on her arms. The days had been long and each hotter than the next as they walked in their unending line. Even so, the coolness of the woods had her looking forward to the bright streak of sun she could see ahead.

Lynn broke into the sunlight first and immediately stopped, the stiffness in her back making Lucy reach for the pistol. Joss slipped behind her.

"What? What is it?"

"It's . . ." Lynn trailed off, disbelief closing her throat. "It's corn."

Lucy relaxed and Joss let out an audible sigh. "Didn't know you were scared of corn," Lucy said.

"Come see for yourself what I'm scared of."

Lucy felt Joss' hand on her elbow and resisted the urge to shake it off. She walked to the break in the trees.

A vibrant green fanned out from the road in symmetrical lines, marching into the distance as far as Lucy could see. The breeze blowing through the knee-high stalks made more rustling than the woods.

"Shit," she said, all cleverness wrung from her. "How many people does it take to plant that much corn?"

"And how many more to eat it all?" Lynn asked, already backtracking into the shadow of the woods. "We're turning around. Right now."

"To go where?" Joss asked. "To do what?"

"Away from here," Lynn said simply, breaking into a trot and leaving the road for the cover of the woods. Lucy followed, holding back branches so they wouldn't whip Joss in the face. They cut into the middle of the woods, where Lucy scrambled up a tree for a better look.

To the south, the road where they had found the hanged men was wide, and she could easily see it from her perch. No houses were in sight, no community capable of sowing the immaculate field of corn.

"Anything?" Lynn's voice, though hushed, carried from the ground. Lucy shook her head and shimmied back down.

"Can't see anything for miles," she said, once her feet hit the ground. "Behind us there's the road we were on. There's another one to the north of us running east–west we could travel. But there's no good cover, just grass on both sides."

"So now what?" Joss asked, nerves cracking her voice. "What're we gonna do?"

Lynn looked at the height of the sun in the sky. "We'll head north for now," she decided. "Cut across the grass to the next road, and the one after that if we have to, 'til we find something that can cover us better than blades of grass."

"And then?"

Lynn sighed. "And then I'm gonna put you in charge, and ask you a bunch of annoying questions."

Lucy squelched a smile as they cut across the road and into the grass, trotting at a decent pace. They hit the next east–west road, a patchy asphalt trek that Lynn didn't care for. They trotted through another stretch of thick grass that danced over their heads as they passed by. Behind her, Lucy could hear Joss panting for breath.

They broke out of the pasture onto another road, this one gravel.

Lynn kept them to a jog and set off to the west, glancing back to be sure they followed. Lucy nodded to her that she was fine, then jerked her head backward and lolled her tongue out to show that Joss wasn't doing so well. The slightest eyebrow twitch from Lynn conveyed exactly what she thought of that, and Lucy could've sworn she picked up the pace. A splash of gray rock in the distance broke the parade of green, and Lucy called out for Lynn to stop when they reached it, feigning a limp.

"Blister," she panted, holding one foot in the air like a wounded animal.

"Want me to look?" Lynn asked, her voice carrying back to Joss, who had fallen behind. Joss slowed to a walk when she saw they had stopped.

Lucy nodded and sat on the boulder, resting her supposedly injured foot on Lynn's knee. Lynn's quick hands undid the laces, and she glanced over her shoulder to see if Joss was approaching.

"Your foot's perfectly fine, isn't it?"

"Those weren't her people back there," Lucy said as Lynn slipped the boot off her foot.

"You guessed that too?" Lynn pulled off Lucy's sweaty sock and pretended to look at the blister that didn't exist.

"That or they were her people and it didn't bother her at all to see them hanging. She's either lying or coldhearted. Whichever way, it makes up my mind as to whether I like her or not."

"Oh, you can like her all you want," Lynn said, wrapping a fresh bandage around Lucy's heel. "Just don't trust her."

Lucy thought of her ash stick in Joss' hands, the spark of interest that had flashed in her eyes. "I don't."

"Good. But my guess is she didn't ever know those dead men."

"Why would she lie about it?" Lucy asked as Lynn slipped the sock over her toes.

"Remember that time you had a tick above your ear, neither one of us noticed it 'til it was big as a grape?"

"Yeah?"

"Joss is like that, I think. Attaches herself to whoever looks like the best bet and sucks the blood out of 'em until they wise up to her."

"She was left behind at Lake Wellesley," Lucy said. "Whoever she was traveling with had her figured out."

"I think so too." Lynn nodded. "And she was lucky enough to come upon our fire. Now she'll say she might as well stick with us, as her 'people' are dead."

Lucy glanced back down the road, saw that Joss had stopped to pull a water bottle from her pack. "So what do we do?"

"Not much we can do, really. Hopefully something looks good enough to make her want to stay in a town we come upon. Or maybe a group bigger than our own that she'd feel safer with. I've tried sneaking outta camp a few times at night. Woman sleeps lighter than a grasshopper. So for now, we put up with her. She's annoying, but she's not a threat."

The next words stuck in Lucy's throat, not wanting to come out. "What if she were?"

Lynn held out a hand and pulled Lucy from the boulder. "Then she's dead. You might have hem-hawed on whether or not you like her, but I never did."

"So why'd you let her come with us in the first place?"

Lynn took a swallow from her water bottle and put it back in her pack before answering, eyes glued to the approaching figure of Joss. "'Cause of the way she came up on us back at the lake, so quiet and still. I figured she might have something to offer other than creeping. Turns out it's her best quality."

Joss was close enough to make out their conversation, so Lucy switched to another topic. "What'd you make of the field of corn?"

Lynn looked to the horizon, and the black storm clouds assembling there. "Trouble."

Twelve

The rain was falling so heavily that their water bottles couldn't stand up in the torrent, and Lucy ran out to collect them. Joss had spotted an ancient brick house standing alone in the middle of a field, the drive leading to it as full of grass as the acres around it. They ran for the house as the clouds opened up, the fat drops spattering around them as they ducked under the eaves of the buckling walls.

Lucy guessed the house had been old even before the Shortage. The open spaces for high windows, broken now, reminded her of home, as did the plaster walls that were crumbling into dust. Miraculously, the stone fireplace still stood, and the soot traces there showed other travelers had used it as they passed. The flames flickered across the walls in the early shadows that had fallen.

The driving rain slipped through the cracks in the roof, dripping down onto their heads and finding their new place seconds after they'd moved. A fresh drop smacked Lucy on the nose, after she'd changed spots for the fourth time. She jumped up in frustration, swiping at her face. "Dammit!"

Lightning flickered, and she spotted an outbuilding in what remained of the backyard, overgrown by a lilac bush. "Building out there," she said to Lynn. "Could be something useful."

"Doubt it," Lynn said. "Looks like people have stayed the night here before. Anything worth taking's probably already took."

"I'll go check," Lucy said, despite the fact that it was still pouring. Joss sat silently near the fire, her wordless presence grating on Lucy's nerves.

Lynn caught her glance and nodded her assent. "If you want to run outside in the rain, that's your choice."

Lucy picked her way down a hallway where chunks of the ceiling lay on the floor, wet and moldy, finally finding a back door that led out to the yard. Another lightning flash lit up the outbuilding, and she dashed into the rain, shivering as the drops slipped past her upturned collar and ran down her spine. Getting inside the building was not easy; the lilac had hugged it for a long time. Lucy pulled and hacked, breaking old limbs and bending new ones until she could kick down what remained of the door.

More lightning revealed that she'd been right—other travelers had missed the little outbuilding. The walls of the shed were lined with rusty tools, a bicycle with rotted tires sat in the corner, and bundles of twine hung from the ceiling. Lucy grabbed what could still be serviceable—a hammer, two screwdrivers with different heads, and some of the twine. A final flash revealed something piled in the corner that made Lucy laugh, despite the wet clothes clinging to her. She sprinted back to the house and into the front room, her tools and twine nestled inside the five-gallon buckets she'd found. Lynn glanced up.

"I thought the buckets might actually make you smile," Lucy said as she stuffed the twine into her pack. As expected, Lynn rolled her eyes, but the corners of her mouth were twitching as she turned back to the fire.

"That was close, anyway," Joss said, watching Lynn's reaction. "What's so great about buckets?"

"These aren't just buckets, lady," Lucy clarified. "These are *five-gallon* buckets. You wanna carry five gallons of something? This is the bucket you need."

Joss turned to Lynn, mystified. "What's the big deal?"

"Where we're from," Lynn answered, "these buckets were kinda hard to come by. They'd get you all kinds of stuff in trade if you were lucky enough to find one."

"Because they haul water?"

"Haul water?" Lucy said in mock exaggeration. "Oh, they haul water, and snow—which turns into water, by the way, or big chunks of ice—which also turns into water. And," she continued, "it's useful empty. Flip it over and set your can on it when you're done hauling water." She dexterously flipped a bucket, clomping it down on the floor and sitting on it with a flourish.

The crack of the gunshot was barely audible over the pounding rain, and Lucy didn't understand why she'd been knocked onto her back until blood blossomed across the front of her shirt.

"Shit! Lynn!"

Lynn was already at the fireplace, dousing the flames with a blanket and kicking the smoking remnants into a corner. Darkness descended and Lucy heard Lynn crawling toward her.

"Where you hit?"

"It's just my shoulder, I think," she answered, trying to control the panic in her voice.

"Can you crawl?"

The acrid smoke from the smothered fire filled her nostrils and Lucy gasped for air. "Yeah, I think so," she said, ignoring the flare of pain that shot through her shoulder as she followed the sounds of Lynn's movement toward a window.

A clammy hand clasped around her ankle. "What's happening?" Joss asked, her voice pitched high with fear.

Another bullet sliced through the plaster wall, mixing a cloud of dust with the smoke that hung low in the heavy air. Lynn growled at Joss to whisper, and the three of them hovered close to a window, heads below the sill. Lucy barely resisted the urge to shake Joss' hand off her leg, and gritted her teeth against the pain spreading through her arm, like hot needles surging under the surface of her skin.

Lynn rose an inch so she could see through the hole where the window had been, but immediately dropped. "It's too dark to see," she whispered. "And too many openings here for me to cover them all."

Lucy felt cold metal in her hand; the butt of the pistol. "Take this," Lynn said, "and you and Joss find the stairs. Go on up if you think they'll hold you, but get out of this room."

"What about you? Where you going?" Lucy asked, a panic darker than the room sprouting in her belly. "Don't leave me here!"

"I'm going outside," Lynn said, her voice pitched low. "I can't see them, but I might be able to hear them out there without the rain pounding on the roof. If we at least show 'em we've got guns, they might back off."

"And if they don't?" Joss asked.

"If they don't, Lucy isn't a bad shot."

Lucy felt Joss' grip tighten on her leg. "Don't you dare get hurt," Lucy said to Lynn, her voice a hiss over the drumming of the rain. "I'll be really pissed at you if you die."

"I'll be fine, and you've been pissed at me before. Now go on."

Lynn was gone when the next flash lit the room, and Lucy spotted the rickety shadow of the staircase. She began crawling toward it without a word, well aware Joss didn't need encouragement to stay close. The needles in her arm surged with movement, and she bit down to keep from crying out. She bumped into the first step and clamped her teeth as the pain shot through her shoulder, drawing blood from her bottom lip.

She crawled up six steps before the wood beneath gave away. Joss trembled a step below her, tangling herself in Lucy's legs in an effort to find cover. Lucy flicked the safety on the pistol and lay very still. The rain let up, the relentless pounding on the slate roof falling back to a low thrum. A rifle crack rang out, and an unmistakable male yelp of pain. Lucy smiled in the darkness.

"How'd she do that?" Joss asked. "How'd she know where to shoot in the dark?"

"Lynn's rifle is another arm to her. Shooting someone in the pitch black is no different to her from you finding your own face in the night."

Joss was silent after that, as was Lynn's gun. The rain spattered on the roof, its inconsistent rhythm fading into a sprinkle.

"I'm here." Lynn's voice cut through the darkness, and relief radiated through Lucy at the sound.

"We're on the stairs," she called. "You scare them off?"

"Seems that way. Come on out of there. We're not staying a second longer."

Joss and Lucy slipped down the staircase, groping in the dark for their belongings. Lucy grabbed the straps of Lynn's backpack and her own. She could hear Joss moving through the blackness to her right, where she and Lynn had been sleeping.

"I've got your two blankets," Joss whispered. "Can you grab mine?"

Lucy felt around for a few moments before realizing Lynn had used it to smother the fire. That bit of explanation could wait for later. When Lucy tried to lift her pack, the weight sent a fresh bolt of pain through her shoulder, and she cried out.

Lynn was beside her quickly, taking both Lucy's pack and her own without comment. They left the house through the back door. Even though it wasn't raining anymore, they were soaked within seconds from the drops clinging to stalks of grass. Lucy followed Lynn, her good arm laced through one of the packs, while Joss held on to Lucy's shirt. The night was utterly dark, and Lynn didn't move them far before stopping.

"Should be okay here," she said. "There's a little cover, and they won't be able to track us in this pitch."

Lynn grabbed Lucy's hand and touched it to a tree. Lucy leaned against it for support, sliding down to the ground in exhaustion. She heard Joss doing the same beside her, and the three rested against the trunk for a few moments in silence.

"Sorry about your blanket," Lynn finally said.

Beside her, Lucy felt Joss shrug. "It's okay."

"We'll get you a new one once we're back on the road."

"Sounds good."

"How's your shoulder?" Lucy felt Lynn's hands wandering up her arm, but she shrugged her off.

"It hurts," she said. "But there's nothing you can do without any light, and I'm not dying."

Lynn's hands dropped from her, and Lucy rested her head on the other woman's shoulder, letting the panic and fear of the night coalesce into a deep sleep that the pain could not penetrate.

When they woke, Joss was gone.

"She must've really been offended when you burned her blanket," Lucy said, ignoring the cold sweat that had broken out on her face as soon as Lynn probed her shoulder wound.

"Mmm," Lynn said, turning Lucy to get the best of the new morning light on the bullet hole. "Doesn't look like it hit too much important, bone-wise. Here, feel this."

She pulled Lucy's good hand around her chest to put it on the right shoulder blade, where Lucy could feel a small, hard lump resting below the skin. "Am I breaking out again?"

Lynn actually smiled. "You're in good humor, for being shot."

"I don't know that it would hurt less if I complained about it."

"I don't know either," Lynn said, unsheathing her knife.

"Never been shot, myself."

Lucy looked away from the naked blade as Lynn circled behind her. "Seriously? I thought you would've been shot at least seven, eight times?"

"Been shot *at* plenty, just too quick to ever get hit."

"So now I'm slow?" Lucy said, baring her teeth as she felt Lynn pinching the trapped bullet between her fingers.

"Hold still now," Lynn said as she hovered over Lucy's back. "No, I'd say you're more like an easy target, what with putting on your bucket show back there."

There was a flare of pain across her back, no worse than a bee sting. "Just trying to make you laugh," Lucy said. "Dammit! I forgot the buckets."

"I think you did more damage to it than it did to you," Lynn said, holding a bloody, smashed bullet out to Lucy.

Lucy rotated her arm, wincing. "Doubt it."

"As for making me laugh, a few more inches to the left and it wouldn't have been worth it."

"Oh, but right where it ended up puncturing me was a fair trade, in your estimation?"

Lynn shrugged. "It was pretty funny."

Lucy smacked at her with her good arm, but Lynn had moved out of reach. "All right, that's enough silliness. Joss took the water bottles we set out in the night. She didn't get into our food, or the full bottles, because we were sleeping on our packs. Otherwise I think she would've gladly left us with nothing."

"So what's she going to do, you think?"

"We came across people stronger than us, with more to offer. She's gone to see if they'll have her. My guess is whoever was doing the shooting last night is the same people attached to that field of corn. They probably don't want anyone spreading the word of their success."

"Why not?"

"'Cause they'll either want to join 'em, or take what they've got. And they can only support so many."

"What about Joss? Think they'll take her?"

Lynn shrugged. "She's not my problem anymore. We're moving on, and quick as possible. Can you keep a good pace?"

"I can try." Lucy struggled to her feet. "You'll have to carry my pack, though."

"Sit back down, we're not done with that shoulder yet."

Lucy groaned but did as she was told. "What now?"

Lynn rummaged through her pack. "Your grandma gave me some honey before we left, said it's good at keeping wounds clean." She looked dubiously at the plastic bottle she produced. "Better than nothing, I guess." Then she pulled a small box from her pack that Lucy recognized as a sewing kit. Lucy shot to her feet.

"No—no way! You're not stitching me up." Lucy had seen grown men down hard cider and still cry quiet tears while Vera sewed them up at her kitchen table.

Lynn pulled a needle from the box and threaded it. "Trust me, little one, this is going to hurt me way more than you."

Thirteen

The gnats hovered around Lucy's shoulder, drawn by the sweetness of the honey mixing with her sweat. Lucy's right arm rested against her chest, cradled in the makeshift sling Lynn had fashioned out of braided twine. The pain from being shot hadn't hurt nearly as bad as being stitched by Lynn's shaky hands, and Lucy walked with her teeth clenched, focusing on putting one foot in front of the other instead of the burning pain in her flesh.

Lynn glanced back, her own face flushed and dripping with sweat. Both packs and two rifles were strapped across her back, and Lucy knew the weight was tremendous. Lynn had kept up a steady pace nevertheless, checking on Lucy often to make sure she was keeping up.

"How you doing?" she called back loudly, even though only twenty feet separated them.

"I'm shot, not deaf," Lucy shouted back.

Lynn halted and drew a bottle from her pack, waiting for Lucy to catch up before handing it to her. "Let's take a rest."

Lucy gratefully collapsed under the shade of a maple and took a deep pull of water. It was warm, but welcome.

Lynn stayed on the road, wiping the sweat from her brow. Lucy watched her as she shaded her eyes against the noon sun. Lynn's water bottle fell from her hand, turning the dirt to mud at her feet.

"What? What is it?" Lucy struggled to her feet and into the road, where a rapidly approaching ball of dirt barreled toward them from the east.

Lynn tore off both guns, tossing the packs into the high grass and handing Lucy one of the rifles. "Take this," she said. "Go out into the grass and lie down."

"No," Lucy said, voice shaking. "I'm not leaving you."

"You're not going to stand next to me useless either," Lynn said. "You try to shoot that rifle with your left and you're as likely to hit me as them."

The ground beneath their feet vibrated, and the foreign sound of hoofbeats rang through the air. Lucy shaded her eyes and could just discern the riders from the horses amid the dust ball. "We've got time. I say we run."

"They'll follow," Lynn said, cocking her gun and resting it lightly in the crook of her elbow. "I heard horses last night too.

Rare as those animals are, I'm betting this is the same bunch. They either think we're a threat or are under the impression we've got something they want."

Lucy clamped her hand down on Lynn's, squeezing hard. "Joss knows I can dowse."

Lynn's eyebrows flew up. "And you were going to tell me this when?"

"I'm sorry," Lucy said, eyeing the riders as they grew closer. "I never thought she'd use it against me."

"That's 'cause you're a decent person," Lynn said. "I would've figured it right off."

The horses were close enough that Lucy heard the front man shout to the others. They slackened their pace, fanning out to face her and Lynn.

"All right then," Lynn said, eyeing their formation. "You talked long enough to earn a spot here on the road. Things go south, you head for the grass and use the pistol. You're better at short range, anyway."

Lucy only nodded, words stolen from her as the men came within thirty feet, then close enough to see one of them wasn't a man at all. "Damn her," Lucy said at the sight of Joss.

"Don't worry about that now," Lynn said quietly. "You keep still."

The horses slowed to a walk, then a halt, as the five men and Joss formed a line. Lucy glared at their onetime companion, the unfamiliar burn of hatred pulsing through her. Joss only stared back.

"Afternoon, ladies," the man in the lead said, nodding toward Lynn, who nonchalantly nodded back.

"Afternoon."

"It's a nice day for a ride," the man continued, crossing one leg over his pommel.

"I prefer to walk myself," Lynn said, eyes roaming over the mounted men as she spoke. "Like to get back to it, if you don't mind."

"That can wait a bit, I imagine," he said, still friendly, though Lucy noticed he was watching Lynn's hands instead of her face. "We hear you shoot like a man."

"You heard wrong," Lynn said coldly. "I shoot like a woman."

A titter swept through the men, and Joss shifted uncomfortably in her saddle.

"One of my men got a little taste of your talent last night," the man continued, smile fading. "He's not feeling so well today."

"Funny, my daughter took a hit and is feeling fine."

"Joss here says that ain't your daughter."

"Joss say anything else?"

The man smiled again, a cold flexing of facial muscles that didn't extend to his eyes. "Enough to get her a nice safe place to live for a while, assuming the young one comes along without any trouble."

The man switched his gaze to her, and Lucy instinctively stepped back, wishing she could puddle into the ground along with the water at Lynn's feet.

"Sorry," Lynn said, a small smile on her own face. "I'll be giving you trouble."

"Why can't we take 'em both?" one of the other riders said to the leader, but his eyes were riveted on Lynn. "I like women with more hair on them than the dowser has got."

"You keep the blond one long enough, her hair'll grow," another one said, eyes crawling over Lucy's body.

"Ain't nobody taking anybody," Lynn said, her voice dropping all pretense of civility.

"I told you she's dangerous," Joss said, nervously watching Lynn. "Take care of her and grab the little one."

"I like 'em dangerous," the one who was interested in Lynn said, walking his horse right up beside her. He took a handful of her hair and tugged on it. "You're awful pretty, to be so mean."

"I been trying to do better about killing people," Lynn said. "Then fate puts you in my path."

Lucy knew the tone well enough to drop before Lynn's rifle cracked, the shot catching his horse in the neck and sending the animal rearing, the rider flying. The horse fell to its knees, lifeblood spilling into the dirt. Lynn crouched behind its flailing body. Lucy rolled to the side and felt the stitches in her shoulder rip as she flung herself into the ditch and pulled her own pistol into position.

The horses panicked at the smell of blood, and the men fired wildly as their mounts struggled against their bridles. Shots rang past Lucy in the grass, but none came close. More blood sprayed from the dying horse Lynn hid behind as she waited patiently to come up for a shot. When she did, the leader fell, a neat black hole in his forehead.

The rider of the dead horse had been bucked off, breaking a leg. He was crawling east as best he could, trying to stay out from under the hooves of the pawing horses. Lucy drew a bead on another rider but hesitated a second before pulling the trigger. Lynn's shot rang out first. The man fell in a heap, his horse trampling his skull.

Joss was screaming, inexpertly yanking on the reins and spooking her horse more. It bucked wildly, frightened by its strange rider, and Joss went sailing over its head.

The two remaining men fired desperately. Lynn crouched behind the dead horse, squeezing herself into the smallest possible target. She came up briefly, fired quickly, and one of the men shrieked and grabbed his arm. His gun clattered to the road. He turned his horse east, disappearing in a cloud of dust, one of the riderless horses following behind.

The last man tossed his gun down and put both hands in the air. Lynn glanced over the body of the horse, saw him unarmed, and rose to her feet. Lucy emerged from the grass and walked to where Joss lay curled in a ball, moaning.

"Don't kill me," the man said, his voice shaking as Lynn approached his mount. "Wasn't my idea."

"I know whose idea it was," she said, looking blackly at Joss, who cowered under her glare. Lynn sighed and looked back at Lucy.

"Don't kill him," Lucy said. "What good would it do?"

"They know you can dowse."

"I won't tell nobody, honest." The rider moved to cross his heart, but Lynn trained her gun on him.

"I really think I should shoot him," Lynn said.

Lucy glanced down at Joss, who was sitting up and cradling her foot. "Save your bullets," Lucy said.

Lynn looked between the rider and the man with the broken leg, who was still trying to crawl east. "I'm taking your horses," she said. "Pick your buddy up off the ground. I see any of your people following us, you're the first person I shoot."

"Understood," the man said curtly, sliding down off his horse and handing the reins over to Lynn. He motioned to Joss. "What about her?"

Lynn looked at Joss with a hardness in her eyes Lucy had never seen before. "She's staying here. Just like that."

Joss moaned and tried to grab Lucy's leg, but she stepped out of reach. Lynn walked away from the fallen riders without another glance, handed the reins of one horse to Lucy, and gathered the two remaining, walking past Joss as if she weren't there.

"Please, Lynn, listen to me," Joss pleaded, as Lynn walked by. "Don't leave me here. I can't walk."

Lynn didn't answer and motioned to Lucy to get on her horse

as she mounted her own, draping the reins of the riderless horse around her pommel. Lucy bit down against the pain as she pulled herself awkwardly into the saddle. Fresh blood broke through the honey coating her wound, the bitter metallic smell mixing with the sweet tang of honey. As they rode past Joss, Lucy glanced down to see a bloody streak of bone sticking out above her foot, already attracting flies.

"Lynn? *Lynn!*" Joss' voice cracked as she pleaded. "Leave me the horse, at least. You've got an extra horse—just *leave me the goddamn horse!*"

Lucy dug her heels into her horse, and it moved faster, Lynn's picking up the pace beside her. A cry of rage ripped the air, and a shower of dirt and pebbles rained down on them as they rode away. Joss kept screaming Lynn's name, but the next fistful of rocks didn't reach them.

"Lucy! *LUCY!!!*"

Lucy jammed her fingers into her ears and began humming the only song Lynn had ever taught her, but Joss' next scream was so strong she could feel the vibrations of it. They were well past the chance of her hearing anything when Lucy finally uncovered her ears.

"Don't look back, little one," Lynn said. "Don't look back, and don't think on it."

Fourteen

Riding jostled Lucy's shoulder less than walking, and the burn of injury faded to the itch of healing before they crossed into Illinois. Lynn's badly sewn stitches had been replaced with much apology and more awkward stitches, but they did the trick. The horses ate up the miles with ease, jauntily switching their tails to keep the flies away as they walked. They acclimated to their new riders much easier than Lucy and Lynn did to riding. Muscles they hadn't known existed were sore after only a day in the saddle.

Heat and humidity fell on them like a blanket, wringing the sweat from their bodies and soaking their clothing through before mid morning. They rested the horses more often, taking the heavy saddles from their backs and nestling under shade trees until the horses wandered back to them, tired of grazing and ready to move once more.

The steady clip-clop of their hooves hypnotized Lucy in the heat of the afternoons, causing her thoughts to stray. Carter weighed heavily on her mind, his illness and the possibility that he wouldn't carry it forever tucked away in a secret spot in her heart. Lulled by the road, she let herself imagine a future where she and Carter sat side by side on a beach. The feeling of hope that blossomed was always stifled by the midday heat, and the heavy air made breathing feel like work.

The heat was their enemy as much as the men with guns had been. The water left their bodies in streams of sweat, evaporating from their hot flesh so quickly that Lucy swore she saw Lynn steaming at one point. Lucy's mind wandered toward home, where the heat wave undoubtedly stretched, giving the polio that lingered a fresh gasp of life in the hot, heavy air.

She saw bodies in her mind as she rode westward; memories of real ones, friends from home whose corpses she'd helped burn. There were imagined ones too. Her mind played with the possibility of death touching everyone she'd known, leaving Stebbs and Vera alone. They were inoculated from the virus, but not the guns of strangers.

Lynn was silent through most of Illinois. Lucy pretended it was the heat stilling her tongue, but she knew better. Lynn had not killed since Lucy was a small child, and though the act was effortless, the effect clearly burned through her conscience. Lucy stayed small in her saddle, aware that the men who had died on the road would never have come for them if not for her.

The horses plodded on without complaint, their equine noses leading them straight to water. Lynn had worried the horses would prove more burden than boon, their need for water outstripping the riders' and making it necessary for them to stop more often. But the horses had won Lynn over by leading them to water each evening, the prick of their ears and a liveliness in their steps the first indication they smelled something their riders couldn't. Lynn would dismount, leaving Lucy with all three horses and a lump of fear in her throat until she returned to report it was safe.

They could drink.

"You really ought to think of a name for your horse," Lucy said to Lynn, as they rested in the shade during midday.

Lynn lazily lifted one eyelid. "Why's that?"

"Because the black horse likes you."

"I don't have time to spare thinking up critter titles. I've got a lot on my mind. We're coming up on Iowa here soon, but we've got to cross a big river to get there. The Mississippi."

Lucy held a hand out to the one she'd named Spatter as he ambled over to her, rubbing his velvety nose when he leaned down. "How big is it?"

Lynn rummaged in her backpack and unfolded the map. "The little streams the horses have been leading us to aren't even on here, and that last one was a decent size."

The last stream they'd crossed had been deeper than it looked, the water flowing over Lucy's stirrups and to her hips as they crossed. At first the cold dousing had been a welcome relief from the penetrating heat, but her fear had risen along with the water, until even Spatter's long legs were no longer touching bottom. She had felt solid ground go out from underneath his feet as the water buoyed him upward, and the flow of the river had carried both horse and rider southward as his strong legs pumped to get them to the other bank.

The watery fingers of the current had tugged at her, trying to pull Lucy from the saddle. She leaned across Spatter's neck and grabbed the pommel, trusting his strength. Beside her, she could see Lynn grimly clutching Black Horse as well, her mouth set in a straight line. They'd reached the opposite bank wet and frightened, both collapsing in a heap and gratefully giving the horses a breather.

"You don't think the horses could swim the Mississippi?" Lucy asked.

"Don't know." Lynn bit her lip as she ran her finger along the curvy line of the river. "River big as that one is, there's gonna be a hell of a current, so I'd say we both better be lashed to the saddles. But if they got halfway across and couldn't make it, we'd be tied to hundreds of pounds of sinking horseflesh."

Lucy brushed her hand up Spatter's long nose, as bothered by the thought of his drowning as by the idea that she'd be riding him when it happened. "So what're our other choices?"

Lynn spread the map across both their laps, pointing to their route. "There aren't any. We can't go around it, and swimming it is too risky. We need a bridge."

"Bridges mean cities, or towns at least."

"I know, so I've been looking for the smallest one I can find with a bridge near our route."

"You're worried that there'll be people along the river, aren't you?"

"It's a water source, a big one. It's easy to find and's got hundreds of miles of banks. There's people, you can count on it."

"Why can't that be a good thing?"

"How many nice people we met so far?"

Lynn gave Lucy a hard look over the map before walking away, leaving her to brood over the thick, threading finger of blue that blocked their way west.

They practiced making the horses run as they moved toward the river. Spatter didn't do much more than flick his ears in irritation when Lucy kicked his sides, but Black Horse would glide into an easy gallop when Lynn urged him, Spatter would follow his lead, and Brown Horse, carrying their packs, brought up the rear.

"I wish he'd move a little faster," Lynn said, rounding Black Horse back to ride beside Spatter. "Once we hit the bridge, I'd like to be running. Somebody wants to stop us, it's the perfect place. Block either end and we're sitting ducks."

"You could try shooting up in the air," Lucy suggested. "It got them moving before, back in Indiana."

"It also made them pitch two of their riders."

"True," Lucy said, thinking of the bloody point of bone sticking from Joss' leg.

Lynn looked morosely at a spot between Black Horse's ears. "These horses attract a lot of attention. Some people might let two women with nothing but what's on their backs walk on by, but two women with three horses is another matter."

"I'm not giving him up," Lucy said, running her hand along Spatter's neck.

Lynn sighed but didn't say anything. They were traveling along a gravel road. A hulking mass of gray clouds blocked the sun for the time being. An overgrown cemetery loomed on the left, only the tallest of the ancient headstones announcing its presence among the grass.

"How far to the river?"

"Not long now," Lynn said. "I wish . . ."

Lucy glanced up as Lynn's voice trailed off. "You wish what?"

"I was gonna say I wish I knew what the hell I was doing," Lynn said, a slight smile on her face. "But I realized that's kind of a stupid thing to say."

"I'd have been dead hundreds of miles back without you."

"You wouldn't be," Lynn said. "You get a light in your eyes now when we talk about California. You want it, and you'd keep going without me in order to get it. As far as me knowing what I'm doing," she continued, "I'm not so used to being the one on the road, you know? I'm accustomed to being the kind of person we're trying to avoid now. People with things to protect."

"Is it weird, being on the other end of things?"

"*Weird's* one word for it," Lynn said, nodding toward the skeletal form of the bridge, looming in the distant haze. "I keep riding and hoping fate doesn't feel like being an ironic bitch today."

The town on the other side of the bridge was Fort Madison, Iowa.

"You like towns with the word *fort* in them, or what?" Lucy asked.

"I don't like towns, period."

Spatter picked up speed to keep pace with Black Horse. Lynn was leading Brown Horse, their packs bouncing along with her steps as they emerged out of the field and onto the main road. Lynn jerked her horse to a halt, and Spatter fell in beside him. The bridge was a mile distant, the haze making it hard to see more than its vague shape reaching toward the sky.

"All right," Lynn said. "I'm going to get Black Horse moving as fast as I can, and yours should follow nicely. If Splatter—"

"Spatter," Lucy corrected her.

"If *your horse* stops for some reason, yell out. If I don't hear you, shoot into the air. We're crossing that bridge as fast as they'll go. Assuming this horse will mind me, I'm breaking south the second we hit the town. The road follows the river a little ways before heading back west. You stay so close you can grab my tail, understand?"

"You don't have a tail."

"And don't get distracted by the river," Lynn added, ignoring the joke. "I'm guessing it's a sight to see, but you concentrate on staying on your horse."

"'Kay."

Lynn gave her a grim smile and looped Brown Horse's reins around her pommel. "Well, here we go."

She slapped Black Horse's rear, sending up a cloud of dust from his rump and the sharp sound echoing over the fields. He only flicked his ears at her. Lynn growled in irritation and dug her heels into his side, getting a slow walk that kicked up into trot when she did it again.

Spatter jumped to follow and Lucy dug her own heels into him, surprised when he immediately bolted past Lynn's mount with his head in the air, flying toward the bridge at a pace she'd never guessed the little horse had in him. She tightened her thighs around his middle, wrapped the reins around her wrists, and closed her eyes against the wind whipping past her face. Behind them, she heard the other horses burst into a matching speed.

At that pace, the bridge came up quickly, and Lucy ignored the bite of the wind and opened her eyes to see the river. Spatter broke onto the bridge at a dead run, his hooves sending out an echo that rang back at them from metal struts and the endless expanse of water.

At first glance Lucy thought Lynn must have been mistaken. This was no river. Water stretched as far as she could see, wider than any field from home. It had to be a lake, or even the ocean itself. It should have made her glad to see a seemingly endless supply of what so many yearned for, but she screwed her eyes shut against it. The sheer terror of something so large existing in the world she had thrown herself into only made her own smallness more apparent, the very fact that she was alive meaningless to anyone besides herself.

She heard Lynn pulling up beside her, Black Horse's hoofbeats ringing out in time with Spatter's, gaining on them, then passing them, followed closely by Brown Horse. Still, she kept her eyes closed.

When the first raindrop fell on her cheek she cried out in alarm, her eyes flying open. The dark clouds that had hovered all day were cracking open and dropping their burden. She could see the far shore now, and the buildings of the river town they were heading toward at breakneck speed. Most of the houses looked deserted; the empty eye sockets of glassless windows stared blankly at their approach.

Lucy leaned low over Spatter's neck, not daring to glance left or right at the endless stretch of water, focusing only on Black Horse's flying tail and the flash of his hooves. They cleared the bridge and Lynn's horses followed her guidance, breaking to the left and following the river as it flowed south. Spatter was losing ground on the bigger horse, his smaller legs unable to eat the distance as quickly.

Lucy clamped down on the urge to cry out to Lynn. Buildings stretched along her right, more than she had seen in a long time, sparking memories of Entargo. Lynn shot a glance over her shoulder, but Lucy waved her on despite the distance opening between them. There were no signs of life, no reason for concern as their mounts sped southward.

The wet smell of the ground opening up to welcome the rain filled Lucy's nostrils, and she pulled it deeply into her lungs, happy for the reminder of home—a place where she had mattered. The buildings on the right gave away to a residential area with houses set so close to the water, it made Lucy shiver to think of every drop of rain falling into the river and swelling it. A brick house flashed past, and she just had time to register the sight of three buckets set out on the sidewalk to catch the rain as she passed.

Soon the houses grew sparse, and the road veered west again. Spatter followed it, a deep huffing in his lungs giving voice to his irritation at Black Horse for leaving him so far behind. Lucy could see Lynn had slowed her mount after breaking into the open. Spatter pulled up alongside him, and they matched each other at a slower pace, the riders not exchanging words until they were well clear of the town, and the river no longer lingered in the air.

"Well," Lynn said, wiping raindrops from her brow and motioning toward the unbroken road ahead of them. "We're in Iowa."

"Wow," Lucy said, still breathless from their ride. "And I thought *Indiana* was flat."

Fifteen

The heat beat down on them, drawing all their water to their skin and killing the grass that filled the plains. An endless sea of brown stretched to all sides, undulating with the wind and reminding Lucy of the rolling Mississippi, but drawn in dead tones. The horses stopped to rest more often, and their riders let them, their own misery trumping the need for progress.

Lynn slid from her horse and nearly tumbled into the shade of a tree. Lucy followed suit, not bothering to loop Spatter's reins around a branch like she usually did. She wiped her face with her shirt and sank beside Lynn, whose eyes were closed against the unending glare of the sun. Her lips were cracking slightly.

"You need to drink more," Lucy said, uncapping her own water bottle.

"I'm fine," Lynn said, her eyelids not even fluttering. "Right now I'm wishing I could take my own skin off and wring it out."

"I know it," Lucy agreed, wiping more sweat from her brow.

"I'm thinking we might consider traveling at night," Lynn said, eyes still closed. "We'd make better time, and it'd be less work on the horses."

Lucy pulled from her water bottle. "Could we even sleep in this heat? Not to mention anybody could see us."

"True enough. There's nowhere to hide out here."

It was impossible to leave the road without creating a trail behind them. Anytime they allowed the horses to wander into the grass, a perfect line of broken stalks followed them. Lucy pictured a group of men much like the ones from Indiana veering off course to follow the curious path of crushed grass, and finding Lynn and Lucy peacefully asleep at the end of it. Even in the heat, she had goose bumps.

"I think we should stick to what we're doing, for now," she said. "The heat has to break sometime."

"You're talking about Ohio weather," Lynn reminded her. "We've got no idea if Iowa follows the same rules."

Lucy took another tug of her water and held it out to Lynn. "You need a drink."

"I've got my own." Lynn waved her off and dug her bottle out of her pack, checking the water level inside before drinking.

"That your last bottle?"

"I got another." She took a sparing sip and shaded her eyes against the glare of the sun. "We'll be out of Iowa in a few days. Farther west we go, all these little springs the horses keep finding will be drying up."

"Right," Lucy said, eyeing Spatter as he cropped off grass with his teeth, flicking velvety ears when flies landed on him. "We won't be able to keep the horses forever."

"No, we won't. But beyond that, since Joss took some of our bottles, we'll be needing to replace them sooner rather than later. We can't walk into the desert with four bottles between us."

"We still all right on food?"

"We're okay," Lynn said. "This heat has been good and bad in that we're not very hungry, so we're not eating. But we're not eating, so we're wore out."

"What do you want to do?"

"I want to get to Nebraska, find a nice out-of-the-way house that hasn't been raided of everything useful, and rest for a few days."

Lucy shot Lynn a sideways glance. "That sounds awfully optimistic of you."

Lynn allowed a rare smile. "Well, that's the happy version of what I want."

"What's the other one?"

"Get to Nebraska without dying or having to kill anybody."

The heat refused to break, and the miles passed slowly. Spatter's head sank lower as they moved westward, his interest piqued only by the smell of water. They filled their bottles at every chance, drank sparingly in between streams, and watched Iowa slip past them as they kicked up dust on unpaved roads. Lucy's fine hair was coated with dirt, her scalp itching as layers of grime and sweat dried on it. Lynn's own heavy mane was so thickly filled with dirt she would shake it out at the end of the day, creating her own dust storm.

It was too hot to talk, and the only thing to talk about was how hot they were, so Lucy kept her mouth shut and her hands busy putting tiny braids in Spatter's mane as he followed Black Horse's lead. The intricate braids held her attention, a convenient excuse to not look up at the all-encompassing nothing that surrounded them. The Mississippi was behind her, but it had been traded for the vastness of the prairie, a river of grass that seemed to have no end.

Looking at the endless road under the limitless sky drove a spike into Lucy's heart. She didn't matter out here. At home she'd been loved by a few, and known by many. Away from there she could easily drown in a river, or lie down to die quietly in the waving grass, and no one would care. She'd be swallowed by the earth as easily as the rain.

Lynn stopped early one evening when they reached a stream. Her legs buckled from underneath her as she slid from the saddle.

"Lynn," Lucy croaked, her voice dry in her throat. She jumped from Spatter to Lynn's side, but the older woman was already waving her off.

"I'm fine, just tired and hot's all."

"We're done for today," Lucy decided.

Too tired to argue, Lynn only nodded. "Too hot," she said weakly. Her face was pale underneath her tan.

"You need to cool off, right now," Lucy said, masking her fear.

"I'll rest here in the shade," Lynn said. "You get the horses unsaddled."

Lucy went to work, glad to have jobs that would distract her from the unfocused look of Lynn's eyes and the pallor of her skin. The horses gathered around her, patiently waiting to be unburdened. She pulled the packs off Brown Horse and glanced at Lynn, whose eyes had slid shut.

She opened Lynn's pack. It didn't look like she'd touched her jerky since Indiana. The dried peas and corn were barely depleted, and the granola container was full. They'd been taking most of their meals on horseback, and it would've been easy for Lynn to look like she was eating, even if she wasn't.

Lucy jammed everything back inside the pack and walked over to where Lynn was resting. She kicked Lynn's foot. "You haven't been eating."

"I'm fine," Lynn growled, without opening her eyes.

"You're not," Lucy argued. "You can't get down off your horse without falling over."

Lynn opened one eye and looked at Lucy, then closed it again.

"What's your plan then?" Lucy felt her anger rising, all the heat her skin had absorbed coming back out of her in a rush. "Die of starvation halfway through so I've got plenty to eat?"

"The second part, mostly."

"That's stupid, Lynn! Plain, flat stupid!" Lucy sputtered, ignoring the tears that rose in her eyes at the thought of Lynn putting empty handfuls to her mouth, pretending to eat so there would be more for Lucy later. "I can't make it alone, even if I had all the food in the world. I'd lay down and die right now if I were alone. I thought I could do it, for a while, you know? It was like I was going on an adventure, and I could jam all the scared parts down inside me and look forward to the end of the road. But now I've seen new things and most of them bad. Horses bleeding out on the road and Joss' bone sticking into the air when it's supposed to be under her skin. I can't unsee it, and I don't want to see any more."

Even as she said it, she knew it was true. She wasn't like Lynn; she didn't have the courage to face the long, empty roads and the cloudless sky without someone beside her. The loneliness of the country they traveled through had penetrated her, opening up a well of fear she'd managed to keep covered at home. The blank fields, the vast sky, all spoke of nothingness.

"God, Lynn." She choked on her fear as she admitted it. "There's nobody out here."

Lynn lifted one hand and rested it on Lucy's shaking shoulder.

"I know," she said. "Here you are terrified we haven't seen anybody, and I'm thrilled to death."

Lucy pulled her handkerchief free from her neck and wiped her face, leaving dirty tracks behind. "I can't stand it," she said. "I can't stand thinking that if something happened and we died, it wouldn't matter. No one would ever find us, no one would ever know. And we'd lie out here and rot and maybe no one would ever even find our bones. It'd be like we never *were*."

Lynn's hand tightened on her shoulder. "But we *are*, little one. And that makes all the difference, whether people know you're here or not.

> *"I exist as I am, that is enough.*
> *If no other in the world be aware I sit content,*
> *And if each and all be aware I sit content."*

Lucy felt a smile tug at the corner of her mouth. "That's down-right cheery, compared to the stuff you usually throw at me."

Lynn shrugged. "I didn't write it."

"Who did?"

"Walt Whitman. You'd know that, and a few things more, if you could've been bothered to listen to me when you were little."

The extent of everything she didn't know washed over Lucy, as deep as the cold waters of the Mississippi. "I feel so small," she said, her voice cracking. "At home I mattered, but out here—you and I both—we're nothing, and we matter to no one."

Lynn pulled herself up to look at Lucy, gripping her face in her hands. "You matter to me, and even if I were gone, you would still matter to yourself. All that time I spent alone before meeting Stebbs? All I mattered to was myself, and I got by."

"I'm not like that. I need people." Lucy took one last swipe at her face with the handkerchief. "So stop thinking you're doing me a favor by not eating."

Lynn settled back against the tree. "Yes, ma'am. I'll promise you that, if you promise me something too. If something should happen, you got to keep going without me. Joss wasn't a good person, but that didn't mean all she had to say was wrong. She's dead-on right when she says you got to *want* something in your life. Me, all I ever wanted was rain and water, wood to get by, and food for the winter. That way of living is so ingrained in me, it's hard to see anything else. But you, little one, you're meant for more and you know it. You want to get to California, but wishing alone won't do it. It's going to be hard—everything worth doing is."

Lucy brushed a tear away but didn't try to deny the truth of Lynn's words. "Why couldn't I want something easy?"

"Because that's not like you. You've always been fond of the difficult."

"True enough. I like you, after all."

Lynn gave her a halfhearted kick and they settled against the tree together, sipping water and watching the birds fly overhead.

Days later, Lucy pulled Spatter up beside Black Horse, no longer content with riding in silence. "How close are we?"

"To Nebraska? Close. But we'll be crossing another river to get there, the Missouri."

"Is it big, like the last one?"

"No"—Lynn shook her head—"doesn't look to be nearly as big. I think the horses could swim it. The closest bridge to our route goes into a city, and I don't like the look of it. What you said earlier is right: there's nobody out here, so where'd they all go?"

"You think everyone is in the cities? But why would they do that, when there's plenty of streams out here?"

"I don't know, but the more I think on it, the more it worries me. We've had no problem finding water, which isn't surprising. But nobody's giving us any trouble about taking it, either, and that's downright weird."

Lucy thought of Entargo, and the rotted emptiness of its streets. "What if there was an illness like back home and there isn't anybody left in the whole state?"

"Then I'm not anxious to hang around and get sick."

Lucy fiddled with Spatter's mane, her fingers burning off the nervousness that rippled through her body. "This river, you think it'll have a strong current?"

"Doubt it, there's not been much rain." Lynn glanced over at Lucy and her busy hands. "It's not as big, kiddo. It won't make you feel so small."

Lucy looked at her fine-boned fingers as she picked a knot from Spatter's mane. "Doesn't take much," she said.

Black Horse picked up his pace, and Spatter jogged to keep up, making her drop his mane for the reins. "The horses smell it."

They rode on, until the Missouri was spread before them like a silver ribbon coursing through the land. It was not nearly the size of the Mississippi, and Lucy's breath left her in a wave of relief. They let the horses drink first and rest in the shade of the trees growing by the bank. The women filled their bottles as well, dousing their hair and drenching their shoulders before refilling for the road.

"C'mere, Mister," Lynn said gruffly, pulling on Black Horse's reins.

"Mister?" Lucy teased. "Your great affection for him is showing."

Lynn surprised her by rubbing him between the ears after swinging up into the saddle. "He's not a bad animal," she said brusquely, and urged him out into the water.

Spatter followed, and the cold water filled Lucy's boots, sliding wet fingers up through her pants and soaking her legs in seconds. Her teeth chattered, despite the heat. When Spatter's legs left the river bottom her stomach churned, lurching along with the current that pulled him southward. She closed her eyes and clenched one fist around the pommel, the other tightly woven in Spatter's mane.

The water flowed over her, much colder than the pond at home.

She didn't open her eyes until his forelegs hit dry ground. Lynn was astride the newly christened Mister, her pride in him overflowing into a neck rub.

"Welcome to Nebraska, little one."

Sixteen

What Lucy would remember most about Nebraska was the graveyards. Some had stood before the Shortage, others were newer. The grass had succumbed to the heat and lack of rain, falling over on brittle stalks and leaving tombstones visible across the flat plains for miles. The few houses they saw Lynn did not trust, and they sought out graveyards for rest, the hulking stones offering more cover from roving eyes than the solitary trees that stood alone on the plains.

Lynn did not rest easy, and although Lucy watched her fastidiously to be sure she was eating and drinking, there was no way to force her to sleep. They kept their guns at the ready, not daring to use them to hunt, as there was nothing to stop the crack of their rifles from rolling across the empty land, into the ears of whoever might be out there.

The emptiness pulled at Lucy, as it had in Iowa. The dark fear that they were the only two people left on earth niggled at her brain, teasing her with the idea that when they reached California it would be no different; the desal plants they were so desperate to find would stand empty, Lucy and Lynn clueless as to their operation.

Halfway through Nebraska she woke from one such nightmare, an image of the ocean stretching into eternity and the empty beach beside it still imprinted on her eyes. Sweat dripped from her forehead, even though the nights had been tolerably cool. She sat up, pulling her drenched shirt away from her body and resting her head against the white marble stone she'd set her pack beside before lying down.

"You all right?" Lynn asked, her voice floating in the pitch black of the moonless night.

"Yeah. Bad dream."

There was a rustling noise, and Lynn appeared beside her, out of the darkness. "Seems like you've been having a lot of those lately."

"Depends," Lucy said. "Not sure sleeping in graveyards helps much."

"Why's that?"

"Well, because . . ." Lucy searched for an answer that would make sense to practical Lynn. "We're sleeping on top of dead people."

"I don't think they mind."

Lucy sighed. "It doesn't bother you at all?"

"Not really. For all you know we've slept on top of unmarked graves many nights and never felt the different for it."

The idea of a body lost in the dirt, not even recognized by a stone above its head, sent Lucy's mind down paths she didn't want to explore. "Never mind," she said. "I'm going back to sleep."

She closed her eyes, barely able to tell the difference from the pitch black of the night. Sleep was fraying the edges of her consciousness when Lynn spoke again.

"It helps if you look at the stones," she said so quietly, Lucy wasn't sure she was supposed to hear. "This graveyard is an old one. Some of the stones are smooth as river rocks."

"What do you mean it helps?" Lucy rolled over, toward the sound of Lynn's voice.

"I was looking at 'em, earlier. You'd already drifted off, so I walked among the stones for a bit. There's a section that's older than the others. Most of the stones are fallen down or worn away, but you can still read some. Those people, they lived a long time ago, but their lives weren't so different from what you and I are living right now."

"Poor bastards," Lucy said, and Lynn snorted.

"It made me think though, about what you said in Iowa—the emptiness of it all. You're right, there aren't many people. I was looking at those old stones, and there was this one woman, buried with her children. By the dates, she wasn't much older than me, but it seems she lost five little ones before she died herself."

"Five?"

"Yeah. Made me think, there's probably people like that now too. Going through the hell of delivering five babies just to lose them all and die."

"Not sure how looking at the most depressing stones you could find is helpful."

"Reminds me of how important it is to keep going, that you're what's mine to protect and keep safe."

A lump formed in Lucy's throat, making her voice thick when she spoke. "You never wanted any of your own?"

"No," Lynn said. "I'd think about it, but then poor Myrtle would go and get pregnant again and I'd see her so big and awkward, she couldn't even get her own firewood. I need my body to do the things I ask it to, and not struggle to do them. And besides, I'm not made for it."

"What do you mean, not made for it? You're a great mom to me."

"Sure, and when I got you, you were half-raised already, determined to do everything on your own and not ask for help. You weren't hard to mother 'til you got older and didn't listen anymore."

"I listen," Lucy said indignantly.

"If you agree with what I'm saying. Mother used to tell me I should be careful, 'cause I'd get a kid same as me someday and pull my own hair out over it. I'm sure you'll get yours one day."

Lucy thought of what Carter had said to her about naming a baby after him, and the lump came back in her throat. "I guess maybe I will."

"You will," Lynn said, with conviction. "You had it about you, even when you were a little one yourself. Red Dog had more mothering than he could stand, and you brought me any injured animal you found, determined to save it."

A smile fought against the lump for control of her voice as Lucy spoke. "Remember the baby skunks?"

Lucy didn't need to see in the dark to know Lynn had rolled her eyes. "Do I ever." They giggled together in the night, the high sounds echoing off the stones around them.

"Anyway," Lynn went on, "what I'm saying is, I don't mind sleeping in the cemeteries 'cause it's a reminder of the generations before, without which we wouldn't be here."

"And without us, there wouldn't be anyone to look back a hundred years from now," Lucy finished.

"Without *you*," Lynn corrected. "You're the one of us that's going to have babies. You've got the temperament for it, and you've not killed."

"What's that got to do with it?"

A long silence stretched out over the tombstones. When Lynn finally spoke, Lucy could hear the tightness of her throat echoed in her voice. "Once you've done that, taken a life someone worked hard to bring about, it sticks with you. Stays close in a dark place you can't quite shake. It's in my blood, and it's not something I want to pass on."

"So it's on me to keep the human race going," Lucy said lightly. "Could you do me a favor and not announce this to every boy we meet?" Beside her, she felt Lynn's silent laugh and the tension that slipped out of her with it. "What's your responsibility then?"

"To protect you, always."

They found each other's hands in the dark, and an angel with chipped marble wings watched over them as they slept.

They found a house on the western edge of Nebraska, just as the gray haze of the mountains made their presence known on the horizon. Lucy had been watching the approaching smear for days, thinking a storm had not quite reached them yet, before Lynn corrected her. The thought of something so massive it could be seen a state away left Lucy quiet and concerned.

The house was a relief, so similar to Lynn's yearnings spoken in Iowa that it seemed it might have grown from the ground on account of her wishes and waited for them to reach it.

It was small, untouched, and close to freshwater. They circled it twice on horseback from a distance, guns drawn and eyes searching for flashes of movement. Lynn and Lucy shared a silent look and moved closer warily, but their caution was unnecessary. It was empty, and the dust they found on the countertop was deep.

Lucy stood on the porch where the horses were tethered, her eyes drawn to the distant mountains, the gnawing worry they caused in her belly distracting her from the happiness she should have felt at the promise of rest. She heard cupboard doors opening, and Lynn joined her outside, a can of corn in her hand.

"The kitchen is even full," she said. "I can't hardly believe it."

"Careful what you say," Lucy answered. "You might wish it away."

"It kinda seems that way, doesn't it? Like what I wanted happened to fall into our path?" Lynn tossed the can from hand to hand.

Lucy deftly caught it in between tosses. "You should have specified creamed corn, and I'd like the creek to move a little closer to the house."

"Yeah, I'd like that too," Lynn said, looking to the north, where the strip of trees announcing the creek's presence was barely visible on the horizon.

A hot wind blew in their faces, bringing with it a smattering of dirt that settled on Lucy's skin. "You didn't happen to wish up a bit of shampoo in that bathroom, did you?"

"I wouldn't be surprised if I did," Lynn said. "I doubt anybody came through here and took the shampoo but left the corn."

There was shampoo, and soap, and even washcloths so soft when Lucy pressed them to her cheek, a memory from childhood flashed so brightly she had to sit down to shake it off. She saw Neva, her long-dead mother, smiling and plastering a wet washcloth to Lucy's pudgy toddler belly, tickling her through the softness. Lucy gasped for breath, still clutching the washcloth to her face and waiting for more.

But none came.

That night they were clean and full of a hot meal for the first time in a long while, and Lucy felt a happiness that even the rising mountains in the west couldn't overshadow. Lynn sat with her on the porch and they watched the stars come out, like pinpricks in the black fabric of the sky. The horses grazed in the yard, their calm mutterings carried to the women on the breeze.

"How far back do your memories go?" Lucy asked suddenly.

"What's that?" Lynn lifted her head from against the post she'd been resting against.

"What's the earliest memories you have, from when you were a kid?"

"I'd have to think about it. It's hard to know sometimes what's real and what's my mind filling in blanks with stories I've been told."

"What do you mean?"

"Well," Lynn said slowly, "Mother was the only person I knew for a good long while. We had to work hard to get things done, and what little time there was together she was pushing me for something else. Like during the winters we'd be in the basement for hours, her teaching me to read when I was little, then memorizing poetry as I got older. Stebbs told me a few stories from before the Shortage, about how Mother looked or acted, that are nicer versions of her, with less worries. Some of those memories I can't help but wonder if my mind is changing it so I remember good things that didn't actually happen."

"So how do you know what's real and what's something you made up?"

Lynn shrugged. "I guess you don't. In the end I know Mother did what she thought was best when it came to raising me. If what I remember fits into that idea of Mother, it's probably true. Why you asking me this?"

"No reason," Lucy said, picking up a stone and flinging it into the night.

"Liar," Lynn said. "Out with it now."

"I don't want you to think . . ."

"If it's something you remembered about your mom, you go ahead and say. It won't hurt my feelings. I'm good at pretending I don't have those, anyway."

"Okay." Lucy took a deep breath. "Certain things will cause a memory to come rushing at me, and I don't know if it's because I need to know she loved me and I'm making it up, or if it really happened."

"I can't tell you whether your memories are true or not, but your mother loved you, very much."

"But she left me," Lucy said, her voice catching in her throat and barely clearing her teeth. "She knew she wouldn't ever see me again when she shot herself."

Lynn was quiet for a long time, long enough for more stars to blaze up and make themselves known. "That was a dark day."

"I know it," Lucy said, trying to ignore the tears creeping down her face. "Grandma told me about how I was sick, and the men from the south traded her for my mom, and my mom went with them because she thought I would die without Grandma to doctor me."

"And you would have, little one. There was nothing I knew to do for you, and your uncle and Stebbs were lost thinking you would be taken from them. Vera saved you, like none of us could have."

"But she didn't have to kill herself!" Lucy cried out, giving vent for the first time to the anger she hadn't known was inside her. "You could have gotten her back from those men."

"Maybe," Lynn admitted. "But maybe by the time I did, the things that had been visited upon her would've changed her for good and forever, and she'd have been no kind of mother to you."

"She could've tried harder," Lucy said. "Held on a little longer."

"Sure. And if Stebbs had shot a little sooner at the man holding a gun on your uncle, I'd have my own babies. But that's life, little one—lots of little *maybes* and *what ifs* all lined up in a row. And if you put your mind to following some of them that never came about, you'll get lost and not find your way back to the way it really is."

"The way it really is sucks."

"It can, from time to time," Lynn agreed. "But there's good things too. Your mom dying means I got to have you, and your uncle dying means you've got me all to yourself."

Lucy scooted across the porch to lean against Lynn, resting her head on the older woman's shoulder and inhaling the clean smell of her hair. "And me losing everybody makes me scared of losing you."

Lynn slipped an arm around her, the strength of it buoying Lucy's spirits. "That goes for both of us, little one."

Seventeen

It really would have been nice to have the creek a little closer, in Lucy's opinion, but she wasn't being picky after the long, dry stretches they'd seen the end of. Perhaps for good. It hadn't escaped her how comfortable Lynn had become with the little house in the week they'd been there. More than once, small comments had trickled out of the older woman that seemed to be her way of feeling out Lucy's opinion without asking for it.

Lynn had always been difficult to read, and more so now that their survival depended on her choices. Continuing to California meant the mountains, and the looming threat of the desert beyond. Staying meant trusting the little creek would never run dry, the winters never cold enough to require more than burning scrub brush to keep them from freezing.

Lucy faced a battle of logic and emotion. The promise of California, and a life less ordinary, was to the west. The possibility of salvation for Carter demanded she continue. But the gray ridge of the mountains that sliced through the map was a weight on her heart, an obstacle to be met. She knew that Lynn was waiting on her to make the call. If she chose to push on, the responsibility for both their lives lay on her.

The creek stayed clear, if not deep, and the wind was warm. Lucy watched as the wind ran its fingers through Lynn's loose hair one day as they went in search of the stream's source. To the west, thunderheads were piling, creating their own impressive mountain range in the sky. Lucy snuck a glance at Lynn.

"I see it," Lynn said. "If it behaves anything like that last storm, we don't have time to make it back to the house. We'll head for the creek and try to find some decent shelter beneath a tree."

Lucy nodded, her thoughts still tangled in themselves.

"In the meantime," Lynn said as she turned Black Horse's head, "I wouldn't mind you letting me in on what's going on in your skull."

"So that you can figure out what to do?"

"More or less. If you're set on staying, we need to gather wood, stockpile food. Wouldn't hurt to set aside as much water as possible. We don't know how reliable this stream is, year round."

"In other words—same life, flatter scenery."

Lynn didn't say anything, and Lucy shot her a glance. "I didn't mean anything by that."

Lynn shrugged. "Sure you did. And you're right. No, your life wouldn't be any different than mine was. Same worries, but with the same satisfactions, too. A place you call your own, to guard and to keep."

"All alone on the prairie," Lucy finished for her.

"You make that sound like a bad thing."

"It is a bad thing, to me!" Lucy said, violently enough that Spatter turned his head to see what was the matter. "I want to be with people, Lynn. I know you don't understand that, but . . ."

"Spit it out."

Lucy felt as if her feelings were roiling in her gut, spilling out in a tide that found a form in words and made her decision for her before she knew it had been made. "I got this feeling, like we talked about the other night. I got this *what if* deep down inside me. If I don't go all the way, if I settle for what we have here, I'll never know what I could've been."

Lynn rode quietly for a few minutes, digesting what Lucy had said. "Well, you have to want something, right? Your momma said once that when you go, you go big. I guess I signed up for this a long time ago without knowing it."

"If you don't want to, Lynn, I can't ask you to—"

"Shut it, I'm going. You want this, right down to your marrow.

All I ever wanted was a rainfall and to live to see the sunrise. I had those, and plenty of times over. Now it's your turn, and I'm with you to the end."

The sky broke around them, the rain masking the tears that ran out of Lucy's eyes at the relief of having made her decision, and the fact that she didn't have to go it alone. Lynn gave Black Horse a solid kick, and he took off for the stream, Spatter racing to keep up. The horses hit the bank and skidded to a halt in the mud. The women dismounted and clustered under the tree, pulling their mounts in with them as far as they could.

The smell of warm, wet horse filled her nose, and Lucy nuzzled Spatter's velvety muzzle. He pushed back against her with a contented grunt and Lucy laughed, but an unfamiliar voice carried on the wind and she fell silent. The look in Lynn's eyes said that she heard it too. She motioned to Lucy, and they slid down the bank to glance downstream.

A bedraggled woman was hunched under a scrubby tree, yelling ineffectually at her children to get out of the creek before the rains made it swell. But the two kids, scrawny yet smiling, were splashing each other without a care in the world.

Lucy knelt near the ground next to Lynn. "What're we gonna do?"

Lynn sighed heavily. "What I always do when I find needy children in creek beds."

The children squealed and ran to the mother as Lucy and Lynn approached, arms in the air to signal they meant no harm. The woman watched them warily, one arm wrapped around each child's head as though her flesh and bone could protect them.

"We're not hurting anybody," she said nervously. "We come to this here crick every now and then for a washing and a taste of water."

"We're not here to fight over water," Lynn said.

"Bullshit," said a man's voice from behind them, and Lucy spun on her heel to see a painfully thin man watching them. Even unarmed it was clear he'd take his chances against them with his bare hands if he thought they would hurt his family. "Everybody fights for water."

"Not us," Lucy said. "It's not our way."

"Then you ain't lived long enough yet," he said to her, then turned his gaze to Lynn. "You've fought for it though. I can see it in you."

"Once or twice," Lynn said steadily. "But not today."

The storm let loose all around them, the wall of rain they had watched leave the mountains overtaking them in a torrent. One of the children whimpered behind them and the woman shushed it, still clutching them tightly to her. "I don't think they mean no harm, Jeff," she said, raising her voice to be heard. "They could've had the better of me 'n' the kids in a heartbeat, but they didn't take it."

"I was watchin'," Jeff said. "Wasn't nothing gonna happen to you and the kids."

"Nothing but pneumonia," she shot back, scooting farther up the bank and against a tree trunk, vainly searching for more cover.

"We've got a house," Lucy said, still facing the man but aiming her words over her shoulder at the drenched mother. "Plenty of food, real beds, a fire to dry yourselves out by."

"Food, Mama," the little girl said, her high voice rising above the drone of the storm. "Food."

"We're going to head on back home," Lynn said slowly. "If anybody here is interested in our offer, you feel free to follow." She nudged Lucy and they turned their backs on the family, ignoring the muted argument that sprouted behind them before they were two steps away.

"Think they'll come?" Lucy asked under her breath as they cleared the canopy of the trees into the full brunt of the storm.

"She will, and she'll bring the children. Him, I can't say."

"I bet he does," Lucy said, thinking of the glances that had passed back and forth over her shoulder, the communication the couple had built over years in each other's presence. "He cares about her, couldn't you see it?"

"I saw a desperate man with no weapons trying to protect an underfed woman and two skinny kids. She better hope he cares for her, 'cause his life would be a lot easier without them."

Lucy broke into a trot to keep up with Lynn. "Is that how you feel? That your life would be easier?"

"Maybe, but it also would've been less interesting." They hit the front porch together, pulling wet clothes away from their skin and peering through the rain.

"Well, I'm glad I could entertain you all these years," Lucy said.

Lynn's sigh was loud enough to be heard over the pounding of the rain on the porch roof. "Yeah, kid, that's it. I took you in because I thought you could give me something to do in all my spare time."

"Why then?" Lucy asked.

"Why you asking me this all of a sudden?"

"Well . . . I . . ." Lucy's voice trailed off as she looked to the east, anxious to spot the dark shadows of the small family finding their way to them. "I guess it never really occurred to me before. You're pretty much all I remember. I grew up thinking that's the way things were—I lived with you, Grandma lived with Stebbs, Maddy and Carter lived with their mom. I never really considered the fact you had a choice in the matter."

Lynn focused her eyes on the horizon, away from Lucy. "My mother had a choice too. There are things women can do to be rid of babies they don't want before they even come to be. Even once I was here, all she'd had to do was walk out to the pond and toss me in it, no one to know the better. One woman, two lives to manage, and everything falling apart all around her. But she did it, and she never said a sideways word to me on the matter. And I did it for you, and I'll keep doing it 'til one of us is gone. In a world like this, you pay it forward, 'cause more than likely you didn't deserve it when you got it the first time."

As Lynn's words faded away, the storm lessened and Lucy spotted four figures slogging toward them in the gray haze of the evening. "Pay it forward, huh?"

Lynn shrugged. "Well, that, and I do kind of like you every now and then."

They left in the dark hours before dawn, sliding between the children's clothing that hung from the rafters, dry but still smelling of rain. The woman was sleeping in the corner, curled protectively around her children even when unconscious. The man sat at the table, slumped forward. They'd left him crumpled there after he'd fallen asleep at his watch, determined there must be some foul trick yet to come that he would protect his family from despite his fatigue. The exhaustion had won out only an hour before, and Lynn and Lucy packed their things quietly, easing the door open only as far as necessary for them to slip outside and find the road again.

Eighteen

The road welcomed them back by laming Brown Horse south of the Kansas border. The land had become unruly, and while the flat plains of Nebraska had frightened Lucy with their unending stretch, the Kansas badlands had her clutching tightly to Spatter's reins, willing him not to break a leg. The horses stayed near a meandering river called the Arikaree that carved its way through the hills, leaving a thin gouge through the land.

Lynn stood by a patch of yucca, inexpertly holding Brown Horse's injured hoof in her hands. "I don't even know what I'm looking for."

Lucy scratched Spatter's nose as he brushed up against her, nuzzling her clothes for the spears of yucca she had hidden in her pockets. "Do you know for sure it's her foot that's hurt? Could it be her leg?"

"Your guess is as good as mine," Lynn said, carefully putting Brown Horse's hoof down and giving the animal a halfhearted pat on the rump. "Even if I knew what was wrong with her, I wouldn't know how to fix it."

"These hills won't do her any favors either," Lucy said, looking out over the rolling land that undulated like sheets on the line in a breeze.

Lynn nodded her agreement. "Only thing I can think to do is let her stand in the water awhile. I know I welcome a good soak when my feet hurt."

Lynn's aversion to traveling alongside the waterways had been overrun by the horses' refusal to leave the path of the Arikaree. More than once they'd fought against their riders' commands, and neither woman was sure enough on horseback to argue with them. The horses had won the day, and Lynn had grudgingly admitted it might have been the best route anyway, as the river they were following would take them nearly halfway through Colorado and in sight of the mountains.

Lynn unburdened Brown Horse and led her down the steep gorge into the flowing river, Mister following her lead. Spatter flicked his ears at his comrades, then looked to Lucy as if in question.

"I know," she said, "it's not like Lynn to go on down to the water without checking for people first, is it? I think your friends might be growing on her. Next thing you know she'll be skinny-dipping."

Spatter snorted.

Brown Horse and Mister seemed content to wade in the shallows near the bank while Spatter stuck by Lucy's side, following her into the shade provided by the wall of the narrow gully. Lynn was resting against it already, keeping a keen eye on the horses as they complacently wandered away from the women. Lucy plopped beside Lynn, surprised when cold water seeped through her pants.

"Bank's not as dry as it looks," Lynn said.

"Thanks for the warning."

"You'll dry off soon enough, once we go back out into the sun."

The heat had stayed with them, although the humidity was gone. It was easy to misjudge whether they were overheating in the thin, hot air, and more than once Lucy had seen black spots in her vision before she realized how close she was to passing out. She'd kept that fact to herself, and her water bottle full.

Lynn cleared her throat. "I wanted to tell you . . . I don't really say it much, but you taking a chance for something, taking a leap like this in the name of an idea . . . Well, not everyone works that way. Including myself."

"Obviously I'm a better person than you," Lucy sniffed, smacking her hand against Lynn's kneecap.

"Maybe, but you could learn to take a compliment," Lynn said, returning the smack lightly to the back of Lucy's head.

Lucy shrugged. "That family needed the house more than we did anyway."

"And they'll have a good life, and you to thank, but that might be cold comfort once we hit those mountains."

"Yeah, the mountains," Lucy muttered, sending a rock spinning out into the stream. "I'm not too crazy about those. I can't quite get my head around it, Lynn. I want this, I do, but the bigness of the world . . . it . . . it kinda scares the shit out of me."

"I can't remove the mountains from our path, little one. Would that I could."

"Yeah," Lucy said, watching Brown Horse favor her leg as she limped away from them. "I wish you could too."

Lucy woke to the sound of strange birds calling overhead, and a man-shaped shadow spread across her blanket.

"Shit!" She leapt to her feet, her cry bringing Lynn upright, gun in hand.

The stranger held Brown Horse's lead, not at all fazed that both women were holding rifles on him.

"Morning," he said.

"You won't be taking that horse from us, if that's what you got on your mind," Lynn said.

"I'm not intending to hijack your possessions," he said casually, pushing his hat up on his forehead and wiping away the faint sweat that glistened there in the morning sun. "I'm asking permission."

"Well, then we say no," Lucy said.

"I don't think you're quite considering the ramifications for this here mammal. She's hurting."

"We know," Lucy said defensively.

"Why'd you go for the injured horse?" Lynn asked, stepping closer to Lucy while keeping an eye on the stranger. "Why not take a healthy one and cut out while we were asleep?"

"'Cause that's hardly in your best interest. Mine either. Or the horse's, for that matter."

Lucy heard Lynn sliding up beside her, felt the older woman's arm brushing against her own as she lowered the rifle a bare inch. The stranger was still regarding them placidly, one hand jammed in his jeans pocket, the other loosely holding Brown Horse's reins. He was unarmed, smiling, and completely in control of the situation.

"Lynn, what the hell is wrong with this guy?"

Lynn shook her head, and the man offered his own explanation. "I suffer from an old-fashioned malady called compassion, though these days it's more likely to be called a personality handicap."

"I don't know there's anything wrong with him so much as he just likes big words," Lynn said quietly to Lucy.

"Ladies, I understand your apprehension. I walked into your camp unannounced, and for that I apologize. Two women traveling alone have the right to be suspicious, but I swear I am a good man."

"Only good men I ever knew are dead or behind us," Lynn said, rifle raised again.

"I didn't figure I'd overcome your misgivings on the spot," he said, sliding one hand up and down Brown Horse's muzzle. "How about you let me administer to this here horse and give her back to you. Would that inspire some trust?"

Lucy's brow furrowed. "What the hell are you? A wandering, cracked-in-the-head, free horse doctor?"

"No, girl," he said, his smile touched with a hint of sadness. "I'm what I claim to be—a good man."

The women were silent for a moment, so still that their rifle barrels rose and fell with their breathing.

"What do you think?" Lucy asked Lynn.

"I think he has honest eyes," Lynn said quietly, lowering her gun. "But don't think I won't blow 'em out of your head if I change my mind," she said to the stranger.

"I'll remember your stipulation," he said, already holding Brown Horse's hoof over his bent knee.

Lucy kept her gun in her hand but stepped closer to see what he was doing. "Do you think you can help Brown Horse?"

"Brown Horse, eh? You girls adhere to descriptive nomenclature. Brown Horse . . . Crazy Free Horse Doctor . . ."

"What's your real name, then?" Lucy asked, unsure whether she was being mocked.

"Fletcher."

"Fletcher?" Lynn repeated, watching Lucy close the distance

187

between herself and the stranger. "What kind of name is that?"

"The kind my mother liked," he replied, running his fingers over Brown Horse's hoof. He glanced up at Lucy. "You're not horse-women, are you?"

"Not really, no."

"Mmm." He gently set Brown Horse's leg back down on the ground and patted her. "From the condition of her, I'll assume you don't have a hoof pick?"

"A what?" Lynn called over the distance.

"If you're interested in overhearing our conversation, you're welcome to join it," Fletcher said. "Feel free to bring your gun."

Lynn hesitated before coming over to stand next to Lucy.

Lucy could feel every muscle humming in Lynn's body, ready to erupt into action if necessary.

"Your mare is experiencing thrush in her frog," Fletcher explained, kneeling back down and pulling up Brown Horse's foot to illustrate.

"A what in her what?" Lucy asked.

"A fungal infection in the soft part here," he said, pointing to illustrate. "Find me something I can use to clean out this hoof and I'll show you."

Lucy looked to Lynn for approval before moving away and breaking a dead branch off a stunted cottonwood clinging to the bank. Fletcher snapped it in two when she handed it to him, and gently pushed the tip into the filth caked around Brown Horse's hoof. She made a low grunting noise as he pried at the inner section of her hoof, and a large chunk of clotted dirt fell away.

"Might want to cover your noses, if you're the delicate type," Fletcher warned.

"Why's that?" Lucy asked, and then the smell hit her and she had to close her mouth before she gagged.

Even Lynn's stoic mask slipped. "Hell's bells," she muttered, backing away with her hand over her face. "Is she rotting?"

Fletcher looked down at the hoof still laid across his knee. "Nah, it's an infection is all. Happens sometimes if they get an irritant up in that soft spot, or a burst abscess from lack of proper hygiene."

Lucy's brow creased. "So it's our fault then?"

Fletcher shrugged and set Brown Horse's hoof down on the ground gently. "You didn't know any better. Even from a distance it's clear neither one of you can sit a horse."

"They're kind of hard to come by in Ohio," Lucy said, catching Lynn's glare at the last second.

Fletcher's forehead crinkled. "Ohio? You might not be horse-women, but I'll call you well traveled nonetheless. How do two midwestern gals come to be in Kansas?"

"Uh . . ." Lucy glanced at Lynn, but the stony look she found there wasn't helpful. "Sightseeing."

"You've seen some sights, coming that far. Of that I can vouch without inquiring."

"What's your interest in it?" Lynn said, cutting through his lackadaisical pace of speech. "You wanted to look at Brown Horse, now you've seen her. You go on your way now. We'll be on ours."

"Not for long," he said easily. "At least, not in the company of the aptly named Brown Horse. She'll founder."

Lucy watched as Lynn debated. The easy answer was they would leave Brown Horse to Fletcher, and their dust would be the last thing he saw of them as they took off on their healthy mounts. But Brown Horse could be used for trade if needed, and Lynn wasn't one to part with an asset. Spatter was easily Lucy's favorite, but the way Brown Horse was awkwardly holding her hoof cut through her soft heart.

"Can you fix her?" Lucy asked before Lynn could open her mouth.

"I can."

"And what would you be wanting for it?" Lynn asked.

"I'd like to know what's going on in Ohio that sends two women west alone, and hear the stories of those you've met on the road."

"What's it to you?"

There was a slight flicker through Fletcher's eyes before he answered. "I'm looking for my wife. We've been separated."

"For how long?" Lucy asked. Images of Carter alone in the moonlight sliced through her mind.

"Doesn't matter," Lynn said, smoothly intercepting Fletcher's answer. "We only met one woman on the road between here and there, and I killed her."

The look on Fletcher's face twisted Lucy's gut, and she was quick to reassure him. "She wasn't anyone you would've wanted to be married to anyways."

"What was her name?" Fletcher asked in a voice laced with fear.

"She said it was Joss, though I wouldn't trust it," Lynn said, rifle fully relaxed now. "The woman wasn't much for telling the truth."

"How long you been apart?" Lucy asked again, her mind far from Joss.

Fletcher looked up at the sun and wiped the sweat from his brow again. "It's a long story, better related in the shade."

"That may be," Lynn said, "but I'm not overly inclined to take a rest with you just yet. You said you could fix the horse?"

"Oh." Fletcher ran one hand lazily down Brown Horse's neck. "Fixing her is the easy part, collecting the necessary accoutrements is the trick."

"What do you need?" Lucy asked.

"Best remedy that comes to mind would be some apple cider vinegar. We might be able to find some left behind in cupboards here and there. It's not exactly palatable."

"Uh-huh," Lucy said, wrapping her mind around the words she knew while trying to figure out the rest. "Think we can find enough?"

Fletcher shrugged, and the simple movement told her everything she needed to know about how life had treated him. "Maybe we will, maybe we won't," he said.

"You don't need to be saying 'we,'" Lynn said. "I'm not about to go running around willy-nilly with you cracking open cupboards, and neither is Lucy."

"Willy-nilly is not a requirement, and it's nice to meet you, Lucy."

Lucy could see Lynn biting the inside of her cheek in frustration at having given away Lucy's name so easily.

"Might as well go on and identify yourself too," Fletcher said to Lynn. "Otherwise I'll be calling you Nice-Looking Lady Who Points Guns at Me."

"Suits me," Lynn said testily, but Lucy saw the whisper of a smile toying with her lips the moment before she looked down at the ground.

"She's Lynn," Lucy said.

"Well, Lynn and Lucy, I'm pleased to meet you," he said, the easy smile cutting a white swath across his tanned face. "I do believe we can be mutually beneficial to one another."

Nineteen

Finding apple cider vinegar was much less of a challenge than Lucy had anticipated. Fletcher rode off astride Mister, his insurance they would stay put while he went searching for the vinegar. Lynn had taken his water jug to be sure he would come back. Which he did, a few hours later, whistling a tune, with a nearly full gallon jug of apple cider vinegar tied to the pommel.

Although Lucy didn't know what *palatable* meant, she understood the second Fletcher took the lid off the jug that nobody in their right mind would even try drinking it. The smell swept up her nostrils and felt like it slid right up inside her skull. She backed away with watery eyes, covering her nose.

"Clears out the sinuses, doesn't it?" Fletcher asked, his ever-present smile lurking around the permanently crinkled corners of his eyes.

"I'll watch the horses closer when we're in the mountains," Lucy promised.

"The mountains? Why would you be taking them through the mountains?"

"We just are," Lucy said, her chin jutting out in anticipation of being told not to.

Fletcher laughed and put both his hands up in surrender. "All right then, little lady. I learned a long time ago not to get in the way of a woman wearing that expression."

"A long time ago? How old are you?" Lucy blurted out.

The surprise that crossed his face caused her to immediately apologize. "Sorry," she said. "I guess that's not something you're supposed to ask people, huh?"

"No, it's all right," he said quickly. "Too many things go unanswered these days. I'd guess I'm a little over forty."

"You'd guess?" Lynn asked, sauntering over in the dying light. "You don't know?"

"Certain things slip away from you when you're on the road as long as I have been," Fletcher said. "You harbor any doubts as to your own age?"

"I'm twenty-seven," Lynn said without hesitation, but Lucy was pretty sure she was actually twenty-six.

"I'm sixteen," Lucy volunteered. "At least . . . I think?" She looked to Lynn, whose brow creased slightly.

"I thought you were seventeen?"

"Either way, your calculations disprove my assumption that you're mother and daughter," Fletcher said, glancing between them.

"Not by blood," Lynn said. "But we are family."

"Family is made all kinds of ways, especially now," Fletcher said.

"What about your own?" Lucy asked. "You said you're looking for your wife?"

"That story is best told sitting down," Fletcher said. "If Lynn here can take a leap of faith and trust me."

Lucy held her tongue for once and looked to Lynn. The older woman was watching Fletcher intently, her eyes boring into his own as if she'd be able to discern his motives by staring him down.

"You come in here and doctor our horse when you could've taken a healthy mount. You hang around all day sneaking our names out of us, and where we're from, though what good that is to you, I don't know. Now you want to stay and tell us a bedtime story. Why?"

A flicker of a smile chased across his mouth, but Lucy saw Fletcher make an effort to squelch it. "'Cause I like you," he said, which made Lynn flinch. "Both of you," he added, including Lucy with a nod of his head, though he kept his eyes on Lynn. "And it's not so much where you came from I'm interested in as your destination. No gentleman would allow two girls from Ohio to cross the mountains alone."

Lynn folded her arms in front of her. "Who says we're going over the mountains?"

"Uh . . ." Lucy almost felt intrusive breaking into the adults' conversation; the tie between their eyes was so strong, it was nearly palpable. "I think I might've let that one slip." Lynn shot her a glare, and Lucy shrugged. "Sorry."

"The little one could use some lessons on obfuscation," Fletcher said.

"Be that as it may," Lynn said so slowly that Lucy realized she didn't know what *obfuscation* meant either, "you expect me to believe you're not looking for anything in return?"

All traces of humor slipped away when Fletcher answered. "I understand you've been on a hard road, and I don't doubt my wife has seen the same trials. I'll help you—one stranger to another—in the hopes that somewhere, someone is doing the same for her. If I can't find her, the best I can do is believe in karma."

Lucy and Lynn exchanged a glance, Lynn's cold blue eyes flashing off Lucy's brown ones and reading her answer in a moment. "All right," she relented. "You can stay, but know that we'll both be sleeping with our guns."

"Wouldn't expect any different," Fletcher said smoothly.

"And keep the karma talk to yourself," Lynn added.

Fletcher raised an eyebrow at Lucy, but she only shrugged and moved to help Lynn unpack their bedrolls from the horses. Brown

Horse was favoring her tender hoof as she stood. The vinegar-soaked wrapping had turned the dust underneath her to a pungent mud. Lucy leaned against her, running her hand along the mare's neck. Spatter took offense and jostled against her, vying for Lucy's affection.

"Don't mean anything by it," she assured him, taking another yucca shoot from her pocket. She scratched Spatter's nose absently while he crunched on the yucca, her gaze drawn over his back to where Fletcher and Lynn were making camp. They moved in circles around each other, his slow and sure as he went about making food, hers erratic and nervous as she attempted to set their beds up while simultaneously keeping an eye on him.

Lucy smiled to herself and rested her head against Spatter, the warmth of his coat soaking into her skin. She knew Lynn didn't want to believe in Fletcher's talk of karma. While he might be doing good for strangers in the hope fate would be kind to his lost wife, Lynn's own past was littered with bodies. And she was always on the lookout for whoever was coming to collect the debt.

"I wasn't much older than Lucy here when the Shortage came about," Fletcher said, the moonlight bouncing off the whiteness of his teeth as he spoke. "I was set up nice in Montana with my brothers and our parents until cholera wiped them out. I couldn't trust our water source anymore, so I moved on, got it in my head that going south was the answer. No winters, right?"

Lynn and Lucy nodded their heads in unison. "We thought the same," Lucy said as she picked stray bits of jerky from her teeth. "Getting away from the snows meant not having to cut wood."

"But leaving somewhere familiar means walking blind for water," Fletcher finished. "And water is the coin of the realm."

"How'd you do it?" Lynn asked. "Did you even have a gun?"

"Started out with one. I've had a lot of things on this journey of mine that are lost now. A gun, some maps. My wife."

"You were married when you were my age?"

"No, that came later. The gun and the maps were with me at the beginning though. Lost the first to a bunch of ruffians, and the second shortly thereafter. I was left for dead and the rains turned my maps into pulp before I came around. My coat grew some mold after that too." He added the second fact as if it had just occurred to him.

"What'd you do?" Lucy asked.

"Found a new coat."

Lynn snorted, and Lucy tossed a handful of dirt in her direction, before continuing. "I mean after that, Fletcher."

"My options were to lie there and die, or keep going." He locked eyes with Lucy, all traces of humor gone. "I kept going."

"And ended up where?" Lynn asked.

"I never *ended* anywhere. I have yet to stop."

"You mean you've been on the road since then?"

"Roads, fields, mountains. You name it, I've traveled it."

Lucy bounced a rock from hand to hand while she spoke. "So you're saying in all that time you never found a place to settle?"

Fletcher said, "There have been plenty with access to water and decent shelter. I even discovered a cellar stocked with canned food, but I took what I needed for a few days' journey and left it behind."

"Why would you do that?" Lucy asked.

"Because I've learned a lesson, and more than once. If you have something, someone will take it from you, and with the loss comes suffering. It's best to be beholden to nothing."

"What about your wife?" Lynn asked, her voice seeming to slice through the air after Fletcher's slow, rolling tone.

Another smile from Fletcher, this one so sad that Lucy felt tears prickling her eyes. "She was the exception."

"You've been looking for her all this time?" The question bubbled up on a wave of emotion, and Lucy's voice trembled to stay under control.

"My best estimate is fifteen years," Fletcher said evenly.

"That is so wonderful," she said. The tears brimmed on Lucy's eyelashes, and she hoped if they fell, Lynn wouldn't notice.

"And stupid," Lynn countered, though her voice didn't carry the same bite as the words. "It's a long shot, walking around hoping to cross paths with her."

Fletcher gave a lazy shrug. "I have nothing better to do."

Lynn looked up to the stars and rolled her eyes, but Lucy thought she detected the faintest hint of tears reflected there.

"So that's why you live on your feet? So you don't get used to having anything?" Lucy asked.

"I find enough to eat for the day, I stay near water when I see it, and I walk. And I rather like my hat," he added. "It's useful."

"We had a place in Ohio, a pond, a house . . ." Lucy's voice trailed off as she remembered her bedspread, Red Dog lying alone in the middle of it the night she'd left.

"Why'd you leave?" Fletcher encouraged her.

"Polio," she said simply, her throat closing entirely over the word and summoning images of Maddy's contorted body, the haunted look in Carter's eyes.

"Escaping a sickness, that's a common story. You leave any behind?"

"Her grandmother and an older man," Lynn answered. "They had been on vacation from it."

Lucy's felt a laugh chasing the tears, and she quickly explained to Fletcher. "Vaccination, she means. Vera and Stebbs were vaccinated against polio."

Fletcher nodded. "Well, that's very similar to being on vacation from it, I suppose," he said, and Lucy giggled, which forced a tear to drop.

Lynn's eyebrows came together. "What'd I say?"

Fletcher skipped her question to ask another of his own. "Why did you come so far? You're a long way from home."

Lynn nodded to Lucy. Whether her reservations about Fletcher were disappearing or she assumed he would finagle the truth out of them eventually, she didn't know. "We decided to head for California," she said, the word tripping off her tongue as if the speaking of it could bring it closer.

"California's a big place. Can you be any more specific?"

"We heard it's normal there, the kind of normal from before."

Fletcher shook his head. "Sorry, ladies, but there's nothing normal about California."

Panic flared through Lucy's system and she looked to Lynn, who had fixed Fletcher with a cold stare. "We heard there were some places where they had desalinization plants." She pronounced the word carefully. "Seems you can get the salt out of seawater if you got the right tools."

"How determined are you to find such a place?" Fletcher's tone was suddenly as careful as Lynn's.

"Very," Lynn said.

"Enough to leave behind a good site in Nebraska," Lucy added. "Enough to come this far."

Fletcher was silent a long while. Lucy was very aware of the horses nickering to one another, the sound of the water tripping over the rocks. When he raised his eyes, he looked to Lynn. "Do you trust me?"

"Not yet."

"And if I said I knew of someplace for you to go, a safe location with water and good people, what would you say?"

"I'd say I need to sleep on it."

Hope chased the panic through her body, making Lucy dizzy. "What do you mean?"

Fletcher looked at both of them before answering, studying their faces. "There's a place similar to what you mentioned—desal plants, safety, a variation of normal."

"This place, it in California?" Lynn asked.

Fletcher leaned in closer to the two of them and dropped his voice. "It's called Sand City. They had a desal plant way before the Shortage and a small enough population to take care of themselves. You have to understand the majority of people didn't think the water situation would prove to be as dire as the predictions, but those with foresight moved to places like Sand City. Out here in the west, water isn't as easy to come across as it might've been for you in Ohio. The few decent people who are left tend to band together for protection."

"You come across these groups of nice people often?" Lynn sounded skeptical.

"Less and less. But last time I was in Sand City, they were doing fine."

"You've been there?" Lucy was filled with the urge to leap up and touch Fletcher just to be nearer to the idea of California.

"A few times," Fletcher said. "If you use my name to vouch for you, it'll gain you a spot there. I'd take you there myself if I could, but I'm headed north after we cross the mountains."

"We?" Lynn said, though Lucy thought she sounded more amused at Fletcher's assumptions than annoyed.

"Indeed," he said. "We're headed in the same direction. And even though I may not be the most imposing figure, even one man in your group will make the two of you a less desirable target."

"And you gain what exactly?"

"A good deed done," he said. "And the full benefit of your whimsical conversation, of course."

Lynn ignored the joke and looked at Lucy. "What do you think?"

"I like having a name to put to it, a place to go," Lucy said. "It feels more real, like we're actually heading for something."

"And him?"

Lucy looked at Fletcher in the white light of the moon, the easy way he'd propped himself against the saddle on the ground, the innocent look of the pale curls his hat had hidden. But his hands were big, and there was no question he was stronger than both of them together. The road had sculpted him into hard muscle, the lines easily seen beneath the worn fabric of his shirt. Placing their trust in him would be a gamble, and she knew it went against Lynn's better judgment.

But Lucy had grown up safe and sheltered, and she believed people were good. "I trust him," she said, holding his gaze.

What she didn't add was that she'd hold the devil's hand if he offered to help her over the mountains.

Twenty

They hadn't been in Colorado long before the mountains asserted their presence, and their low line on the horizon could no longer be explained away as an ever-present storm front. The fact that their goal now had a name—Sand City—had buoyed Lucy through their first few days of traveling with Fletcher. But as the slim line of the mountains made itself evident, the weight in her stomach settled again, and she could not sleep.

Lynn was less worried about the mountains and more concerned with keeping one eye on Fletcher at all times, which had interfered with her rest. Hours after they had made camp Lucy would awake to find Lynn lying facing their companion, both eyes open and alert. Lucy knew Lynn's mistrust was rooted in a lifetime of self-preservation and had only been reinforced by their unfortunate friendship with

Joss. So far Fletcher had been everything he'd promised: a guide and a gentleman. But for all his effortless attempts at conversation, Lynn had remained aloof and disinterested.

Lucy would've been amused at Fletcher's vain attempts to corner Lynn's attention, but there was no room in her mind for anything other than the mountains. Whenever Lynn produced her well-worn map with their new route traced in faded pencil, Lucy's heart never knew whether to be elated at their progress or dismayed as the continuous battle between *what if* and *I can't* raged.

She almost missed the humid heat of Illinois and the long, flat stretches of land. There she'd looked into the distance and seen heat rising up off the road in liquid waves. In Colorado the heat mirages couldn't hide the fact that the mountains lay ahead of them. The sun disappeared behind their black peaks long before the rays were truly dead, and Lucy would covet the moments of sun the impassive mountains stole from her. At night she felt their presence as keenly as if she could see them. Although she knew it was only her imagination, it seemed every noise bounced back off those far walls and reverberated in her ears. The night noises of insects and the far-off calls of coyotes filled the dark hours.

The first night they heard the high-pitched yips of the wild dogs, Lynn bolted from her blankets, gun in hand. Fletcher was upright in a second, producing a knife Lucy had never even known he carried from his bedroll.

"What?" He searched Lynn's face, but she shushed him viciously. Lucy huddled under her blankets, the tiny corner of sleep she'd managed to find shattered.

The calls came again, the leader barking loud and long, the rest of the pack joining in a continuous howl as they ripped apart an animal out in the darkness. Fletcher slid his knife back into his bedroll.

"Coyotes don't interfere with people," he said. "Don't let them steal your sleep."

Lucy didn't know how Fletcher could possibly believe Lynn was getting any sleep in the first place. Dark hollows were sculpted under her eyes, and her brows had been scrunched together for the past two days, something Lucy knew was a sure sign she had a headache.

Lynn moved over next to Lucy and laid her gun between them without speaking to Fletcher. He shrugged and curled back into a ball, dropping off to sleep in a moment. Lucy reached out and touched Lynn's dark hair, offering comfort as well as searching for some. "He has no way of knowing how you lost your mom," she said softly. "Don't hold it against him for thinking coyotes don't hurt people."

"What I hold against him is how fast that knife came out, and one I didn't know he had on him."

Lucy rubbed some of Lynn's hair between her fingers, letting its inky darkness entangle her hand. She didn't want to think of Fletcher as anything other than friendly; his easy smile had won her over miles ago, and she wasn't blind to the way he looked at Lynn, even if Lynn was.

"I don't think it's anything to worry about," she said.

"And he doesn't think coyotes are anything to worry about," Lynn shot back. "Here's hoping you're both right, 'cause I'm tired as hell."

"Get some sleep," Lucy said. "I'm awake."

There was a long silence in which Lucy thought Lynn might have done exactly that. "I know you're awake," Lynn finally said, her voice low and heavy. "I almost believe you have been ever since we crossed into Colorado. Thought you trusted him?"

Lucy let Lynn's hair fall from her fingers. "It's not Fletcher keeping me up."

"The mountains then?"

"Yeah," Lucy said, drawing out the single word as if she could pour all her anxiety into it and find escape.

"I wouldn't have agreed to Fletcher coming along with us if I didn't think there was some use for it," Lynn said. "He'll get us through those mountains better than I could have on my own, trust him or no."

Lucy smiled a little to herself in the dark. "I think he would've followed us whether you said he could come or not."

"Whatever the case is, he's with us now. You don't think on those mountains anymore."

Lucy surprised herself by laughing aloud. "Yeah, right. I won't think about the mountains. How about you start trusting Fletcher?"

The second she said it, she wished the words back into her mouth, and the tight silence enveloping their little camp made her think Fletcher was awake too, and listening for the answer. But instead of getting angry, she felt Lynn's light touch on her cheek, and soft words came out of the darkness.

"I don't understand when you started being so scared of everything, little one."

It was a question Lucy didn't have an answer for, even though the road gave her plenty of time to ponder it. She remembered days from long ago, when her legs seemed too short to take her all the places she wanted to go, and Lynn had fought to keep her within a safe distance of their house. The ripples of fish in the pond would send her leaping into the water before she could swim, the call of a hawk drew her to the fields to see what it was hunting.

Then she lost Eli, her uncle, whose face was clearer in her memory than her own mother's. He had left one evening from Grandma Vera's cabin by the stream with a light kiss on her forehead. And then he was gone, with a pile of stones in the clearing to replace him, resting forever beside the infant brother she had never known.

Her mother lay there too, nestled between them in the grave of her own making. Lucy's curious wanderings had taken her all over as she grew older, with Lynn's protective warnings ringing in her ears when she stayed out too long or strayed too far. But the graveyard was one place she always skirted in order to keep the dim memories safely cornered in the recesses of her mind.

People could be lost. People could leave. People could be taken from her. This idea had taken root in her childish mind and delved deep, sending dark thoughts that made her clutch more tightly to Lynn with her heart. Though she would wander far, there was never a time when she opened the door of their home without a sharp stab of fear: What if Lynn wasn't there?

Lynn had gone to the graveyard often, Lucy knew, spending equal time with Neva and Eli alike, though she'd been bluntly honest when Lucy had asked long ago if she and Neva had been friends. Uncle Eli was another story, one Lynn clearly hadn't found the end to yet, Lucy thought, as she walked along, glancing sideways at Fletcher.

He sat astride Brown Horse, who he'd cheekily renamed Terra Cotta after her foot had healed. Lynn was riding beside him, Mister barely a nose behind. Lucy guessed Lynn would rather have died than admit to Fletcher he was actually leading them, and she kept her face impassive whenever she spoke to him, which was not often. Lucy had to nudge Spatter to keep up every now and then, as he was always leaving the road to investigate what edibles might be hiding from him in the Colorado dust. Her own thoughts roamed along with her mount, as if discovering the moment in time she had lost her courage might help her reclaim it.

Whether it was Neva's abandonment, Eli's death, her own realization that Stebbs and Vera were getting older, or the terror on Carter's face when he had accepted his fate, the seed of fear had been planted inside of her. And it had grown, filling all her corners and finding an answering echo in the dark line of the mountains. Forcing Spatter forward felt like inviting terror, and even the calm, straight lines of Lynn's and Fletcher's backs as they rode ahead of her held no comfort.

The day finally came when they rode into the shadow of the mountains, and Lucy fought the urge to bolt as the shade swallowed first Fletcher, then Lynn, and finally herself. Goose bumps stood out starkly on her skin even though she was sweating, and she felt Spatter falter in response to her own wariness. She leaned forward and patted him to reassure them both, glad that she was behind the adults so they would not see the struggle it was for her to keep from wheeling Spatter's head around and running back east as fast as he could take her.

The first night beside the mountains stole any semblance of sleep from Lucy. The chill that had started on her skin penetrated to her bones. Lynn had consented to a small fire after Fletcher mentioned it in passing. The heat had lulled the exhausted Lynn into a sleep Lucy envied, and she watched Lynn by the light of the flickering flames.

"It's good she's finding some peace," Fletcher said. His voice jolted Lucy from her reverie, and she looked over to where he was propped on his elbows, his eyes on Lynn as well. "I doubt that poor woman has had any true sleep since I joined you."

Lucy scooted closer to him so they could talk without disturbing Lynn. "Take it as a sign she trusts you now."

"And leave poor unassuming you to my infernal devices?" Fletcher asked.

"I don't think I'd put it that way, mostly 'cause I don't know what you said."

"What it breaks down to is, it may seem she trusts me not to harm you, but really the woman is exhausted and sleep is a biological imperative."

"Lynn's been known to outsmart her own body once or twice," Lucy said. "If she didn't want to sleep, she wouldn't. Take heart."

Fletcher smiled, an easy action for him, but this one was quiet and personal, and Lucy felt intrusive even watching him. "Regardless," he said. "Her trust would be a lovely thing to have, but a man such as myself can't ask for anything more."

"A man like you?"

"One who's got nothing to give."

They were silent together for a moment as they watched the flames play across Lynn's face, darkening the shadows under her eyes still further. Lucy broke the silence. "How did you meet your wife?"

"She was on the road, same as me. We crossed paths and it was simply serendipity. The chances of finding someone you can truly love were small, even before this dark and broken time of ours. What are the odds two people left in this vast emptiness would find each other and be soul mates?"

"It's a long shot," Lucy agreed.

"We found each other once. I'll find her again."

Though his eyes were still on Lynn, Lucy could see his thoughts were elsewhere. "What was her name?"

Fletcher was still for a while before answering, as if considering imparting a secret. "Rose," he finally said, and she could hear the long years of loneliness embedded deep in the single syllable.

"I had someone," Lucy said after a moment.

"You had to leave him behind, didn't you?"

She nodded as an answer, her throat too tight for words.

"I can see it. There's a worry that surrounds you too mature for your years."

"Yeah, well," Lucy said, "I got lots of worries."

"Tell me about this boy, for starters."

"His name was—*is*," she corrected herself, "Carter."

"And what happened? Why isn't he traveling with you?"

"He got sick. Well, actually, he *never* got sick, which was the problem. Turns out he was carrying the polio that wiped out our people. Lynn said I couldn't see him anymore, and back home he was . . ."

"Exiled?"

"He was turned out, yeah," Lucy said softly, remembering the lost look in Carter's eyes as he left her underneath the trees.

"That's a hard life, when it's not voluntary," Fletcher said.

"He didn't want to go," Lucy said, lost in her own story. "But he knew it was best for everyone, best for me. I've seen Lynn do all kinds of brave things my whole life, but I've never seen anything like Carter walking out into nothing all by himself."

"Sounds like he was a good fella."

"*Is* a good fella," Lucy insisted. "For all anyone knows, he's still alive. I'm sticking to that, the same as you're sticking to Rose."

"Even though he's back east and you're headed west as far as the land can take you?"

"This place, Sand City, does it have doctors?"

"Some, as I recall." Fletcher looked into the fire before continuing. "I don't know if they were doctors in the modern sense of the word though, and I don't want to mislead you."

"Mislead me?"

"Meaning that I don't want you to have Sand City set up in your head as a utopia—a place where everything is perfect," he added before Lucy could interrupt with the question. "The folks there are kind, and life is easier, definitely. But there's still illness and accidents, and different kinds of work to be done every day."

"Life is work." Lucy shrugged.

"And here I thought you had the optimism of youth." Fletcher laughed softly to himself, then held up his hand to reassure her that he wasn't mocking her. "No offense meant."

"My grandma Vera is a doctor—a real one," Lucy said. "But she didn't know if Carter would carry the polio forever or if it kinda faded out."

"So you're hoping you can find someone who does know? What if you walk toward the sunset thinking you'll find all your answers in Sand City, and they're not there? Or shall we consider the opposite? What if someone tells you what you want to hear—that this boy is no longer infectious—yet you're separated by all the miles you just crossed to hear those words?"

Lucy felt the pit of hopelessness opening in her stomach at such direct questions. To speak her half-made plans out loud made them sound feeble and childish, the product of a lovesick mind that had no room for logic. "If he can be rid of it, I'm going to find him. I won't leave him for dead."

"And how do you imagine that scenario playing out with Lynn?"

"Not well," she admitted.

"I'd say not," Fletcher agreed. "She crosses the country on foot to keep you safe and you do an about-face and head back?"

"You do it," Lucy said, letting the edge in her voice cut through the air even though Lynn was asleep. "You wander around with no

215

idea where to go without a second thought."

"And beholden to none," Fletcher added, weighting each word. "I can do it because there is no one who cares for me. Those who reap the blessings of freedom must undergo the fatigue of supporting it."

Lucy could feel her jaw tightening into the stubborn set Carter had always teased her about, the tiniest flare of irritation firing along with it. "If I say I'll do it, then I'll do it."

"No reason to get heated, though it's refreshing to have a philosophical conversation," he said.

Lucy let all her breath out in a rush. "Sorry. I didn't know I had that in me."

"I imagine there's a lot of things you don't know you have in you, little Lucy."

Lucy shook her head. "You don't know the half of it, Fletcher. My mom, my *real* mom, she killed herself rather than have to face her fears. That's who I am. It's in my blood."

"Maybe. But Lynn's been teaching you her ways, and I think one or two of them might've taken. It's an old argument you'd know nothing about, but whether it's the nature of your mother that wins out in the end, or the lessons of the one who's nurtured you, the choices are your own."

"Yeah," Lucy said. "That I know."

"The other side of the coin, my small friend, isn't all that shiny either."

"What're you saying?"

"I'm saying Sand City has things to offer you haven't even thought of yet, things you might not want to forsake in exchange for a long, hard road back to where you came from."

"I grew up in a city," Lucy said. "I remember electricity and bathrooms. It's not like it'll be all that much of a shock to me."

"And people?" Fletcher said quietly. "You'll be welcome in Sand City. A whole group of new people, kind ones, people who'll take to you—and you to them. It's apparent that you form attachments quickly. Will you walk out on a whole city of new friends for the sake of one old one?"

"Is it right for me to leave Carter alone forever because my grandma didn't know the answer to a question? Is it right that he should be hated and feared if there's really nothing wrong with him, and I'm too comfortable to come back?" Lucy's voice was rising; Lynn twitched in her sleep, and Fletcher motioned to her to shush.

He patted her shoulder awkwardly. "Don't get all discombobulated, now. I'm just planting some thoughts in your head for you to ruminate on while we travel. Get some sleep. Tomorrow we're into the work of the journey."

"'Kay," she said absently, but didn't lie down. Long after Fletcher had drifted off, Lucy stared into the mesmerizing comfort of the flames.

Twenty-One

"I was not expecting that," Lynn said as she stared down the rock slide as if willpower could move it.

"What were you expecting? Smooth sailing?" Fletcher asked, as he slid off Terra Cotta's saddle.

"I would've been content with smooth walking," Lucy muttered, joining Fletcher on the road.

The pile of rocks, dirt, and twisted roots had been there awhile; Lucy could see fresh spikes of green growth emerging from the broken trees that had re-rooted themselves in the rubble heap. What she couldn't see was the other side of the road. The heap was piled well over their heads, and a few rainfalls had settled the dirt solidly.

Lynn put one hand on her hip and surveyed the earthen wall. "Well, shit," she said. "Now what?"

"Not a lot of options, ladies. We dig, or we go back."

"Back how far?" Lucy asked.

Fletcher pushed his hat up off his forehead and scratched at his blond curls while he thought. "Last turnoff I remember would lead us too close to a little town I'm not entirely in favor of. One before that might take us where we need to go to get back on the highway, but I've not traveled it myself and don't know who we might meet on the way."

"Then we dig," Lynn said.

"With what?" Lucy asked.

"You got hands?"

Lucy was doubtful their hands would do much damage, but going against Lynn when she used that tone of voice wasn't in her best interest. Fletcher didn't complain, digging in with a smart, "Yes, ma'am."

It wasn't long before a million tiny cuts from the brittle shale had sliced open Lucy's hands, but never deep enough to draw blood. Dirt filled them quickly, bringing with it a persistent itch she didn't start scratching for fear of never stopping. Her fingernails bent backward, most of them snapping clean off as she dug, leaving the soft white skin underneath unprotected against more cuts and more dirt.

Lucy continued to claw at the pile, working alongside Fletcher, who did most of the heavy lifting. Lynn had scrambled to the top and was pushing boulders too heavy for her too lift and rolling them down the opposite side, the thunderous *cracks* of their landing sending vibrations through Lucy's feet. Loose dirt slid down from Lynn's efforts, settling into Lucy's scalp and mixing with her sweat to create a thin mud that covered her like a second skin.

The sun climbed, bearing down on them as Lynn slid to the other side of the road and began digging from there. Fletcher wordlessly touched Lucy's shoulder and motioned to her that she should drink. Too tired to speak, she only nodded and went to where Spatter stood listlessly, his ears flicking away blackflies in the midday heat. Her water bottle was warm from being next to his body, and she swished the first swallow around in her mouth before spitting it out.

She went back to work, and Fletcher took a break of his own to get a drink and clean the horses' hooves. He returned to her side, tugging a rock as wide as his chest from the rubble.

"Careful," he warned, right before it became dislodged and hit the ground in between them, narrowly missing her toes. "You okay?"

"Yeah," Lucy said, "it missed me."

A drop of blood fell onto the boulder in between them, and they both looked at each other in alarm before Lynn's voice, unrecognizable in its weakness, came from above.

"I'm not feeling too great," she said through the blood dripping from her nose, right before she toppled and Fletcher deftly caught her.

Lucy had seen Lynn's blood before. The nature of their lives left them open to scrapes and cuts. Lynn had always brushed off Lucy's concern and sewn up her own wounds, no matter how deep, with awkward stitches. But Lynn wasn't conscious to tell her not to be worried, and the blood wasn't stopping.

"What is it?" Lucy crouched at Lynn's feet, peering over Fletcher's shoulder as he rolled Lynn onto her side. "Why isn't it stopping?"

"Don't know," Fletcher said brusquely, tilting Lynn's head forward and pulling a clean rag from his pocket to stanch the flow from her nose.

"Will she be okay? You can't bleed to death through your nose, can you?"

"Doubt it," he said. "Though I wouldn't say it's impossible."

They sat in silence for a few minutes, watching the red bloom spread across the rag. "Shit," Fletcher said quietly, and handed it over to Lucy. "You got anything else we can use?"

"An extra shirt in my bag."

"Go get it."

Lucy glanced to Lynn's face, where the blood was now seeping between Fletcher's fingers as he tried to stop the flow with his hands. She ran toward the horses, startling Spatter and sending Mister into a concerned trot in the opposite direction. Lucy yanked sharply on Spatter's reins to hold his head down and rifled through her bag with one hand. Spatter stomped his foot at her but she ignored him, all her thoughts focused on Lynn and the blood spilling onto the road.

When she got back to the adults, Lynn's eyelids were fluttering and Fletcher was trying to get her to answer him. She pushed him away with little strength, her hand sliding off his shoulder and resting against his chest as she lost consciousness again. Lucy shoved a long-sleeved shirt, packed in anticipation of colder days, into his hands.

"She soaks through this and we're in trouble," Fletcher said, holding it to her face and resting Lynn's head against his chest.

"What happened?" Lucy asked again. "Did she get hit with a rock or something?"

"Don't think so," Fletcher said. "There are no bumps on her head, and we didn't hear her cry out. We didn't even know she was hurt until she came to tell us herself. My best guess is she's not responding well to the elevation."

Lucy's eyebrows crinkled. "Elevation? What d'you mean?"

"Certain areas of land are higher than others. You don't necessarily notice it as you travel, but you're much more elevated in relation to sea level right now than you were back in Ohio. The air is thinner, especially here in the mountains."

"I don't feel any different."

Fletcher shrugged. "Some people respond to it differently than others. Most only get a headache."

Lucy thought about the permanent line that had formed on Lynn's face over the past couple of days. "She didn't tell me. She wasn't feeling well and she didn't tell me."

"Why am I not surprised?" Fletcher looked down at Lynn, who appeared to be scowling even though she was unconscious. "If it's been bothering her for a while, her body is disagreeing with the thin air. She's probably been weak and dizzy too."

"And then the damn fool went over the rock slide to move boulders where we couldn't see her," Lucy mumbled, more angry with herself for not noticing Lynn's sickness than she was with Lynn.

"Hard labor was a poor decision, I'd say. And she won't be improved by the loss of so much blood," Fletcher said. He pulled Lucy's shirt away from Lynn's face, and Lucy was relieved to see the flow had dropped to a trickle.

"So what do we do? How do we make her better?"

"The only thing that'll help her is getting down off the mountain. That means pushing through and going on over, hoping for no more delays—"

"Or going back," Lucy finished for him.

"Or going back," Fletcher agreed.

Lucy looked at Lynn while Fletcher wiped the smeared blood from her face, dipping the shirt in what little was left of their fresh water. Turning around was appealing for so many reasons. Fletcher looked to Lucy, patiently awaiting her decision.

"If Lynn wakes up to find us pointing in the wrong direction, she's apt to kill us both," Lucy said.

Fletcher pushed his hat back on his head and looked at the woman still cradled in his arms. "Well, she does have a fondness for pointing guns at me."

They worked into the night by the light of the fire Fletcher built near the rock slide. Lynn was rolled in their blankets, watching them work with a glare in her eye Lucy swore she could feel penetrating right through the rocks when she climbed over to work from the other side.

Lynn had not been happy when she woke to find herself resting beside the fire while the two of them labored on. She'd been even less happy when they refused to let her help, or even stand. All her arguments had landed on deaf ears, and she'd finally relented when Fletcher threatened to tie her up.

Either the rocks were responding to Lynn's willpower, or Lucy had found a renewed strength. After a quick meal by the fire with a sullen Lynn, Lucy had returned to work determined to clear a path before morning. She knew more than rocks and dirt stood in the way of getting Lynn somewhere safe, but it was the obstacle in front of her, and she tore into it with ferocity.

By the time the morning sun was streaking the horizon with pink, they'd cleared a passage Lucy could slip through if she inhaled and held her breath. An hour later, Fletcher could slide through, and full morning found them leading an anxious Spatter through the narrow crevice, his grunts letting Lucy know he was not happy with her but willing to follow. Terra Cotta backed out when she felt the rocks brushing her sides, and it took another couple of hours of labor and strained patience to get the finicky mare through. Mister, by far the largest of the horses, flatly refused to walk through until Lynn stood and took his reins. He put his head down and followed her, meek as a kitten, and Lynn shook her head at him.

"You're a dumb animal," she said, but Lucy caught the older woman rubbing his nose when she thought no one was looking. They traveled until the rock slide was out of sight, lost in a bend in the canyon. A stretch of road lay ahead, reassuringly clear. The highway sliced confidently through the mountains, despite the looming peaks on both sides that seemed to Lucy to silently threaten to topple upon them at any moment.

Lynn had slid off Mister's back the moment they stopped, even though they hadn't even traveled a mile. Her legs seemed to buckle, and Lucy saw Fletcher watching her out of the corner of his eye, poised to help. Lynn sank to the ground, Mister's reins still in her hands. The black horse nuzzled her, and she pushed her head against his.

"I'm exhausted," Fletcher announced loudly, glancing at Lucy. "We should all rest up."

Lucy nodded, ready to ignore the fact that even though Fletcher had worked throughout the night, he didn't look any worse for wear. Her own limbs were heavy, and her knees kept threatening to give out beneath her.

"I'll find a stream, fill our bottles," Fletcher said. "Be right back." He tipped his hat to Lynn as if looking for her approval and she nodded, but her eyes slid shut moments after he'd left.

Lucy plopped to the ground beside Lynn. "How you feeling?"

"Shitty."

"Oh."

A rare smile, though weak, played across Lynn's face. "Sorry, kiddo, I don't have it in me to reassure you right now."

Lucy's heart skipped a beat, and she felt the pulse in her neck jump. "You're okay though, right? There's not, like, anything really wrong?"

"I'm not going to die, if that's what you're asking," Lynn said, though her voice was thready and her eyes remained closed.

"Fletcher said it's probably the mountains, something about how we're higher than you're used to."

"Guess he would know."

"Yeah he's . . . he's a decent guy."

Lynn's eyes flickered open, and she watched Lucy for a moment before letting them close again. "He seems to be," she said.

"But . . . ," Lucy began, anticipating the word before Lynn could waste any of her hard-won breath on it.

"He's still a stranger. Don't you get too comfortable, with me feeling this way." Her eyes struggled open again, and Lucy saw what she'd never believed possible: fear in Lynn's eyes. "I don't think I could even raise my rifle if I needed to," Lynn admitted, and her eyes slid shut again.

Lucy pulled her knees into her body and let Lynn rest, her mind reeling. Lynn without a rifle was like the sky without stars. And if she couldn't trust Fletcher, it was almost like being alone.

Twenty-Two

The first rainstorm came three days later, drenching the hot horses and creating a wet animal smell so thick, Lucy sometimes felt she was choking. They plodded on, determined to reach lower ground where Lynn could recover, until hailstones the size of Lucy's small fists were pounding them. Terra Cotta, always the most nervous of their mounts, reared onto her back legs and nearly threw Fletcher.

Unable to shout over the storm, he signaled the women, and they coaxed the horses into the shelter of an outcrop after dismounting. The horses huddled together, as did the humans, and Lucy tried to ignore the fact that she seemed to be holding up most of Lynn's weight.

Fletcher peered out at the storm and then back at Lynn, who was nearly dozing on her feet. "Might as well rest here. It doesn't seem inclined to desist."

Lynn leaned against the rock wall and slid to the ground without argument, and Lucy joined her there. The hail fell around them, coating the road and creating the illusion of snow, something Lucy wondered if she would ever see again.

When the storm passed they saddled up again, and the crunch of the hailstones underneath the horses' hooves made it impossible to make conversation. Lucy stayed near Lynn, idly brushing Spatter up against Mister as they walked companionably alongside each other. Lynn was quiet, her eyes focused on the road ahead, which was not unlike her. What set Lucy's nerves on edge was the blank look, the permanent daze that had settled over her ever since the nosebleed.

That night Lucy made their food, ignoring Fletcher's insistence that he could do it and she should rest. "I've got it," Lucy said stiffly, when he rose to take Lynn's plate from her hand and carry it to her. She slept nearer to Lynn than necessary that night, curled close despite the heat.

The days went by slowly, and Lucy doubted they would ever be able to get the bloodstains from Lynn's shirt. The first errant drops had been nothing new; most of their clothes had blood on them from themselves or someone else. But Lynn's shirt was now streaked, and they stopped often to give her the chance to rest and stanch the flow.

"Dis ib ridicklob," Lynn muttered through the rag she had

pinched around her nose, eyes glaring over the dried stains.

"This is ridiculous," Lucy translated for Fletcher.

Their mounts were circled in the middle of the highway, heads hung low in the heat. Lucy glanced up at the rocks above them, unable to escape the fear that any moment a boulder could land on one of them.

"Ridiculous or not, it remains a fact." Fletcher watched Lynn out of the corner of his eye to see how she reacted. "Facts are stubborn things."

"Doe am I," Lynn said, and Fletcher waved away the translation when Lucy was about to offer.

Spatter shuffled closer to Mister, sensing Lucy's concern for Lynn. Lucy reached out and touched Lynn's shoulder. "Should we camp?"

Lynn shook her head ferociously, sending scarlet droplets onto Lucy's hand. Lynn dragged the handkerchief across her face, leaving a smear that went all the way to her earlobe. "I'm fine," she said, voice thick with blood. Lucy looked away from her teeth, which flashed red when she spoke.

"Not to be argumentative, but you're not," Fletcher said, refusing the handkerchief when Lynn tried to return it to him.

"I'm not going to be until we get lower, isn't that so?"

"That's my theory."

"And we ain't getting any lower, all of us standing here watching me bleed outta my face," Lynn said, and delivered a kick to Mister's ribs that sent her out ahead of them.

Fletcher sighed and looked at Lucy. "What do we do?"

"Nothing we can do," Lucy said, wishing it weren't the case. "She's right. Getting down out of these mountains is the answer, and standing here isn't getting us there."

The two of them stood together, silently watching Lynn round the bend and move out of sight. Fletcher cleared his throat. "I want you to remember well what you've seen here."

Lucy gave him a cold stare. "You think I can forget her blood dripping everywhere and the fact her rifle is on her back more than in her hands? It isn't right. That isn't Lynn, and I'm not about to forget it."

"You keep it close in your mind though, little Lucy," Fletcher said, all traces of his familiar smile gone. "I know you've got convictions same as she does. I won't be with you to speak reason if you get it in your head to drag her back across these mountains for the sake of someone you don't even know is still alive."

Anger stirred in her stomach, sending her scalp prickling. "I didn't tell you about Carter so you could use it against me."

"And I'm not saying it to fill the empty air. Don't ask her to do it."

Lucy kicked Spatter harder than usual, and he hurried to catch up to Mister, his steps not slowing until he was safely nestled in the shadow of his leader.

◆ ◆ ◆

Guilt nibbled at Lucy as they pushed on, often traveling through the night if the heat of the day had not overly tired the horses. Lynn's condition remained the same, but Lucy's own body never wavered. The thin air actually felt good in her lungs, and she could feel the difference as they descended, a certain heaviness that required some forgotten effort to breathe as they wound their way down. Fletcher never commented on their progress, though Lynn had given the map over to him after a particularly long-lived nosebleed had soaked one of the corners.

It took resolve to not ask Fletcher to pull out the map every night and show Lucy how far they had come during the day, gauging to see how close Lynn's safety might be. She watched Lynn like a hawk during a downward descent that had nearly made her dizzy, but Fletcher only shook his head at her when he saw the direction of her gaze.

"Doesn't work that way," he said quietly to her.

"What's that?"

"I see you watching her for signs of improvement every time we come over a steep hill. Her headaches might recede soon, but her body has been stressed for a long time. She'll need to recuperate once we're on level land again."

Lucy's heart leapt in fear at the thought. Fletcher had said he was heading north after they crossed the mountains. "How long?"

He followed her thoughts. "I won't leave you in my wake until she's all right."

232

She let out a breath as if she hadn't been holding it. "Thanks."

"Surely you knew that by now, that I wouldn't leave?"

"But you will," Lucy argued. "When it's time. You've got your own life to lead."

Fletcher smiled to himself and looked back at the road.

"What's so funny?"

"You and Lynn," he said. "Always looking for people to let you down, but for different reasons. She doesn't trust me enough to believe my motives are altruistic. You think I'm more devoted to someone else than to you two."

Lucy snuck a glance at Lynn, whose body was swaying with each step Mister took. "Well . . . aren't you?"

"Rose has been waiting on me for years. A few more days doesn't make any difference."

"But for us it might, is that it?"

Fletcher nodded once, slowly, not taking his eyes off the road. "It may."

"You don't think we'll make it, do you?"

"I think women traveling alone face a unique set of challenges, and it's best if Lynn is feeling well when I leave you."

His last few words echoed through Lucy's mind, bringing with them the faces of all those she had lost through death or separation: her mother, Uncle Eli, Maddy, Carter. Her heart faltered, missing a beat when she realized that even Vera and Stebbs could be lost to her now. With the mountains between them, it was a real possibility she would never see them again, or hear their voices. She took a ragged breath and looked at the horizon.

"When you leave us," she repeated, giving each word the weight it deserved.

The day they came down out of the mountains was one Lucy had always pictured in her mind as warm and pleasant, with a clear blue sky and the weight of the world removed from her shoulders. Instead she was picking her way around another rock slide in the rain, and ankle-deep mud had sucked one of her boots clear off her foot.

Spatter was shaking his head against the downpour of rain, refusing to step over the guardrail even when she yanked on the reins.

"Damn it," she shouted, dropping Spatter's reins in frustration. "He won't move," she shouted over the downpour to Fletcher and Lynn, who had already coaxed their horses off the highway and around the guardrail that had stopped the rocks. They hunched over their own mounts, miserable in the rain.

"That's helpful, thanks," Lucy muttered to herself, and turned back to Spatter with her hands on her hips. He had never willfully disobeyed her before, and she was at a loss. She dug her boot out of the mud while balancing on one foot. Spatter pushed against her with his nose, offering support from behind. She accepted his apology and scratched behind his ears with her free hand. "What d'you say, buddy? Think you can do this for me?"

He nickered deep in his throat and she rested her head against him for a moment, ignoring the warm smell of wet animal. Vera's kitchen had smelled like that whenever she allowed the neighborhood stray in the house during a rainstorm. The dog had never allowed anyone to touch him, a low growl warning away anyone who tried. Vera was the only person who could come within five feet of him, her kind voice pitched low and melodious as she cut mats from his coat, or treated whatever new wound he'd been visited with.

Vera's voice rang in Lucy's ears and she matched the tone, whispering in Spatter's ear and running her hands up and down his neck. He muttered back to her, low and sweet, and she took the reins in her hand once again. Spatter balked at the railing, but instead of yelling, she comforted him with Vera's voice and Vera's words, feeling the massive muscles calming under her touch. On the third attempt he stepped over the rail, gingerly testing the gravel on the other side. It was loose and gave under his hoof, but she kept a low drone of talk going that allayed his fears.

His second foreleg cleared the rail, and his back legs followed easily now that he was moving. He followed Lucy docilely along the gravel ridge until they were past the rocks. Getting back over onto solid ground was much more attractive to him, and Spatter nimbly crossed the rail back onto the road without complaint. They joined their companions on the far side of the rocks, and Lucy swung into the saddle.

"You may be a horsewoman yet," Fletcher said. "How'd you talk him into it?"

Lucy ignored the question, looking instead to Lynn. "I miss my grandma," she said suddenly, and the heat from the tears rolling down her cheeks contrasted sharply with the cold rain sliding down her back. Lynn only nodded, the understanding of loss buried deep in her eyes. They traveled on together, ignoring the weather as they put the mountains behind them.

Twenty-Three

"I'm not leaving him," Lucy said, legs spread in a fighting stance as she stood between Spatter and Lynn. Her small hands were curled into fists, and she could feel adrenaline coursing through her veins, filling the deep gouge of betrayal.

"You get to feeling better and the first thing you want to do is take my horse from me," she yelled at Lynn, hating how childish her words sounded and the way her voice was weak and lost in the arid land.

"I'm not taking anything from you," Lynn said calmly, her hands out to either side. "I'm talking sense." She looked to Fletcher, who was kicking sand over the ashes of their fire from the night before. "Wanna help me out here?"

Fletcher didn't even glance in their direction when he spoke. "A man comes across two she-bears fighting in the woods, he does best to go around them."

Lynn's answering scowl ended up aimed at Lucy, as Fletcher was ignoring her completely. "Lucy, it's for his own good. This here isn't even the real desert. Once we go out into the nothing, we'll be hard-pressed to find enough water for ourselves, let alone the horses."

Lucy felt her throat tightening at the thought, the image of a frothing Spatter slicing across her eyes. She uncurled her fists. "Not yet," she said, the rod of tension gone from her voice. "There's still streams from the mountains, enough water for us. We'll make better time with mounts, and there's no point giving up our one advantage until we have to."

If emotion couldn't carry weight with Lynn, logic did. Lynn's mouth went into a flatter line than usual, and she gave Lucy a heavy glare before turning her back. Lucy relaxed against Spatter, relishing the velvety feel of his nose brushing against her arm. She'd won the battle but knew the war would go to Lynn.

Lucy kept her distance as they packed up their camp, rolling their blankets, refilling water bottles from the nearby stream, and checking their guns. Once astride her horse, Lucy took a deep breath and avoided the eyes of the adults as the heavy silence that hung around them lasted longer than necessary.

Fletcher cleared his throat. "Well, ladies," he began.

"No," she cried instantly. "You can't leave yet."

"You knew this was coming, little one," Fletcher said, eyeing her carefully. "Sooner or later I'm going to have to go."

"Make it later then," she shot back.

"Lucy," Lynn said quietly, "it's time. He's got his own cares."

The way the two watched her, gauging her reaction, caused a resurgence of temper. "You talked about this beforehand, didn't you? The horses too, I bet."

"We thought it best if I took all three horses with me at this juncture, yes," Fletcher said, using the same tone he did with Terra Cotta when she was finicky.

"But we agreed if you couldn't handle losing him and Spatter on the same day, we'd settle for one over the other," Lynn finished.

"You plan anything else for me while you were at it?"

"If I had a son, we would've arranged a marriage," Fletcher said.

"He made that bit up," Lynn added, and Lucy felt her face flush at the fact that they were sharing a joke at a time when she felt like crying.

"Lucy." Fletcher edged Terra Cotta closer to Spatter, and the two horses nickered to each other. "You started this without me; no reason to think you can't finish it in the same manner."

Her anger melted into tears and she gave in to the lump in her throat, allowing it to find release through a choked sob. "It's not that I'm scared of going on without you. I'm *losing* you, don't you get that? You're gone, just like everyone else."

239

Fletcher put a hand on her shoulder, one of the few times he'd touched her. "Losing people, that's something I understand right down to my soul." He leaned forward in the saddle and she slumped against him, crying so hard Spatter turned his head to glance at her quizzically, which only made it worse.

Lynn nudged Mister over to them, holding a water bottle out to Lucy. "You're wasting your water," she said.

"You would be practical right now," Lucy said, pulling back from Fletcher and taking the bottle.

"Somebody has to be," Lynn said, doing an exaggerated eye roll toward both Fletcher and Lucy.

Fletcher smiled back and tipped his hat. "So," he said. "Sand City?"

Lynn patted the map tucked inside her pocket. "Seems that way."

"Maybe I'll . . ." He trailed off, an uncharacteristic blush spreading across his features. "Maybe I'll find my way back there someday."

"Maybe that'd be all right," Lynn said, and Lucy could see the muscles in her jaw twitching in an effort to stop a full-fledged smile.

Fletcher had no such compunction, and his ear-to-ear flashed once again before he spurred Terra Cotta and they headed north.

Lucy's sorrow was lost in a sudden rush of curiosity. "Shit, Lynn, how much talking did you two do?"

But Lynn had already urged Mister into a trot, and Spatter hurried to catch up.

Lynn had called it "the nothing" long before they reached it, a land where even the brush tapered off and the red rocks reached for the sky. The mountains had frightened Lucy with their vastness; their towering heights had persevered for thousands of years, reminding her she was a breath on the wind. The desert made her feel like even that breath was stolen, and the dust filling her lungs taunted her with the reality that one day she'd be reduced to the same.

The highway stretched to the horizon, an unbroken black strip that burned so hot in the afternoons, the heat shimmer reached upward for miles. The landscape was equally monotonous, the stray breezes blowing up dust storms to compete with the mirages. The only thing that broke the view was the marching electrical poles, skeletons from a different world whose veins had been emptied of their power long ago.

Lucy reined in Spatter next to Mister and looked to Lynn, wondering why she had stopped. But the other woman's eyes were rooted on the horizon, focused on nothing. "Lynn? What are you thinking?"

Lynn startled and seemed to struggle to focus on Lucy. "Just this—

"And I will show you something different from either
Your shadow at morning striding behind you

Or your shadow at evening rising to meet you;
I will show you fear in a handful of dust."

"I think I like Walt Whitman better," Lucy said.

"You would."

Spatter and Mister ducked their heads low in the heat, their noses leading the party to the ever farther springs of water, some of them nothing more than a brackish trickle. For nearly a week after Fletcher had left their company Lynn kept her mouth shut, and Lucy knew she was waiting for her to make the right choice and unburden the horses. Her silence made Spatter's nickering all the more precious. She twirled his rough hair in her fingers while she rode, putting off the inevitable for as long as she could. She was so focused on every aspect of Spatter—the sound of his hooves, the feel of his movements underneath her—she didn't notice the speck on the horizon behind them until Lynn pointed it out.

"You're lost in your head over there," the older woman said.

Jerked from her reverie, Lucy was suddenly very aware she hadn't spoken since they'd saddled up that morning. "Sorry," she said, clearing her throat of the dust first. "Just thinking."

"I'm not pointing it out for the sake of talk," Lynn said. "There's been someone behind us for a good two hours, and you've not spotted him."

Lucy turned in her saddle, shading her eyes against the harsh midday sun. There was a black figure, barely discernable among the heat shimmer. "You're sure it's a person?"

"I been watching. Wasn't much more than a dot, but he's moving faster than us."

"So he's mounted?"

Lynn nodded gravely. "And on a horse that's better suited to the desert than our own, I imagine."

"Any chance it's Fletcher? Maybe he changed his mind about going north."

"Don't think so. Terra Cotta was the slowest of the three, plus he knows where we're going. No reason to push his mount to catch us."

Lucy turned back in the saddle. "So who is it then?"

"Nobody we know. And if we can see him, he can see us."

The fear of the unknown swooped back in to trump the nothingness of the desert. Anything could be done to them in the emptiness, and their bones left to be buried in the dust with no one the wiser. "So what do we do?"

Lynn's brows drew together, and Lucy understood she'd been thinking over their options long before starting the conversation, weighing the choices that could end in life or death while Lucy had been making fine braids in Spatter's mane. "I'm sorry I didn't see him," she added quickly.

"Don't be sorry you didn't, just be glad I did." She looked to the bleak landscape around them, devoid of even a tree for shelter. "As for what we do, we can try to outrun him, which'll likely kill the horses and land us helter-skelter in the middle of nowhere with no idea where we're going. . . ."

"Uh, there's an 'or' coming, right?"

Lynn inclined her head toward Lucy. "*Or* we hide."

"Hide?"

"We need to get off this main road. There's been unpaved ways breaking off here and there, but a lot of 'em aren't on this map. Don't know if I'm more comfortable being lost than being followed."

Lynn unfolded the map as she rode, looping Mister's reins around the pommel. "If we split off to the south up ahead, we'll come across some canyons before long. I know you don't like the idea of the rocks hanging over your head, but if we got down in one of those little mazelike canyons, he'd be hard-pressed to ever find us."

"And we might be hard-pressed to find a way out."

"That's where me asking you to start paying attention comes in."

A flush crept up Lucy's cheeks that had nothing to do with the sun. "All right."

Lynn watched Lucy for a second before continuing. "I want to get over the next ridge, and then we'll cut to the south. I can't imagine it'd be easy to track us down in the rocks, 'specially if that cloud there graces us with a bit of rain."

An unassuming storm cloud was rolling in from the west, and Lucy licked her parched lips as she glanced at it.

"Let's hope so," she said.

They broke away from their path once they crested the ridge. Without the baking road reflecting the heat back in their faces, the horses picked up the pace. But without the familiar snake of black-top, the sameness of the desert made the word *lost* seem too short to capture the enormity of their situation. The only hint of the road they were traveling was an old fence that ran parallel to it, remnants of a pasture devoid of animals.

"If someone kept their herds here, there must be a creek nearby," Lucy offered, hoping perhaps the horses had sped up for more reason than one.

"Makes sense," Lynn said, her lips pursed so tightly the words came out in a growl.

The road met up with the creek shortly, and the horses stumbled wearily into the cool water, Spatter wading in up to his knees. Lynn and Lucy slipped off their saddles as well, filling their near-empty bottles and thirsty mouths. Coaxing the horses out of the stream was tricky, and Lynn caved in to their mournful eyes.

"Our friend behind us won't be able to track us in the stream, and it'll lead us down into the canyon besides," she said.

The shadows of the towering steeples of rock striped their path as they moved silently southward. Then the stripes disappeared as the rocks reached for one another, forming a sheer wall on either side.

"Just breathe easy," Lynn said softly, though Lucy noticed she also looked to the bright-blue strip of sky above them as she said it. "This is mostly a straight shot. When the canyon dumps us out, we'll be able to backtrack to the highway."

Lucy nodded her assent, too spooked by the sound of Lynn's voice bouncing off the nearby walls to answer. The innocent splashing of the creek rebounded as well, echoed and magnified. Spatter's ears flicked backward, then forward in an effort to make sense of this new phenomenon. She scratched his neck, and he made a deep mutter she could only too well agree with.

"I don't like it either, boy," she whispered as she leaned forward.

At first she thought the goose bumps were caused by fear. She'd become all too familiar with the rushing prickle of them in the long, lonely nights. But a cool breeze was playing with her hair as well, and the first cold drop that splattered on her skin was as big as a shotgun shell. Ahead, Mister startled to the right when another drop struck him, and he brushed against the close canyon walls that made it impossible for the horses to ride abreast any longer.

"Guess the rain is coming," Lynn said, the calm that carried back in her voice soothing Lucy, though she suspected it was on purpose, as she saw Lynn dig her heels into Mister a little deeper, urging him forward.

The thin strip of sky above them was no longer blue, and the swirling clouds moving past weren't the comfortable shade of gray they'd been when Lucy first saw them, but a menacing black that contrasted with the red rock so sharply that her heart skipped a beat.

Another drop fell directly on her face, as if scolding her for looking so closely. She wiped it away, trying to ignore the increased pattering of the rain falling into the creek and seeping through her clothes. A streak of lightning shot through the sky, and the answering thunder was so loud that shards of rock were knocked loose from the walls. They rolled down to the path, spooking the horses.

Lynn had pulled Mister into a trot, her gaze sweeping the rock on either side and the widening water rivulets that were pouring into their hiding place. "Lynn?" Lucy called out, alarmed that she had to raise her voice to be heard over the rain.

Lynn looked back and said only one word. "Faster."

She kicked the already skittish Mister and he took off, hooves splashing in the water that was now creeping up his legs. Spatter needed no coaxing; he leapt to follow. Lucy wondered if he could sense the danger of the rising water as it touched the tips of her boots.

They cleared a turn to see Lynn and Mister only paces ahead of them, and no end to the canyon walls in sight. A slight whimper escaped Lucy, but she could see only grim determination in Lynn's face when she glanced back to check on her. Lucy waved that she was all right and urged Spatter to go faster, although he was beginning to lose his footing. A near panic had settled into Mister, and Lucy watched as he slipped, nearly unseating Lynn. She jerked back on his reins and brought his head around, but the horse was wild, and the splashing his struggles brought around them didn't help. He took off at his own frenetic pace, anxious to find a way out.

Spatter answered in speed. Seconds later Lucy felt him lose contact with the ground as the rushing water buoyed him above it. He neighed in fear and she wrapped her arms around his neck, unable to control him with the reins any longer. She called out for Lynn, but Mister had the upper hand on his rider as well, and the two of them were out of sight.

She felt Spatter's legs pumping beneath her, working with the current to move them forward. His courage gained them precious minutes until the first swell came, rushing over his back and plucking Lucy from the saddle as easily as she pulled overripe pears from the trees at home.

The water enveloped her, shocking in its coldness. She kicked upward to break the surface, managing a single gulp of air before the strong current took her in its own direction and slammed her against an outcrop. Her head struck rock, and she felt the thin skin of her temple parting easily, the hot blood releasing from her head to mix with the cold flow of rainwater.

Lucy clutched the outcrop and managed to drag herself on top of it. She swiped at her eyes only to realize a darkness was seeping into her vision that wasn't blood, the ringing in her ears overwhelming even the rushing of the river sweeping by only inches from her face.

"This isn't fair," she managed to say weakly as she slipped into unconsciousness, knowing she was about to drown in a place where little water could be found.

Twenty-Four

She was out long enough that her clothes were dry when she woke, as was her mouth. Lucy tried to sit up, but a wave of vertigo forced her back down, the lump on her head pulsing in time with the nausea. She vomited over the edge of the outcrop, into the serene water below. The angry rolling white froth was gone, but Lucy knew enough about moving water to know that didn't mean the current wasn't strong. She rolled onto her back to glare at the mockingly blue sky above, clear of any trace of the storm. She had no way to judge how long she had been out. It could be the same afternoon, or two days later. The only gauge she had was the scratch of dehydration in her throat and the gnawing hunger in her belly.

She sat up by inches the second time, letting her pounding head adjust to the change. Once upright, she leaned back against the canyon wall, which soared at least a hundred feet above her head. Climbing out was not an option. Neither was staying and waiting for the river to recede more. If she waited too long, she could die of thirst, hunger, or even the drop down to the shallow water. Jumping now meant a drink, and the very real possibility of drowning. In the best of health she would've jumped without question, trusting to the strength of her body. As it was she couldn't move more than a foot at time without feeling dizzy.

She swallowed once, ignoring the thickness of her own saliva, before calling out. "Lynn?" The single syllable echoed off the walls, bouncing back and forth as it traveled upward toward nothing, to the endless expanse of desert. There was no answer.

It was what she had always feared.

She was alone.

An hour later the water had receded another five feet, and there was still no answer to her increasingly panicked calls. Her heart beat so quickly, she could feel the answering pulse under the thin scab that had formed on her temple. The sun had dried her lips, and as she thought, she chewed on the thin strips of skin that flaked off.

Delay would only increase the drop as the river fell, and Lucy knew it was time. Her legs were still shaky, but her weakness would grow along with hunger pains. She shimmied to the edge and swung her legs over, meaning to dangle and drop after taking a deep breath.

But she'd misjudged the strength left in her arms, and the sudden weight was too much for them. Her hands scrambled for purchase as gravity yanked her over the edge. She had a pristine moment of clarity as one fingernail was ripped off, the pain standing out like a sharp moment in time.

And then she was falling. She gasped deeply and closed her eyes. The water was so cold it felt like hitting rock as she sliced through it, her heart stilling for one second at the shock. Her feet struck bottom for one moment and she pushed upward with the strength she had left, scissor-kicking to propel herself to the surface. She gulped the air, which tasted sweet and made it seem like her lungs were the only warm part of her body.

The current had her, but its fingers lacked the cruel grip that had ripped her from Spatter's saddle, and she allowed herself to relax until her foot was caught up by something beneath the surface and she was pulled under. The water closed over her head before she was able to take a lifesaving breath.

Darkness came again, calling with a comforting numbness she knew had little to do with the cold water. It was the same futility she'd seen in her mother's eyes, in the few memories Lucy still had of her life in the city. Dark days with curtains drawn and Neva lying in her bed though the sun was high in the sky outside. Even as the current forced her lips open and the cold water slid into the crevices of her lungs Lucy thought of Neva, and the living death that had been in her eyes years before she put a pistol to her head.

And she thought of Lynn, who had forced herself to survive even with Mother's blood on her hands and no meat stored for the winter. Lynn, whose faith in her own strength kept her going beyond all limits of endurance in order to provide for herself, and later for Lucy. Giving up now meant betraying Lynn's effort, the years of her life she'd given over to raise a child not her own. Lynn, who might be looking for her at that very moment.

Lucy screamed underwater, bringing more water into her body as if challenging it to drown her. She broke the laces of her boot with willpower rather than strength and, kicked for the surface, buoyed by thoughts of how disappointed Lynn would be with her for losing a boot. She broke through to warmth and a dark shadow riding the current alongside her, a scruffy tree that had been torn out by its roots, still clinging to the dirt it had depended on.

She made a lunge for it, twining herself around the pale, water-logged roots. They encircled her like a thousand arms, grasping her waist and tangling in her legs. Water warmed by her own body gurgled from her lips, and the next breath of air felt like daggers pulling her apart from inside. She gasped and choked, sending more water through her nose and bringing on a coughing fit that crushed her chest and stole the last ounce of energy she had. Lucy fell forward against the tree trunk, her bare foot trailing her body in the dark current like a tiny ghost.

◆ ◆ ◆

A day later the river water was a pleasant memory, longed after like the wet days of spring in the middle of summer's drought. The sun was merciless as Lucy dragged herself across the desert, the toes of her bootless foot curled under to keep the burning dust from her sensitive sole. She'd tried switching her remaining boot from foot to foot, but a blister had formed and burst only minutes after she'd forced the left boot onto her right foot.

The raw spot on her toe had quickly filled with dirt, and it throbbed as she forced herself ever onward, eyes scouring the vast nothing for any sign of Lynn or Mister. Spatter she'd found the day before, caught up in a bend in the river where debris had piled. Even though the current had carried her past him mercifully quick, the bulging of his blank eyes and the image of his long, lifeless tongue dangling in the water for a perpetual drink had brought a fresh grief that spilled new tears from her swollen eyes even as she was pulled away from him.

Weariness had taken hold again, not relenting until the canyon fell away and the log she'd lashed herself to with its roots came to rest on a sandbar. The peacefulness of the undulations tugging at her feet had urged her to free herself and continue on with the river, to a place where pain and grief would bother her no more. She'd pulled her legs up onto the tree and slept through the cool night, taking what rest she could before facing the desert.

Leaving the river went against all her instincts, but if Lynn were alive, she would head north to return to the highway, and expect Lucy to do the same. The rising sun had felt good as it baked the chill from her bones, and Lucy had a flicker of hope as she rested on the sandbar before leaving. The idea of Lynn dying at all was so foreign to Lucy that she rejected it wholly. Lynn would live if the canyon itself were to collapse on her, the tenacity of the life inside of her finding a way to survive against all odds.

But the odds felt longer as the day wore on and the last few mouthfuls of water she'd taken from the river had long since been spent by her body. The heat shimmer began to play games with her head, showing shadows in the form of horses and people who urged her to stray from her northward path with promises beyond her reach. Lucy pushed on in as straight a path as she could, though she feared the dragging pain from her injured foot was pulling her to the left.

She sat down at midday, unable to ignore the pounding in her head any longer. The wound on her temple had reopened, and she licked at her own blood as it streamed into the corner of her lips, but her tongue came back coppery and salt covered. Lucy touched the wound and studied the blood on her fingers, reveling in the beauty of the red rivulets against the underside of her hand.

"Lynn," she said weakly, though she knew there was no one to hear. "I understand that poem now. It's what I've been saying all along about being scared of the bigness, and me being so small. Only it says it better. All I'm going to be here soon, after the sun and the animals have their way, is just a handful of dust. I'll be even smaller than I am now. I'll be nothing, and no one will ever know what became of me. Lynn, I think . . . I think I'm dying."

But there was no one to tell her this was not the case, no strong hands to pull her to her feet and force her to go on, no gentle touch to bring a cool cup to her lips and bring her back from the brink. There was nothing, and there was no one.

Stebbs was not there to tell her any water she witched would be too deep to reach. She'd seen him witch without a stick before, and she called to mind his steady pace and calm demeanor as he would walk with his arms outstretched. She reached out for water with her entire being, eyes closed tightly against the baking sun. Her heart leapt along with her pulse a few paces later, and she fell to her knees.

She dug with her hands, the hot sand packing the tiny cracks in her knuckles, first only irritating the skin but finally breaking through and dotting the ground with black drops of her own blood. She kept on, digging through the pain. Her fingernails peeled back from her dry nail beds and still no water bubbled up, no earthy smell of water filled her nose. There was only the dull, endless wafting of arid air.

Soon she collapsed beside a hole barely two feet deep, her body so dry she could hardly blink her eyes.

And still, she smelled no water.

She had lived rough her whole life, but hunger had never been a true enemy. Lynn's gun and Vera's garden had kept food on the table, and the slight gnaw on her stomach she'd always called "hunger" seemed almost pleasant compared to what she was suffering from now. In the overwhelming burn of a desert day, she understood the difference between hunger and starvation. It felt as if the rough rock under her back had bitten through her spine and was making a meal of her stomach lining. The pain curled her body into the fetal position, and Lucy cried tears that never gained the weight to fall.

Night brought a wicked chill, the desert playing its cruel trick of burning her to death during the day and leaving her to freeze at night, along with a moon so bright it made the hills of sand seem like snowdrifts. Images of her long-lost uncle Eli floated by, teasing her with snowballs and a smile that made the brightness of the moon seem insignificant. The sharp pain of a grief remembered brought her back to full consciousness, and in the white light of the cool desert she could see what the mirages of the baking day had hidden from her. The road. The dark spine of the desert stretched before her east to west, and what had once held nothing but fear for her was now welcome.

She crawled the last few feet to the pavement, her cracked and dry skin absorbing the heat of the road the desert night had stolen from her body while she slept. The warmth invigorated Lucy, bringing her to her feet and reminding her there were worse things than pain. If there was a trail of red blood behind her on the road from her dragging foot, it meant she still had blood to shed, and her veins weren't rotting under the sun, noticed by no one. If she was going to die, she would do it where someone would see, and the trail of blood behind her would show how damn hard she'd tried to make it.

"Like Lynn would," she said to herself through shredded lips as the road pulled the blisters on her naked foot open. "Like Lynn."

She'd anchored her mind so deeply onto the idea of Lynn that when she came upon the actual woman, she thought she was a mirage and nearly walked past her. Lynn sat sprawled in the barest shade offered by an electric tower, the black lines of its shadow zigzagging across her legs, her pack and half-full bottles scattered at her feet. Her eyes flickered when Lucy shuffled past, but there was no disbelief in them once she'd focused.

"Hey there, little one," she said, her voice dry and shaky.

Lucy fell to her knees in the dust. "I didn't think you were real," she said, touching Lynn's face.

"I'm real enough," Lynn said, breath hitching in her chest as she pulled herself to her feet.

"Drink," Lucy said quickly, twisting a cap off one bottle and offering it to Lynn before gulping it herself.

"You drink."

Water spilled down Lucy's neck and chest as she gulped, sweeping through the dirt that covered her like a shroud.

Lynn gently pulled the bottle away from her, finally taking a drink herself. "You'll make yourself sick," she warned.

The water pooled into her tightly clenched stomach, forcing it open and bringing on a gag reflex that Lucy struggled against futilely. The water came back up, as warm coming out as it had been going in.

"Uh-huh," Lynn said as she watched Lucy retch.

"Sorry," Lucy said, spitting out the last gritty mouthful. "I wasted your water."

Lynn pulled up the edge of Lucy's shirt and cleaned the girl's face as best she could. "Don't know that it matters much now," she said.

The finality of her tone brought a swift despair that overwhelmed Lucy, causing her now-empty stomach to convulse again. "So now what?"

Lynn held out her hand to help Lucy to her feet, the long, tanned fingers casting dark shadows in the dust below them.

"We keep walking."

The simple act of walking had never been more impossible, and Lucy missed Spatter with her heart and her feet as they struggled westward. Mister had fared better than his companion, and Lynn had done what Lucy could not, letting him go once they had reached safety. She'd left his bridle and saddle piled next to the canyon, a useless mound of leather with no mount.

With Lynn at her side and what little provisions had remained in her pack, hope had bloomed in Lucy like the desert flowers around them, subsisting on nothing more than heat and dust. But the flowers had hidden wells of moisture Lucy did not, and days later her energy was flagging to the extent that she no longer lifted her injured foot at all, allowing it to drag.

Lynn had given her a sock and replaced her boot over her own naked foot without complaint, even though Lucy saw the glistening smear of burst blisters when she slipped it off later that evening. The river had swept Lynn from Mister's back, but she'd managed to hold on to his reins and her pack. What little food was left tasted like the rain that had nearly drowned them both.

They traveled at night and sought shade in the day, waking and moving with the patchy shade the power lines offered as the sun made its arc. Lynn spoke little and Lucy kept her own mouth shut as well, pooling the energy inside of her for the next step, and then the one after. The road stretched forever, marching toward a goal that seemed unreachable. But Lucy's newfound will to live and Lynn's refusal to die kept them both moving. The red rim of the sun greeted them and brought an end to the night's travels, and the women curled beneath an electrical tower, this one no different from the day before except for the fact that it was farther west.

Lucy woke to the familiar pain of hunger and cracked lips.

Lynn did not wake at all.

Lucy was screaming, but it did no good. Lynn would not answer. Her throat burned as she screamed Lynn's name over and over, sweat sprouting across her brow with the effort. She yanked Lynn into a sitting position and her head tipped backward, the deep circles underneath Lynn's eyes no lighter for being under the sun's glare. But she did blink, the tiny fraction of movement sending Lucy into a relief so great it felt as if her heart had fallen into her remaining boot.

She held the other woman's face in her hands. "Lynn, come on now. Don't do this."

"'Here is no water but only rock,'" Lynn choked out. "'Rock and no water and the sandy road.'"

"Lynn!" Lucy shrieked into her face. "You're not making any sense."

Lynn's eyelids fluttered, and the tiniest of smiles snuck into her words. "T. S. Eliot often doesn't," she muttered, and then fell still. Her mouth was open, and her swollen tongue remained out, the cracked lips refusing to close back over it.

Lucy let go of her, and Lynn's head slumped to the side again. Frantic, Lucy ripped at the pack and pulled out the bottle of water they'd pooled together from what remained. Only two inches were left. The rays of the midday sun bounced off it, sending tiny gorgeous rainbows across Lynn's gray face.

She dropped to her knees beside Lynn, jamming her fingers deep into the hair at her temples and jerking her head backward so fiercely they both went over into the dirt.

"Open your eyes," she screamed at her. "Look at me when you're telling me you're leaving me alone." Lucy peeled Lynn's eyelids open and her pupils dilated in the sun.

"Can't close 'em again . . . ," Lynn said. "Too dry."

Lucy realized there was no reflection on Lynn's eyes of the tower above, no answering glint from the burning sun. Tears poured from her own eyes as she realized how far gone Lynn was, and she tore the cap from the bottle, pried Lynn's teeth apart, and dumped water down her throat.

Lynn gagged and convulsed against the force, but Lucy jammed her jaws together and pinched her nose, not pulling her hand away until she saw Lynn swallow. She curled the other woman's hand around the bottle.

"You're not dying without me dying too," Lucy said sternly. "This is one decision you don't get to make alone."

The barest suggestion of a smile stretched Lynn's flaccid lips. "It is what it is," she said.

And the sun moved across the sky.

◆ ◆ ◆

Lucy dismissed the flash of light on the horizon as nothing more than a spasm of her dying brain. All her senses felt sharpened as she struggled on, distinctly feeling each contour of the road beneath her, the sound of her frayed and bloodied jean leg dragging against it. Taste alone was elusive, her own tongue now swollen to the point that the idea of fitting food into the increasingly small area of her mouth was ludicrous. Her saliva was gone; her eyes felt like apples left to wither on the tree.

The flash came again, this time bearing with it the faintest hum that in her delirium Lucy mistook for an insect. She waved her hands around her head to fend it off, and the movement sent her to the ground, tearing a hole in her jeans at the knee. The knobby white skin of her kneecap poked through and she stared at it, amazed at how easily her dry skin had peeled away from the lower layers, how slowly her thick blood rose to the surface.

The sound grew louder, and she felt vibration underneath her that seemed to pierce through her skin and rattle her bones. The light on the horizon was gone; in its place a dark shadow hurtled toward her. Her fevered brain struggled to find a word that would make the phenomenon sensible.

"Car," she croaked, the word sticking in her throat and resisting her enlarged tongue. The single syllable roared through what was left of her logic, and she said it louder, hoping to cut through the fog of fear that had immediately swirled around the one word.

"People," she said, rising to her feet, not knowing whether to run into the desert and hide or toward them with her arms uplifted. Then she remembered Lynn's still body left miles behind. Lucy straddled the yellow line in the middle of the road and put her hands into the air, wishing she could touch the light-blue dome that stretched above her and pluck down the merciless yellow glare of the sun.

The car came to a stop in front of her, the waves of heat rolling off its hood so thickly Lucy feared they might knock her over. With her hands still in the air, Lucy said in the strongest voice she could muster, "My name is Lucy, and I can witch water."

Part Three
CITY

Twenty-Five

L
ynn's skin was so dry, it didn't dimple around the needle when the woman put an IV in her.

"She'll be fine," Lucy said. "She's too proud to die."

"Pride won't keep your mom hydrated," the nurse said simply, and hung a bag of liquid next to the bed Lynn lay in. A thin pulse pressed against Lucy's fingers, light as the wings of a butterfly. Lucy pressed back against it, not bothering to correct the woman's assumption that Lynn was her mother.

There had been no time for details when Lucy had crawled into the car with the help of the two men who had found her. Unconsciousness had been calling, but Lucy was frantic to explain they had to go back and get Lynn. Fever and fear had driven all words from her brain, and Lucy had only been able to point back in the direction she had come, and then to her own heart.

The drive into the city had seemed nearly obscene to Lucy, the speed at which the car ate up the miles of road mocking the hard-earned progress they had made on foot. Lynn's head had rocked in her lap, unresisting. The driver had braked suddenly, and Lynn had rolled with the momentum, dropping to the car floor like a bag of rocks. The men had looked back at the noise and shared a glance even Lucy couldn't miss.

But Lynn had defied them without uttering a single word. Her heart kept beating, her breath kept coming, and Lucy's pride in her had soared to new heights. Lucy stayed in a wheelchair by her bed-side, her own IV trailing behind her, snaked with Lynn's.

"You should get back to your own bed," the nurse said. "You weren't in much better shape than your mother twelve hours ago."

"I need to stay where she can see me," Lucy said, not glancing up.

"She's not been conscious since they brought her in, little girl. She's not seeing you, or anyone else."

"It's best I be here when she can though," Lucy said. "Otherwise she's likely to start killing people."

There was a disgruntled snort; then the woman was gone and Lucy sighed with relief. "I hope she's here when you do wake up," she muttered to Lynn. "You should definitely meet."

The nurse who had been on shift when Lucy was carried into the hospital was an older woman she had mistaken for Vera. She'd struggled from the arms of the man carrying her and fallen forward into the nurse's arms, weeping for joy. When her wits had been restored to her hours later, Lucy was not sure how her mind had made the leap. The only similarity between Nora and Vera was age and the ability to heal, but Lucy was thankful both for the proof that people could live long lives in the desert, and that someone was around who could save hers.

Lynn's hand twitched underneath her own, and Lucy leaned forward, eyes searching Lynn's face for any sign of movement. "Lynn? Can you hear me?"

One eyelid flickered, opened slowly, and focused on the needle in her arm. Lynn licked her lips before trying to speak. "Cold."

"That's your IV," Lucy said, rubbing her hands up and down Lynn's arm to warm it. "Mine was cold too, at first, but you get used to it."

"IV?"

"Yeah, it's like a vein with water in it, and they pour it into your body, kind of," Lucy said. "So don't try to move a whole lot, 'cause you're connected to it."

"Hurts," Lynn said, weakly lifting her other arm.

"That's 'cause they started the IV over there yesterday," Lucy said, trying to remember everything Nora had explained to her as she had rolled her over to Lynn's bedside. "Your veins were flat like . . . like a worm that's been stepped on, you know? They switched over to this arm today, and had a little more luck."

Lucy brushed her hand over the deep purple bruise that had formed in the crook of Lynn's other elbow. "You relax for now. There's no reason for you to be worried, or . . ." Lucy trailed off, searching for the right word. "Or scared," she finished.

Lynn struggled to open both eyes and gave Lucy a brief glance before they slid shut again. "Why do you look scared then?"

Lucy tightened her grip on Lynn's wrist. "You were so close, Lynn. You were damn close to dying."

"Close to nothing," Lynn said vehemently, though it cost her breath to do so. "You said I wasn't allowed to die without you. I'm still here."

Lucy's throat closed in on itself, and she fought against the tears, not wanting Lynn to open her eyes again only to see her crying. "Yeah," she said. "You are."

"Where the hell is here?"

"It's a city called Las Vegas."

"Well," Lynn muttered as she dropped back into unconsciousness, "shit."

Nora showed up later, her warm hands soothing in the dark.

"Lucy, are you asleep, little one?"

"Grandma?" Lucy asked, her groggy voice heavy with sleep and hope. There was a reassuring pressure on her arm, but the answer was disappointing.

"No, it's me, Nora," she said. "I'm here to check on you. You fell asleep in your wheelchair." Clarity descended, and though it was pitch dark inside the hospital, Lucy could feel Lynn's alertness in the bed next to her.

There was the screech of the brake being taken off, and then Nora was rolling Lucy toward her own bed, the unexpected movement making her nauseous in the dark. She put her head down and felt Nora's hands moving over her hair. "You all right?"

"Wasn't ready to move is all," Lucy said, taken aback by the easy familiarity with which Nora touched her. Though Lynn's affections were true, she rarely showed them through touch.

"I'll warn you next time," she said gently, and Lucy felt strong arms beneath her as she was shifted over to her bed, the neglected sheet shockingly cool.

"Did your mother wake?"

"No," Lucy said, relieved the dark masked her lie.

"I'm sorry."

Lucy didn't know what to say, so she lay still in the darkness.

"How are you feeling?"

"Better," she answered. "Not well, but not nearly as bad."

"That's to be expected. You lost a lot of water."

"Water, always water," Lucy repeated. The wave of nausea returned as she remembered the river of rain closing over her head and sweeping her away.

Nora's hands brought her back to reality as she checked Lucy's pulse and felt for a fever. "The men who brought you in said you can witch it."

"I can," Lucy said, and felt the hand on her forehead tense at the answer.

"That's good, little one, good for everyone."

She'd begun to slide back into sleep before Nora's words trailed off, but she jerked herself awake. "Why'd you call me that?"

Nora's hands were gone, her voice suddenly distant in the dark. "Call you what?"

"Little one."

There was a pause, and Lucy strained her eyes against the black to see if Nora was still there. "I had a child that was built small, like you. Now get some sleep."

Footsteps retreated, and Lucy heard a door shut behind them. Moments later Lynn's voice cut through the black.

"You told them?"

The words hung between their beds like a weight, and Lucy fought hard to sound confident when she spoke. "There wasn't any choice. I'm sorry."

"Who all knows?"

"I don't know. The men who found me, Nora apparently."

"So let's assume everyone," Lynn said, and the quiet descended again. "How many people are here?"

"I don't know, Lynn," Lucy said. "I've been awake about five more hours than you."

"And what'd you learn in those five hours?"

"That we're lucky we're not dead, you especially. Nora and the bigger lady have some kind of medical training. We're in a real hospital, but apparently they don't have electricity."

Lynn was silent again, but Lucy could feel her thinking in the dark, and her own mind ran over the thousand things she should've noticed while Lynn lay comatose.

"Those men that found you . . . did they hurt you in any way?"

"I'm fine, Lynn," Lucy said.

"You understand what I'm ask—"

"I'm. Fine. You don't need to assume that—"

"Everyone we meet is bad?"

"Yeah," Lucy answered. "There are good people in the world, like Grandma. Like Stebbs and Fletcher."

"There are," Lynn said carefully, "but we'll start with the assumption most people aren't, and let them earn their way up."

Nora's warm touch and concerned tone flickered through Lucy's mind. "Nora seems all right," she said tentatively.

Lynn grunted in reply.

"What do we do?" Lucy asked, even though her foot ached horribly and sleep was toying with her brain again.

"I don't know that there's a lot of *we* involved. I'm draining myself just talking."

"You've never exactly been chatty," Lucy said. "So I think you'll be fine."

Lucy heard something sailing toward her through the dark, and a pillow hit her in the face.

"Nice shot."

"I have my gifts," Lynn said, and Lucy would've mistaken it for a joke if not for what came next. "Though they don't seem wanted here."

"What do you mean?"

"Where's my gun?"

"It's—" Lucy's tongue was quick to supply an instant answer to the all-important question, but she couldn't. "I don't know."

"The men who picked us up, did they take it?"

Lucy racked her brain, forcing the fevered car ride from the desert into high detail, but all she saw was Lynn's limp body, her head lolling endlessly. "I don't remember."

"Nobody in this world leaves a high-powered rifle lying beside the road," Lynn said. "They took it."

A chill crept beneath Lucy's skin that had nothing to do with the IV. She curled into herself under the thin sheet and tucked the edges under the sharp contours of her body.

"So what happens next?"

"We're in your territory now, little one, and me without my gun. You tell me."

Lucy lay in the dark, her mind at odds with her heart once again. Lynn's innate distrust of people might be leading her into paranoia.

These people had saved their lives, filled their bodies with water again. She was in a bed for the first time in months, her head resting on a pillow.

"I'll keep my eyes open," she finally said. "People like to talk about themselves, especially if they've accomplished something. And they have, Lynn. We're in a city in the middle of a desert, and they're giving out water to strangers."

"Don't be afraid to show them how smart you are," Lynn said, her voice fading further into weakness. "You've got a sharp mind; that's of value anywhere. Watch and learn."

"And then?"

"And then I get my gun back."

The other nurse was there in the morning, and Lucy resisted the urge to ask where Nora was. The bigger woman did everything brusquely, as if Lucy were a life-size doll whose plasticized limbs could bend in any direction while being dressed.

"Ouch," she said as her head was forced through a T-shirt much too small for her.

"You're fine," the woman said dismissively, though Lucy pulled the ribbed collar away from her neck and looked with dismay at the outlines of her ribs showing through the fabric.

"Um . . . I think this might be for a little kid," she said.

"Mmmm" was all the nurse offered in reply.

"What's your name?"

"Bailey."

"Hi, Bailey, I'm Lucy," she said as politely as she could manage.

"Uh-huh." Bailey finished folding the gown she'd taken off Lucy and moved over to Lynn's bed. "Your mom wake up yet?"

"I'm awake," came Lynn's voice, though her eyes stayed closed. "And if you try to take my clothes off, we'll have issues straightaway."

Bailey stood at the foot of Lynn's bed with her arms crossed over her chest, but Lucy noticed she made no move to touch Lynn. Even with her eyes closed and her voice pitched low, Lynn looked and sounded dangerous.

"You going to be the one to give me trouble then?"

"You an important person around here, Bailey?" Lucy suddenly asked, switching the big woman's attention back to her.

"'Scuse me?"

"I asked if you were an important person around here. I'm guessing you're not, since you're cleaning up the piss of wandering strangers. So Lynn will give as she's getting, and there will be no kind words for anybody until you bring me someone who matters to talk to."

Bailey glanced at Lynn, then flushed three shades of red as she backed out the room, arm muscles twitching.

"Well, that was a nice bit of sass. I've heard that tone on more than one occasion as I caught you sliding out the window in the middle of the night."

Lucy stuck her tongue out at Lynn, but her reservations outlasted her sarcasm. "I don't know how well I can keep it up."

"It was a solid start, anyway," Lynn said, tipping her a wink before they heard Bailey's heavy footsteps in the hallway. Lucy glanced up to see a boy standing in the doorway, his anxious face torn between amusement and interest as he glanced at her.

"Uh, hi," Lucy said, highly aware of the fact that the shirt she was wearing clung to her in more places than her ribs.

"You're requesting to speak to someone important?"

"And that's you?"

He visibly tried to make himself taller. "Kind of. My dad is . . . important."

"So where's he?"

"Out. He told me to come and see if you can really do the witching."

"I can," Lucy said. "Didn't know I had to prove it."

"What's your name?" Lynn asked.

"Ben," he answered, without taking his eyes from Lucy.

"Well, Ben, bring my daughter a willow switch and she'll show you."

"Willows aren't easy to come by," Ben said, his eyes still roaming over Lucy in curiosity.

"Doesn't have to be a willow," Lucy said, feeling the challenge in his gaze. "Just bring me something wooden, three blankets, and a bottle of water."

Ben left, and Lynn's sigh filled the room. "I don't think you're going to put much over him. Nasty little weasel, that one."

"How old do you think he is?"

"Younger than you, by a bit."

"He acts older."

"People act lots of ways."

Ben was back moments later with a pencil, an IV bag, and three hospital gowns. "This'll have to do."

"Good enough," Lucy said, taking the pencil from him. "Now hide that bag under one of the gowns. I won't look."

She buried her head under the pillow, taking comfort in the dark and the memory of Stebbs that the game brought rushing back. Long winters had been spent in the basement while he taught her to hone their shared ability to the point that she didn't even need a switch to point the way. The hum of water called to her fingers, the vibration of life answering in her veins with a voice few could hear.

When she opened her eyes, she saw Lynn had turned her head, unwilling to see her giving away her grace so easily to strangers. Lucy made a show of deliberation even though she felt the pulse the moment her hand passed over the middle pile, strong and sure.

"That one," she said, and Ben lifted it to prove her correct. Bailey's white face floated in the door window like a curious moon.

"You really can," Ben said, his voice breaking on the last word.

"Yes, I really can," Lucy said, and forced herself to smile at him.

Twenty-Six

"It's called *failure to thrive*," Ben said as they walked into the scorching sun. Lucy tried to ignore the feeling that her skin was trying to creep off her bones upon being reintroduced to the heat. Nora had warned her against walking too much on her injured foot, but she wasn't going to let Ben know how badly it hurt her to keep in stride with him.

"What's that?"

"That's what's wrong with me," he clarified. "Up here." He pointed toward the building that was their destination, mercifully near.

"I didn't realize there was something wrong with you. Physically," she added.

"Oh, there is. Failure to thrive," he repeated, as if naming it provided an enemy. "I'm eighteen years old."

"You're not," Lucy contradicted. "You don't even hit my shoulder."

Ben shrugged. "That's why it's called failure to thrive. We do very well for ourselves here now, but that hasn't always been the case. When I was little, I didn't get everything I needed, nutritionally speaking."

Lucy was about to point out that he was still little when she stopped in her tracks, awed by an eerily familiar sight she couldn't quite place. "I feel like I've seen that before." She gestured at the building across the street, which rose into a graceful point in the sky.

"Not that, exactly. At least I doubt it," Ben said. "That's a replica of the Eiffel Tower. The original is in Paris, France. Do you know where that is?"

"Europe," she immediately shot back, suddenly grateful to Lynn for forcing an education on her, even if it was only culled from encyclopedias during the long winter months when their hands could be idle.

"You can't catch my disease." Ben changed tracks quickly, obviously surprised that she knew the answer.

"I wasn't going to ask that."

"Maybe not, but you were wondering."

They walked on in silence, the towering presence of the empty buildings silencing any retort she might have come up with. Even though her memories of Entargo were limited by time and the fog of childhood, she could recall uniform skyscrapers like rectangular siblings. The buildings here were different, each a vibrant explosion of glass and cement, their colors dulled by time and the joy of life they strived to express stilled by the emptiness of the streets.

Ben veered to the left, steering her by the elbow toward a huge building, bleached bone white by the sun. "Careful," he said. "The railing is starting to give in a few places. You don't want to fall in."

"Fall into what?"

"That used to be a lake," Ben said, nodding toward what looked like a miniature desert trapped by white barriers. "We can't keep the sand out of everything, though we try to keep the streets clean. You step out onto it and you'll sink."

Lucy looked over the undulating plains of sand, carved by the hot breeze that felt like a blast from a wood fire. "Would it go over my head?"

"No, it's not that deep, but digging you out would be a job. I'm not strong enough to pull you out, and everyone else is busy enough as it is."

She didn't ask who "everyone else" was, as they had passed no one on the streets. The shadow of the building they approached stretched out toward her, and Lucy resisted the urge to run the last few feet into its inky coolness.

"A lake, huh?" She glanced back over her shoulder at the miniature desert. "Where'd all the water go?"

Ben opened a door for her, and she stepped through into the heat of the building, its trapped air stuffy with the exhalations of generations. "It was all taken out and stored by my grandfather a long time ago," he said, his chest swelling with the importance of his ancestors. "The pools too."

"What's a pool?"

"It's—" Ben stopped and looked at Lucy as condescendingly as possible, since he was a foot shorter than her. "Exactly how country are you?"

"Very," Lucy said, her voice lost in the faded opulence that surrounded her. The lobby stretched for what seemed like miles, far past the daylight streaming through the sand-grimed windows behind her. The rounded arcs of light cast by the windows were quickly eaten by the depth of a darkness so complete that Lucy could only guess at the height of the ceiling or where the walls ended on the far side. The heat from the outside had tapped the last of her rebuilt strength, and her lungs struggled to pass the weighty, warm air in and out of her body. Her foot throbbed so deeply she could feel a pulse in her knee.

"I need to sit," she said weakly, seconds before falling to the floor, the impact softened by a rug so deep her fingers sank into the fibers, and she wondered if it would close over her head like the sands outside, and the raging waters of the river.

Ben walked into the shadows and she heard the scraping of

furniture, followed shortly by the reemergence of his face, puffy with exertion, as he pushed a padded chair to her. "Have a seat," he said grandly, then dropped to the floor next to her, falling back onto the carpet and staring into the emptiness of the far-reaching ceiling.

Lucy could almost forgive his attitude when she saw how much it had cost him to bring her the chair. She lifted herself into it, studying his pasty, pale face while he had his eyes closed for a moment. "Thank you for the chair," she said.

"Dad says I need to make sure I'm polite. He says a boy built like me won't get a girl who wants protection. So I've got to aim for one who wants someone to be nice to her."

"So you're nice on purpose, not because you want to be, is what you're saying?"

"Is 'nice' a naturally occurring trait?"

Lucy didn't answer, since she doubted failure to thrive was a naturally occurring trait either. Ben sat up and pulled himself to his feet using her chair. "C'mon. Dad's in the gardens. He'll be wanting to see you."

She followed him through the cavernous lobby, their footsteps echoing out and above them, bouncing off the unseen walls and ceiling. They emerged from the darkness into a garden so bright Lucy's eyes ached from the contraction of her pupils. The garden stood in stark contrast to the hollowness of the lobby, every inch covered with light and green growth. Lucy's words did not echo endlessly there, instead absorbed by the life around her, drinking in her voice instead of throwing it back at her in defiance.

The loamy smell of good, wet dirt filled her nose and made her soul ache for home, and lengths of green fields drenched with rain. The sudden whiff of life was so direct and strong Lucy felt woozy again. She settled onto the cold marble floor with a soft sigh as her skin drank in the moisture around her, her body answering the life in the room with a response of its own as she felt every pore in her skin opening up to drink air cleaned by green leaves.

"I think she likes it," said a deep voice, and Lucy startled from her reverie to see a man among the vegetation, his smile a glaring white against the backdrop of green.

"Dad, she can do it," Ben said by way of introduction.

The smile slipped for a second as he shot an irritated look at his son, and then returned when he glanced at Lucy. "Hello, little one," he said. The endearment sounded so natural in his deep voice that she felt comforted.

"Hi," she said shyly, suddenly aware that Ben's father had a handsome face to match his voice. "I'm Lucy."

"Lucy, welcome."

She ducked her head in response but could think of nothing to say. Ben backed away as his father came toward them, emerging from the garden like a god of life. He was a massive man, the biggest Lucy had ever seen; he would dwarf Lynn, and Lucy herself only rose to his elbow. Feeling more childlike than ever, she reached up to shake his hand.

"I'm Lucy."

"You already said that." He winked at her, and her hand was immediately lost inside his, which was coated with the rich blackness of the soil.

"I'm Lander," he said, releasing her hand and clasping her shoulder, turning her away from Ben. "Impressive, isn't it?"

Lucy's eyes were still riveted on Lander's bicep, so she didn't realize he meant the garden until Ben sighed heavily. "Yes," she said, redirecting her gaze. "It's . . . is that a *tomato?*"

The inviting flash of red among the waves of green brought Lucy out from under Lander's protective arm, her mouth watering at the sight of a favorite food so long denied her. "You grew a *tomato?*"

"More than one, actually," Lander said. "That's the first ripe one of this crop."

Nearer the plants, Lucy could see the bunches of green tomatoes, swelling with life and drinking in the sun from the glass ceiling above, the moisture from the thick air around it. The one that had caught her eye had just turned, the skin a deep orange that would turn to overripe redness in a day or two.

"It's yours, if you want it." Lander's voice was at her elbow.

She reached for it, her hand barely glancing the thin skin pulled taut over the meat of the fruit, vibrant with life. It snapped off the vine easily, the spicy scent of the broken stem delivering the taste to her mouth before she'd touched it to her lips. "You're sure? It shouldn't go to someone else, someone who—"

"I grew it," Lander said. "What's here is mine, and that is for you. There's plenty more where that came from."

Needing no more urging, Lucy bit, her sharp teeth breaking the skin and sending the red juice spilling over her lips and dripping to the marble floor at her feet.

Lynn looked mistrustfully at the green tomato Lucy had brought her as proof of the garden down the street. "You ate one?"

"A red one, yeah," Lucy said, flooded with guilt that it hadn't occurred to her to save part of the ripe one for Lynn. "I thought you could set that one in the windowsill, 'til it's ready."

Lynn sniffed it, closing her eyes in a replica of Lucy's moment of bliss at the smell. A small smile tugged at her mouth, but it was tinged with sadness, and Lucy knew she was thinking of home instead of the small miracle in front of her.

"Once you feel good enough, you've got to see it," Lucy said, unable to hide her enthusiasm. "I guess it used to be a botanical garden." She pronounced the word slowly so it came out correctly, unable to shake the thought of Ben's mockery even when he wasn't around. "They had all kinds of weird plants and things there people would come to look at, so when the Shortage hit, Ben's grandfather pulled up all the flowery plants and they used that dirt for vegetables."

"Uh-huh." Lynn ran her thumbnail over the tight green skin of the tomato. "And how do they water this garden?"

"I didn't ask. But Ben said Lander's dad took all the water out of the fountains and swimming pools—and there were a ton of pools, Lynn, you should see this place—and stored it in the hot water tanks of all the hotels."

"You sound impressed."

"I can't *not* be," Lucy said. "We're in the middle of the desert and you're holding a tomato."

Lynn sniffed the skin one more time and handed it to Lucy to set in the windowsill. "Who is Lander?"

"That's Ben's dad. Wait 'til you meet him, Lynn—good God. He's massive." Lucy felt herself warming at the memory of his smile. "He might even make you feel feminine."

Lucy turned from the windowsill to see Lynn staring over her shoulder out at the bright-blue sky. "I've never felt more or less of a woman because of a man."

"I didn't mean . . ." Lucy stumbled over her words, but Lynn waved them away.

"Don't worry about it. I'm just sick of being in this hospital bed."

"It's actually not a hospital," Lucy piped up. "This is a hotel, same as the other where the garden is, but they took some of the first-floor rooms and brought over equipment from the hospital so everyone isn't scattered all across the city."

Lynn nodded, but her eyes slid shut as exhaustion claimed her again. She licked her lips before trying to speak. "Everyone?"

"Yeah . . . well, that's how Ben put it. Everyone."

"No idea how many?"

"So far I've just met Ben and Lander, Bailey and Nora."

"I doubt it's the four of them, if they've been hoarding pool water for generations. What else did you see when Ben took you outside?"

"Not much, really," Lucy admitted. "It's a city that's falling apart. Ben said they all live in the first one or two stories of the hotels along the strip here because the heat is unbearable if you go any higher, and the sand is blowing back into the city on the edges. They try to keep the main road clear for the cars they send out, but they can't keep up with much else."

"Yeah, that's what has me thinking."

"Thinking?" Lucy had to prod Lynn when she didn't volunteer more information. "Thinking about what?"

Lynn opened her eyes again, the strength in them outshining her weary body. "If they've got all the water and food they need, why they sending patrols out into the desert?"

"Why question it? We'd be dead, otherwise."

"Right, but why? Just to find half-gone people like ourselves, bring us back from the edge of death with tomatoes?"

"Why not?"

"'Cause this is a dark world, and I've yet to see those who have helping those who have not unless they've got their own reasons."

"We do," Lucy pointed out. "We gave that family a perfectly good house with a freshwater source back in Nebraska."

"That was your choice. And you had a *reason*." Lynn's eyes flashed, all her strength pouring into her words. "This ain't California, little one, and don't you forget it. These people were driving way out of their way, burning gas without knowing we were out there to save. And I want to know why."

"Next time they offer to save my life or give me something to eat I'll question that, okay?"

Lynn ignored Lucy's tone, her eyes sliding shut again. "Thing is, you've got something to offer in return. Me, I don't matter here. They ask you to show them where water is, you do it."

"I would anyway," Lucy said. "We owe them."

"That's right, we both do. But you're the only one who can repay the debt. You're the one they need, the one they're going to listen to. You understand?"

"Yeah, I get it," Lucy said, her voice lacking the conviction of her words. "I'm the one in charge now."

Twenty-Seven

Nora insisted Lynn remain in bed, a rule Lynn disobeyed until Bailey tried to enforce it. The resulting match of wills ended with a broken wheelchair and the remnants of Lynn's uneaten overripe tomato running down Bailey's face. After that Lucy tried to be in the room whenever Bailey was around, but Lynn's increasing unhappiness and the alluring call of freedom under the bright sky kept her away more than she had intended.

Ben was not ideal company, but his short shadow dogged her footsteps no matter where she went in the city. She soaked up the incessant stream of information he supplied, and regurgitated it for Lynn at night in the darkness of their shared room. She learned much and met new people, always cataloging their names, descriptions, and duties within the city to report back to Lynn in the evening.

Lynn listened carefully, but Lucy's mind was whirring away, analyzing the oasis of a city.

The long, deep pools full of sand fascinated Lucy, and she spent time lounging by their sculpted tops, watching the hot breeze make new patterns and imagining what the world had been like when crystalline waters lapped the concrete banks. But she was not asked to find freshwater, or prove her abilities again. Ben brought four bottles full of water, her allotment for the day. People in physically demanding jobs received six, as did the ill.

"Ugh." Lynn grimaced, holding the bottle up to the light. "Doesn't taste right."

"Ben says that's on account of the chlorine," Lucy said, sipping her own water. "He says it breaks down after a while, but there's an aftertaste."

"That's one word for it," Lynn said, twisting the cap back onto her bottle.

"You drink that," Lucy said. "Nora says you need to stay hydrated."

"I've drank so much already I feel like I'm pregnant with a water baby."

Lucy crossed her arms and mockingly raised one eyebrow. "Do I need to get Bailey in here?"

Lynn made a nasty noise in her throat but drank what was left in her bottle and handed it off to Lucy. "Happy?"

Their fingers brushed as she took the empty from Lynn, and Lucy thought hard before answering. "Yeah . . . actually. I am. This place, it feels good," Lucy said. Even though Ben's constant presence grated on her nerves, there was food and water. People had time in their days beyond their duties, playing pool in the rotted-out lobbies of the crumbling hotels in the fading daylight. "It might not be California, but if it's got what I wanted . . . why not stay?"

Lynn settled back into her bed, eyes closed against the glare of the setting sun and the weight of Lucy's words. "Let me meet this Lander fella before I even consider anything, okay? The only people that cross my path over the course of the day are Bailey and Ben, and it doesn't seem fair to judge the whole city by those two."

"And Nora," Lucy reminded her, trying not to sound too hopeful. "Nora's great."

"And Nora," Lynn admitted. She played with the edge of her blanket, focused on the simple task of folding it into a fan, the ridges poking through her fingers. "Let me meet Lander," she repeated, "and have a little conversation about my gun. We'll see how that goes."

"Yeah, we'll see," Lucy agreed. For the first night since their arrival in Vegas, she did not sleep well.

The heat was oppressive the next day, the air creeping into every cranny of her skin and opening her pores to bring out each drop of hard-fought-for water she'd drunk in the morning. Lucy peered back into the dark of the lobby.

"You sure you want to go out today?" Lucy asked.

"It ever cool around here?" Lynn asked, as she shuffled out of the shadows.

"Not that I've noticed."

"It's time for me to do something," Lynn said, though Lucy noticed the sheen of sweat that popped up on her forehead. "I can't sit in that room forever, letting you take all the risks."

"I'm not so sure there *are* risks," Lucy reminded her, as Lynn walked down the strip toward the hotel where Lander and Ben lived and managed the garden. Lynn was out of breath by the time they reached the hotel, and Lucy tried to steer her toward the chair Ben had pulled out of the shadows, still sitting alone in a bright arch of sunlight. Lynn brushed her off, though Lucy could feel her tightly wound muscles shaking even in their brief touch.

"I'm fine," Lynn said. "Where to?"

Lucy led her to the gardens, hoping for a few minutes in which Lynn could absorb the life around her and restore her spirits. But Lander was there, moving quietly among the crop despite his size. He emerged from the tasseling sweet corn, golden fronds tangling in his stubble as he passed.

"Lynn, hello," he said, his voice carrying the same reassuring resonance that had lulled Lucy's fears when they met. "It's good to meet you, and looking much stronger than I expected." His eyes moved over her body in a way that made Lucy suspect he wasn't just appreciating Lynn's skills of recuperation.

"Uh-huh," Lynn said, her interest focused on the corn rather than Lander. "So where's my gun?"

"Your gun is somewhere safe."

"Safest place for my rifle is in my own hands."

Lander spread his hands in front of him, still smiling. "And I'm open to that. Your daughter has shared her abilities with us, and I understand your own lie in a more . . ."

"Violent," Lynn provided. "You can say it."

"A more violent path, then," he finished.

"True enough."

"So this is your gift to the world?"

Lynn's eyebrows flew up, and Lucy felt herself bracing for the backlash. "I don't remember ever getting a gift in the first place, or signing up for any kind of exchange."

"Did we not give you life?"

"My mother gave me life; saving it was your choice. The only gift I give is death."

Something flickered across his face, and Lander moved closer to Lynn, graceful as a cat. He towered over her, muscles rippling in his arms as he put a massive palm against Lynn's throat, slim and pale after her illness. He leaned in to whisper to her, "Even now?"

Lucy breathed quietly in the shadows, tensing herself to spring, should she have to.

Lynn looked up at Lander, the strength of her voice vibrating his fingers where they lay. "Even now, you big son of a bitch."

He burst out laughing, a sound so overpowering that not even the living air of the garden could soak it up, and it rolled out into the lobby to echo off the dark walls and back to them. "I like you," he declared, and slapped Lynn on the back, which pushed her forward a foot. "I like you a lot."

Lynn shot Lucy a look. "Fantastic."

His hands fastened onto Lynn's shoulders, and he beamed into her upturned face. "Then let's see what you can do."

Lynn's rifle seemed to have missed her as its bullets sang out over the city, dropping targets at growing distances as Lander pointed out signs, car windows, anything that caught his eye. Nora had insisted on following them to the roof when she learned her patient would be climbing steps. Lander had carried Lynn the last hundred or so, cradled in his arms like a doll, while she likewise cradled the rifle.

It was soon clear exactly how novel gunshots were in Las Vegas. Bailey appeared shortly after the sharp cracks of the bullets, puffing her way to the roof as if she expected an insurrection she would single-handedly end. Her amazement at seeing Lynn with her gun in hand turned to bitterness in seconds flat, and Lucy kept her eye on the big lady, noting how her pinched face contracted even more with every compliment Lander paid to Lynn.

Ben was hot on Bailey's heels, his cheeks flushed and any assistance he might've been able to bring to the imagined threat spent on the climb itself. He collapsed at Lucy's feet and began lecturing her on how the long-dead elevators had operated. She made semi-interested noises at the appropriate times, which she'd learned was the only encouragement Ben needed to keep talking.

Lucy could see people in the streets shading their eyes against the glare and looking toward the gunshots. Lander waved to let them know all was well and continued to point out targets for Lynn, whose frail arms could only hold the rifle for so long. Eventually she lay down prone on the roof but kept shooting. "Lucy," she called out, "some water."

Lucy came forward and dropped next to Lynn to swap the bottle for the rifle, the easy feel of the weapon changing hands so familiar they could've been on the roof of their own home.

"Take a look," Lynn said, pointing toward the west. "Something new."

Lucy leaned into the rifle, her eyelashes brushing against the scope and bringing back memories in a flood. It wasn't the green fields of Ohio she saw, but the burnt-out streets of Las Vegas, with drifts of sand invading the areas people had surrendered back to the desert. Sprawled in the sun, amid the broken buildings and rusted cars, was a huge cat, its tail twitching with pleasure as it soaked up the rays.

"Lord above." Lucy blinked and pulled away from the scope. "How big is that thing?"

At home there had been a few feral cats, generations removed from their domesticated ancestors and mean as hell. Lucy remembered them as half-starved, hissing balls of fur, nothing like the majestic, well-muscled animal sleeping in the middle of the abandoned city.

"Big. It's a mountain lion," Nora said. "Group of them moved into that side of town years ago."

Lucy rolled onto her elbow to look at Nora. "They a problem?"

"*Yes*," Nora said.

Lynn took the rifle back from Lucy. "Why don't you run them off?"

"Because you're holding the only gun in this whole city," Lander answered.

"And it's time you handed it back," Bailey added.

"No, shoot it first." Nora had come up to the edge of the roof beside Lander, her shadow falling across Lynn and Lucy. "Shoot that one lying out there like she owns the place."

To Lucy's surprise, Lynn looked to Lander before sighting the cat again, and she found her gut twisting at the thought of Lynn's crosshairs on the unsuspecting creature. The rifle cracked, and in the distance Lucy could see a streak of color as the she-cat fled for cover.

"Damn," Lynn said, shading her eyes. "I missed."

"Let her have the gun, Lander," Nora said. Lander was about to object when Nora raised her hand to stop him. "Let her come up here while you or someone else is with her. You know as well as I do there are some buildings we can't even get to anymore because of the cats and the coyotes. If she picks them off, we can recover all that water."

Lander gave Nora a hard look but she didn't drop her gaze, and her next words were directed at Lynn. "I'll give you part of my water ration for every cat you drop," she added, defiant eyes still on Lander.

Lynn looked between the two of them and unloaded her gun. "No need. I don't find myself liking the taste of your water."

"And why's that?" Bailey bristled, as if personally insulted.

"Tastes bad," Lynn said, handing the unspent bullets over to Lander.

"Can I be the one to stay up here with her?" Ben spoke up. "I want to see her get some of the coyotes."

"Since everyone is assuming she will in fact be shooting," Lander said, "I'd like to be the one who accompanies her."

"And you're all assuming I'm staying here in the first place," Lynn said, her words casual but her tone stopping the very breeze.

Lander's smile was back, warm and caring. "Where would you go? Even if we gave you water, once you walk out of here there are no guarantees."

"You can't walk anywhere, in your shape," Nora added. "I wouldn't let you leave."

Lucy saw Lynn bristle. "I'm not sure you *letting* me is—"

"We plan on staying until I can find you a good source of fresh-water," Lucy interrupted. "We figure by then Lynn'll be feeling well enough we can get along and I'll have repaid our debt to you."

"That so?" Lander said, holding out his hand for the rifle. "Well, I hope we can convince you to stay, between now and then."

Twenty-Eight

"**S**o how bad is it, really?" Lucy asked Nora as they stripped the beds she and Lynn had been using.

"What do you mean?" Nora asked, all attention on the sheets.

"If Lander's willing to give Lynn a gun to free up the route to water you've been cut off from, you've got limited supplies."

Lucy moved her small pile of belongings before tearing the dirty sheet off her bed. The clothes she'd been wearing on the road had been washed and returned to her, folded into a tight square so thin she could feel her thumb rubbing her forefinger through it. Her single boot she'd kept, and it stood sentinel on top of her threadbare clothes, waiting to be moved to the new room Nora had cleared them for now that Lynn no longer needed an IV.

"I wouldn't say they're limited," Nora answered.

"You wouldn't say that 'cause you're too scared to, or because that's not the case?" Lynn asked from the corner, where she rested in a wheelchair.

Nora turned to Lynn, irritation chasing manners from her features. "Look, I don't know why you've got it in your head the whole world is made to harm. We're good people here, and if saving your life without knowing the first thing about you isn't proof enough, I don't know what is." She snapped the final clean sheet onto Lucy's bed. Lucy could see her teeth digging into her lower lip as she worked.

"That's great and all, but you didn't exactly answer the question," Lynn said, but Nora ignored her, lost in her work.

"That mountain lion was something else," Lucy said, searching for a different subject. "We've got coyotes back home, but I've never seen anything like that."

"They're a menace," Nora said through gritted teeth as she moved to Lynn's bed. Lucy watched as a clean white sheet sailed overhead. "It began with only one or two down in the residential area. Some of the men would see them when they raided the homes.

"The smaller critters, like skunks and raccoons, came into town shortly after all the water went off. Smelled all the food rotting, I guess. Cats followed them, coyotes too. We all hoped enough human activity would keep them away from the strip, but . . ." Nora broke off to tuck the corner of the sheet tightly under the mattress.

"We started seeing coyotes in the main roads after a bit, and the lions followed them into the city."

Nora stood straight and surveyed the bright white of the empty beds, as clean as if Lynn and Lucy had never been there. "I'll show you your new room," she said.

They went up a floor, the heat rising enough for them to notice. Lucy cracked the balcony door of their new room to see black clouds piling in the distance. "Might rain," she called to Lynn, but Nora was the one who joined her outside, the long curtains flapping in between them.

"She's out of breath," Nora said. "Your mother is weaker than she looks."

"She'll be fine."

Nora came to the railing beside Lucy. "I know you've counted on her for a long time, little one. But the type of bodily injury she suffered . . . some people never come back from that, not fully. I don't know that leaving would be wise. Ever."

Lucy nodded, her eyes trained on the darkness rolling in. "I won't let her leave, if I don't think she's able. And if she's never able, then it is what it is."

Nora followed Lucy's gaze to the storm rolling in and reached for the younger girl's hand. "I know she doesn't trust us yet, or our ways, but the fact that Lander would let her touch a gun speaks volumes."

Lucy's spine stiffened, and she took her hand away from Nora's. "It's her gun."

Nora sighed as a hot wind blew through the city, whipping the curtains around them. A dark streak shot across the road in the face of the storm, and Lucy smiled at the familiar sight of a striped tail. "Never thought I'd miss seeing one of them."

"Raccoons give you trouble back home?"

"Always. I thought Lynn was going to tear her hair out one year over the sweet corn. Stayed up three days in a row picking raccoons off from the roof, but it didn't matter. She fell asleep for five minutes and it was a done deal. They stripped every stalk."

"Lander and Ben keep them out of their garden, though I don't know how," Nora admitted. "We do see coyotes up here on the strip occasionally, so they probably keep the population down."

"But not lions?" Lucy asked, trying to keep her voice casual.

Nora's mouth tightened. "No, not them, thank God."

"You hate them."

The clouds passed over, covering what was left of the sunset and leaving the women in darkness. The air was close and hot, the rain refusing to fall. Lucy could barely see the outline of Nora's face in the last rays of sun.

"Before the world ended I used to *try* to find them, ridiculous as that seems now," she said. "I'd go out hiking overnight, make animal distress calls, anything I could do to call them to me. I loved the way they moved, like liquid under fur. They made me realize some animals are better than others, that the food chain in all of its barbarism is exactly what nature intended."

"So?" Lucy asked, the hot wind pulling her words from her mouth. "What changed?"

Nora looked at her as the clouds scudded across the sky and the last red rays of the setting sun brilliantly lit her eyes. "One of them ate my daughter."

Lucy grasped the older woman's hand, covering it completely with both of hers. "I am so, so, sorry. I wouldn't have asked . . ."

Nora waved the apology away but took her hand back to wipe at some stray tears. "You had no way of knowing."

"Was this . . . in your time? Before the Shortage?"

"No. It was a few years ago. I had a child very late in life, here in what's left of the world. I mentioned her to you, do you remember?"

"Little one," Lucy said quietly. "You called her little one."

"I did." Nora nodded, wiping at another errant tear. "She was built small like you, and wiry too. She used to make Lander laugh by showing off how much she could lift. They made a game of it.

"She was twelve when it happened. Her job was scavenging on the western end for food, clothes, little things we needed replaced in the day to day, like scissors or can openers. Lander was going to teach her how to manage the garden, and Ben was going to fill her post as a scavenger. She was showing him some of the areas that hadn't been picked over yet.

"I don't know if you've ever seen a cat hunt, but a lion will stalk its prey same as little tame cats. No matter how many times I tell myself it's helping nobody, I've played it through my head a million times how that cat must've followed the two of them, sliding through the shadows and waiting for the chance to pounce."

Lucy pictured it in her mind as well, drawn in by the grieving mother's words and the image of two small bodies picking through rubble, hunted by a gliding shadow. She'd seen it in miniature at home before, the silent paws that could deal a crushing velvety blow to the slowest of the stalked.

"But why wouldn't the cat have gone for Ben?" Lucy asked. "Predators always attack the smallest or the weakest. He would've been both."

The clouds pulsed overhead, refusing to break. Lightning flickered and the thunder rolled in the distance before Nora answered.

"The way he tells it, my girl was outside and he was indoors when it attacked."

Lucy carefully watched the play of muscles across Nora's face as they waited for the rain to fall, the flashes of lightning contorting her expression and making it unreadable. "You believe him?"

Nora's shrug was barely perceptible in the darkness. "Ben wants nothing more than his father's love and respect. Working that garden with Lander day in and day out is how he thinks he'll get it. I can't say for sure what happened the day my daughter died, and knowing wouldn't change it anyhow."

"It is what it is," Lucy said, turning to stand shoulder to shoulder with Nora as the storm passed them by.

Twenty-Nine

Lucy felt a distinct sense of unease when she went out to witch with Ben the next day. She could easily picture him sacrificing Nora's daughter, allowing her to be taken by the big cat to further his own ends. Lucy struggled for nonchalance as they walked out of the shadows of the city's buildings, into the bright white stretch of desert.

The rain had refused to fall the night before. The clouds had taunted the city as they slid past. The sky was as clear as glass when Lucy stepped out of the shade and into the sun, the sand throwing the heat back up at her and baking her skin from below.

"C'mon then," she said testily to Ben, who was struggling with an armload of flags. Lander had been overly optimistic when giving them a hundred of the wire flags used to mark buried water lines, but Lucy hadn't wanted to crush the hope in the big man's eyes.

"I'm coming," Ben shot back. "These keep poking me. I don't see why you can't carry some."

"I need my hands free," Lucy said.

Ben caught up to stand next to her. "So how's this work, anyway? You walk around 'til you feel it?"

Lucy stifled a sigh. "Something like that."

"No, really, tell me. I want to know how you do it."

"It's not something I can teach. People either can, or they can't."

Ben made a face at her and she walked away from him, closing her eyes and holding her hands outward, hoping the show of concentration would keep him quiet. Lander had cut her a forked stick from one of the trees in the garden, and while it lacked the smooth contours from years of her grip, it would do the trick.

The power to find water was so sacred that Stebbs had lowered his voice when he spoke to her about it, even in private. Lynn would prefer to never speak of it at all, keeping Lucy's gift in a quiet place where it would draw no attention. But Lucy had always reveled in the spasm of power that water sent toward her, crying out to her it was there and wanted to be found.

"Here," she said. "It's not very deep though."

Ben pulled a flag from his bundle and jabbed it into the ground. "That's good, right? Easier to get to."

"Easier to get at, yeah, but if it's shallow, it might not last long."

Lucy wandered off in another direction, letting her feet go, her mind drift while waiting for the water to talk to her. The heat was drawing her own moisture straight out of her skin, dotting her pores with beads of sweat. A rifle shot echoed across the flat plain and Lucy jumped, drops falling off her forehead and evaporating on the hot sand.

"Shit," she said. "Scared me."

Ben looked back at the city, the flags slung across his shoulders. "Your mom. She's rather basic, isn't she?"

"What do you mean?" Lucy asked, her sudden clench making the stick jump in her hands.

"That water?"

"The stick wants to hit you and I'm stopping it."

Ben smiled, whether he thought she was funny or because he enjoyed getting under her skin she didn't know. "I mean she's one-sided. She wants her gun, and she wants to shoot things, and that seems to be about where her interests stop."

"Well, she's good at it," Lucy said, repositioning the stick and walking away from Ben.

"You ask questions about the garden, and our people. You want to know how we manage, but all she wants to do is get her gun and move on."

"Yes, she does," Lucy agreed. The stick leapt in her hands, viciously jabbing downward, but she felt no rush of pride. "Here."

Ben planted a flag, eyes still on Lucy. "What if she wants to go, and you don't?"

"What about it?"

"Would you stay?"

"I don't . . ." Lucy looked off into the distance at the blue mountains not unlike the ones Lynn had nearly died getting across, all because Lucy had asked her to. She dropped her stick and glared down at Ben, unsure how he could look so smug when he had to look up to meet her eye. "Lynn and I go together or we stay together. End of story."

"That's a shame."

"What do you care?"

Ben dropped his armload of flags to the ground. "I wouldn't say I *care*. It's obvious you like it here and your mom doesn't. Did you mean what you said about finding us a clean source of water and moving on?"

"Yes," Lucy said, taking the bottle of water Ben handed to her from his backpack.

"Because that's what she wants, or what you want?"

The odd-tasting water slid down her throat, coating her tongue with the residue she could never quite wash away. But it was water, and two weeks ago she would've licked puddles off the hot road to save her life.

"I don't know," Lucy said, handing the water back to Ben.

His smile was honest, and it nearly made his awkward face handsome. Lucy smiled back, unable to help herself. "You almost looked like your dad there for a second."

Ben rolled his eyes. "Better than my mom."

Lucy dried her palms on her jeans before taking the stick back up. "What's she look like?"

"Bailey's my mom."

"Bailey? The nurse?"

Ben sighed and re-shouldered his backpack. "Oh, I know. How did such a little shrimp of a guy come out of Bailey and Lander? It's a genetic joke that gets trotted out for a laugh all the time, so go ahead and have your giggle."

"I wasn't thinking that so much as . . . ugh," Lucy said, turning red for reasons that had nothing to do with the heat.

"Well, yeah, there's that too," Ben agreed, falling into step beside her with his armload of blue flags. "But my dad can't exactly be picky, you know? He had a kid with Nora and that didn't turn out so great—"

"Wait, Nora's daughter was Lander's?"

"She told you about that?"

"Yeah." Lucy looked away, answering the tiny vibe the earth had thrown her. "Here."

"There was nothing I could do," Ben said stiffly as he planted the flag.

"So she was your sister then?"

"Half sister, yeah," Ben answered as they veered away from the smattering of blue flags waving behind them. "Anyway, after Rachel got killed by the lion, Dad started showing me how to manage the garden right, measure the acid in the dirt for the different vegetables and make sure they each have the proper sun exposure. It's not an easy thing, if you want to do it right."

Ben was swept away in the surge of importance as he talked about his duties, and Lucy let him go on through the next two flags before asking a question. "So was your dad hoping he and Bailey would be able to . . ." She trailed off, unable to finish the sentence politely.

"Make a big, healthy baby?" Ben asked, his eyebrows raised in two mocking points. "Maybe. That or by then he'd realized Nora wasn't going to be having any more kids and he realized it was Bailey or bust." He giggled at his own joke, but Lucy didn't join in.

"What do you mean? Surely there's someone else willing to . . ."

All humor slid from Ben's face as he looked at her. "You seriously didn't know? Jeez, Lucy, open your eyes. How many women have you seen around here?"

A cold tremor passed over Lucy despite the heat, and her witching stick jumped even though there was no water beneath it. "I thought . . ." Her words gave out as her mind jumped back to Lynn's first shooting session from on top of the hotel. People had littered the streets, staring up at them with their eyes shaded. But none of them had been women.

"Thought what?"

"I don't know. I guess maybe that they were out . . . you know, just doing things."

"Doing things?" Ben laughed outright. "You're something. No, it's been Bailey and Nora for a long time. Then here comes your mom into town with her long hair and her birthing hips—"

"You can't be serious," Lucy interrupted. "Lander wants to get Lynn *pregnant?*"

"Sure, why do you think he's the one that's sitting with her while she's shooting? You really think he doesn't have better things to do?"

Lucy looked to the city, shading her eyes against the glare and searching for the flash of the rifle among the thousands of panes of glass. "He wouldn't force her, would he?"

"What, rape her? My dad? Nah." Ben dismissed the idea with a wave of his hand. "He likes to get people to do what he wants, not make them."

"No danger of that then," she said. "Lynn's not interested."

Ben reached up and awkwardly patted her on the shoulder. "Don't worry, I don't like the idea either. I might be small, but I'm still my dad's son. And right now, I'm the only one he's got. I'm hoping he'll realize you turned out small, and kinda stupid too, so he'll give up the idea of making a baby with your mom."

"Well, let's hope so," Lucy said through gritted teeth, and swept her stick across the sand. The rush of surprise and anger was sending tremors through her skin, making it impossible to listen for the quiet pull of water.

"Oh, and speaking of rape," Ben said casually, taking his backpack off again. "I have something for you."

The stick jumped in her hands, and Lucy rested one end on the sand. "You are the worst person in the world to try to do this with," she said.

"Sorry," Ben mumbled as he dug in his pack. "Here, these are for you and your mom." He handed Lucy two black rectangles with prongs at the top.

"What's this?"

"Push the button on the side," Ben said.

She did, and a bright-blue arc of light jumped from one prong to the other. The rectangle buzzed in her hand and Lucy yelped, dropping it to the ground. "What the hell?"

"It's electricity," Ben explained. "Nora and Bailey carry them too, although I don't think any of the men would ever consider touching you while my dad forbids it."

Lucy toed the black object in the sand mistrustfully. "So it shocks people?"

"Yeah, anybody gives you trouble, you—*ZZZZZZ*—" Ben imitated jerking motions. "Zap 'em. It's really pretty neat. Catch a turtle and I'll show you how it works."

"I think I'm okay," Lucy said, putting both in her own backpack. She picked her stick up and looked behind them at the handful of blue flags spotting the desert. "We should keep going."

"Dad wanted us to place all of these," Ben said, looking doubtfully at the pile still at his feet. "We should stick some in random places."

Lucy shook her head. "And then people would be digging for no reason. I can't always be sure what I find is a solid bet, but I won't set people looking where I know there's nothing."

Ben blew out his cheeks in frustration. "Have it your way then."

She flapped her arms about her, muscles cramping from holding them straight for so long. "Give me a sec, I'll be ready soon."

"Whenever," Ben said, flopping to the desert floor.

"So, were there ever other women? Has it always been just Nora and Bailey?"

"Huh? Oh no, there used to be a whole lot more people here, in general. Then cholera swept through right around the time I was born, and it wiped out a lot of us."

"Cholera's bad stuff."

"We'd taken in some new people and one of them was falling sick but hiding it. Probably one of the females, because not long after that their water supply was infected."

"The women drank from different water?"

Ben shaded his eyes to look up at her. "Dad said it caused too much trouble and distraction to have everybody doing as they pleased, so men and women lived apart."

"And people were okay with that?"

"I guess they had water and food, so they were okay with anything."

Lucy dropped down next to Ben in the sand, pulling out her water bottle. "So one of the women was sick with cholera?"

"Yeah. Whoever it was, they were all drawing out of the same tank in the women and children's hotel, and a few days later most of them were dead. Dad said it was such a stink they ended up torching the place, hoping to kill off the bug."

"It work?"

"Seems so. We haven't had a case of cholera since then, although it made Nora straight paranoid. She made Lander take her out to the hospital—the real one—and the library to get medical books so she could know all there was to know about waterborne illnesses. She had groups of men carrying boxes of books that weighed more than me up into her hotel room for days."

Lucy's hand stopped cold on the cap of her bottle, as a bubble of hope rose from her long-dormant heart. "She know about polio?"

"She knows about damn near everything. Even if she doesn't, I guarantee you anything anybody needs to know is in those books."

Lucy jammed her bottle into the depths of her pack to hide the quaking of her hands. "All right then, let's get moving."

Ben remained where he was, lying in the sun like the big cat she'd seen through Lynn's scope. "So it doesn't bother you?"

"What's that?"

Ben's smile was slow and measured, nothing like the spontaneous one that had burst across his face earlier. "You gave up your secret way too early."

Lucy's eyebrows came together as she looked at him, comprehension only dawning as she remembered the look on the men's faces as they'd carefully bundled Lynn's nearly lifeless body into the backseat of the car. In her own state she'd not questioned why perfect strangers would be scared at the thought of Lynn dying.

"You would've saved us anyway," Lucy said slowly, "whether I could witch or not. Because you need women."

"Well," Ben said, "you're not so stupid after all."

Thirty

"**G**et that away from me," Lynn said, when Lucy offered her the zapper in their room that evening.

"It's not such a bad idea," Lucy argued. "Lander keeps your gun locked up when he's not on the roof with you, and you're weak like a fish on shore."

"Maybe, but that thing's no good unless somebody is in arm's reach. My rifle keeps them farther even when it's not loaded."

"Fine." Lucy put both zappers into her pack. "But I'll point out *again* that you don't have the rifle, period."

Lynn threw an arm over her face, and her voice came out muffled by the crook of her elbow. "I'll get it back. Lander's not the most charming man in the world, but he's not stupid either. If it helps them to arm me, he'll do it."

Lucy unlaced her boots carefully, weighing her words before speaking. "I found quite a few veins today."

"Viable ones?"

"Think so. Ben was pretty distracting, so I couldn't get a feel for how deep they were, but there's water out there."

Lynn grunted, but offered nothing more.

Lucy stripped off her clothes and slid into her own bed. Darkness had filled the rest of the room, but she could see the outline of Lynn's arm tented over her face in the moonlight. "Ben said Nora and Bailey were the only women here before we showed up."

The eruption of panic she'd been expecting didn't come. Instead Lynn sighed, the simple exhalation a measure of how trapped she felt. "I know."

"How?"

"Lander can't always know what I'm looking at through the scope, and I see plenty, but never once a woman. So asking a few of the right questions to Nora today opened her up a bit. She even told me how come there's no guns around here except mine." Lucy rolled onto her side to hear Lynn better as her disembodied voice floated through the darkness.

"I was wondering," Lucy said. "Seems like a city this size there'd be guns somewhere."

"There was, back when the Shortage first happened. Plenty, to hear Nora tell it. But people were panicking here, same as back home. Mother said when things first went down it was chaos. In a city this size, with the hotels filled with those who didn't belong, it turned downright nasty. Those that lived here claimed their water for themselves."

"So what happened?"

"Those who didn't belong were tossed into the desert, but they didn't go easy. Nora said there was so much blood the sand was like mud, and people sinking into it up to their ankles while they begged to stay."

Lucy reached for the bottle she had beside her bed, though she hadn't adjusted to the taste of the water yet. The burning heat of the desert was a fresh memory, and the image of desperate people driven to madness made her clutch the bottle all the more tightly. "They all die?"

"Seems someone among the outcasts was no idiot, and they made their way over to a place called Lake Mead. Lost a lot on the walk. Nora said there were buzzards in a straight line in the sky. People must've been dropping every few feet."

Lucy had seen enough buzzards in her time, their black wings and long, slow descents marking the final resting place of someone unlucky. "That's horrible."

"They weren't the only ones who headed to the lake. There were plenty of people those days that didn't like everything this city stood for, and the things that went on in it. So when the people who lived in the City of Sin made judgment calls about who got to survive after the Shortage, it didn't set well with those who had took up at the lake. When the exiles straggled in, there was no sympathy for the city dwellers among either group, and a common enemy makes for fast friends.

"They came back at night and went after those who had killed their loved ones. Nora said if she had thought the sand was mud before, then the streets were rivers that night.

"The people from the lake scoured the city, took every gun they found, adding to their own strength and ensuring any revenge the people of Las Vegas tried to take would be of the unarmed kind. Nora says still if anyone from the city tries to take the pass to Lake Mead, they get a warning shot. But only sometimes."

"So all the water they've got access to is what's in the hotel tanks, the stored pool water and such. If they run out . . ."

"If they run out, they're dead, and I've got no idea how much is left. But the fact they'll let a stranger like me clear areas where there's old water stored says a lot."

Threads of thought spun webs in Lucy's brain, and when she spoke again it was with a hesitant voice. "Ben says there was a bad wave of cholera back when he was born. For all they know the water in those hotels they've been cut off from is infected with Lord knows what all."

"There'd only be one way to find out."'

"That's what I was afraid you were going to say."

"Well, cheer up. They won't risk losing us—we've got wombs," Lynn said darkly.

"You really think Lander would have one of his own men drink water that could kill them?"

"I think Lander would pour poison down his mother's throat if it served his purposes."

The thin bank of clouds moved on and the moon shone into their room, shining brightly on the two women so far from their home. Lucy swallowed hard, fighting back tears.

"Ben says I spoke up too early, that I shouldn't have told I can witch. He says the men on the road would've helped us anyway, on account of us being women, and I was stupid to give away my secret so soon."

The words tumbled out into the darkness, hot and sticky in her mouth, leaving as much of an aftertaste as the Las Vegas water. "If I hadn't told, they might not try so hard to keep us here. They'll never let us go now. Not when I could be the only thing that keeps them from dying."

"Well, Ben's a short idiot. Letting us go is one thing and us leaving is another."

The giggles started in Lucy's midsection and worked their way upward, erupting only when she pictured the look on Ben's face if he knew Lynn had called him a short idiot. Lynn glanced over.

"Not a lot to laugh about."

"No," Lucy admitted, wiping the last tears from her face. "There's not. Shit, Lynn, what're we gonna do?"

"We're gonna get out of here before I'm pregnant and you're failing to thrive."

Lucy did not sleep well. Dreams filled with bloodied sand and dark drops on black pavement kept bringing her back to consciousness to take deep breaths of the fetid hotel air.

"I'm getting up," she said to Lynn, moments before the sun began to streak the sky pink. Lynn muttered something from the other bed but didn't stir. She was not the type to sleep in, and her fatigue was a measure of how drained her body still was.

Lucy dressed in clothes Nora had given her, ones that fit better than Ben's castoffs from when they first arrived. Lucy's clothes from the road were so choked with bad memories she couldn't believe the threadbare fabric could hold up under the weight. She slipped out the door and closed it softly behind her, not wanting to steal whatever moments of sleep Lynn might have left before Lander came calling to take her to the roof.

The hallway air was even heavier than in the room, where at least a window could be opened. Lucy exhaled sharply, and a door down the hall opened. Nora stepped out and Lucy called to her, glad to see she wasn't the only one awake.

"Hey, Nora," she said as she walked toward her, and the older woman jumped. "Sorry," Lucy said quickly. "I didn't mean to scare you."

"It's okay," Nora said, but her hands were shaking as she pulled her hair up off her shoulders into a ponytail. "You couldn't sleep?"

"Nope." Lucy glanced into Nora's room out of curiosity and saw what Ben had promised. Medical books lined the walls on shelves clumsily set at awkward angles, sagging beneath the weight. "You a reader?"

Nora pulled the door shut but smiled at Lucy, motioning for her to follow. "Those aren't the kinds of books you read to pass the time, little one. What's in those books keeps me sleepless, like you."

They walked out of the hotel into the warm morning. A stiff breeze peppered with sand picked at them as they walked toward the indoor gardens. "Not a good day for your mom to be up on the roof," Nora observed.

"No," Lucy said, "but Lander will probably take her anyway. She's a good enough shot to account for the wind and still hit her target."

They picked up the pace as they passed the sand dunes in front of the garden hotel. The breeze was sculpting intricate tops and tossing the extra sand into their faces. Nora held the door open for Lucy and they stood inside for a moment, listening to the sand hitting the glass windows.

"That's quite the ability your mom has. I'm surprised she has no problem doling out death, when her own mother was a healer like me."

Lucy splayed her hand on the glass window and studied it to buy some time as she made up a lie. "My grandma was trained in the city as a doctor, but when she had to leave, Lynn learned a harder way of life."

"And which one do you take after?"

"I don't know enough about myself to know," Lucy said honestly. "I guess I could kill if I had to, but Lynn's made sure I haven't had to."

Nora spread her own hand on the glass next to Lucy's, equally small but with wrinkled skin. "I think you've got potential as a healer. You have small hands and a quick, gentle touch. Your mom said you were helping your grandmother back home when polio went through."

"Yeah." Lucy pulled her hand away from the warm glass, a sudden vision of familiar faces contorted with pain filling her mind. "My best friend was the first one to go."

Nora touched her arm, her hand warm and sure. "I'm sorry."

Lucy watched the pattern of her hand fading from the window, the tiny amount of moisture she'd left behind evaporating quickly on the hot glass.

"Ben said you know a lot about water sicknesses, that you gathered up those books and learned all you could. Is polio something you know a lot about?"

"I do, yes." Nora smiled at her. "Is that the first thing you would like to learn about? The illness that drove you from home?"

"Definitely," Lucy said, smiling back despite the nervous churning of her stomach. "I was wondering about something in particular. I know someone can have polio and not show any symptoms, but still pass it on to other people, right?"

Nora nodded. "Yes, they're called carriers."

Lucy's words came out in a rush, the miles of road in between her and Carter insignificant in her mind if she could deliver him from the hell of loneliness. "So will that person always have polio? Can they continue to infect people until they're dead?"

"No," Nora said automatically, and Lucy's heart leapt in her chest. "The carrier's body will pass the virus out within a few weeks. They'd definitely need to be quarantined for a while and monitored, but after enough time, the carrier would pose no more danger."

Lucy shut her eyes against the pounding heat of the lobby, her heart beating in her chest so loudly, she wondered if Nora could hear it.

"Morning, ladies." Lander's voice bounced off the glass in front of them to reverberate back through Lucy's bones, reminding her there was still a game to be played, and with more consequences now than ever.

She turned with a smile. "Good morning."

Thirty-One

Witching with Ben was more tedious than ever, now that Lucy knew she would never benefit from the wells she was marking. Fletcher's warning about dragging Lynn back over the mountains echoed in her mind, drowning out Ben's complaints about the blowing sand. With each quiver of the stick Ben drove a flag, and Lucy didn't stop him even when she was well aware it was the quickness of her own pulse and not the call of water.

"Can we be done already?" Ben whined. "This sand is getting everywhere, and I mean everywhere." He pulled the band of his pants away from his stomach to illustrate his point.

"Don't forget this stick still wants to hit you," Lucy teased, her spirits high enough to put up with Ben's misguided humor.

He was concocting a smart remark when Lucy spotted a flash of light over his shoulder. "What's a car doing out there?" Lucy framed her hands around her eyes to keep the sand out and squinted. "The highway's the other direction."

"It's nothing," Ben said, jamming the diminishing stack of flags under his arm. "C'mon, I'm done with this."

"What if it's someone lost, like I was?" Lucy argued, still staring into the distance.

"I *said*, it's nothing," Ben insisted. "But if it'll get you moving, I'll tell Dad once we get back and he'll send a car out."

"All right," Lucy agreed, readjusting her pack. "Don't forget, though."

Ben's eyebrows shot up. "You can tell him yourself if you don't trust me."

"No. I need to get back and talk to Lynn."

"About what?"

"Just to check on her," Lucy lied quickly, alarmed at how easy it was becoming. "She wasn't feeling well this morning."

Ben stopped in his tracks and grabbed Lucy's arm. "Do you mean she was vomiting? Like morning sickness?"

Lucy jerked out of his grip. "No, moron, just like, you know, I-nearly-died-in-the-desert-and-don't-feel-so-great-yet kind of sick."

"Okay, good," Ben said as they started walking again. "You'd let me know if she was, right? Pregnant?"

"Oh, you'll be the first person I tell," Lucy said. "Another good indication would be your father's slit throat."

"Lynn?" Lucy burst through their door, the news of her early morning discovery about Carter on the tip of her tongue.

"What?" Lynn was resting in the chair, her head leaned to one side, eyes ringed in dark circles. Lucy's words died on her lips.

"Are you all right?"

"I'm fine," Lynn said. "Though I could do without Lander watching every move I make. I've got a gun and all he's got is his eyes, and somehow I feel like he's got the drop on me."

"Is there . . . did he . . ." Lucy trailed off, unaccustomed to being the one asking after the other's safety.

"He didn't lay a finger on me," Lynn answered the unasked question. "Though he's not very good at hiding the fact he'd like to try."

"Well, he probably doesn't have a lot of practice with flirting."

Lynn smiled. "It worries me though. Him and Ben both are used to getting what they want and probably don't know how to handle it when it doesn't come easy. We need to get out of here."

"I need to talk to you about that," Lucy said, sitting on the end of the bed.

"You want to stay?"

"No," Lucy said. "I want to go home. For Carter."

Lynn sat back in the chair. "What the hell are you saying?"

"I talked to Nora this morning," Lucy said. "She knows all about polio. She said a carrier—like Carter—they don't have it forever. It passes out of their body."

Lynn's eyes slid shut, her body suddenly so still the only movement was the pulse in her throat. "Christ," she said after a while. "Oh, Christ."

"Carter is out in the wild by himself. I owe it to him to go back and let him know. I can't—" Lucy's voice cracked as she thought of the few hours after she'd left Lynn behind on the road, her footfalls no longer echoed by someone else's. "I can't imagine anything worse."

Lynn was silent in the chair, the last red rays of sun hitting her hard and showing lines Lucy had never noticed before, as if she'd aged in the last few minutes. "Lynn?"

"I can set your mind at ease about that," Lynn said. "Carter's not wandering alone by himself. I killed him."

"You . . ." Lucy stared at Lynn blankly, all reason having left her. "You're kidding."

Lynn shook her head slowly, and opened her eyes to fix them on Lucy's.

The hope that had gathered in Lucy all day was sucked out of her so forcefully it felt as if her lungs collapsed, leaving the only word she could think of weak and flat as it escaped her. "Why?"

"He was following us for a ways, and back at Lake Wellesley I went out and found him. He was ready to go, Lucy."

A white heat leapt from Lucy's gut, igniting her muscles and driving her up off the bed before she knew what she intended to do. Her hand cracked against Lynn's cheek, and the older woman's head bounced off the side of the chair with the force of Lucy's blow.

"No!" she screamed at Lynn, tears erupting from her eyes. "You shut up! Don't you say it, don't you tell me it was a mercy!" Lucy beat at Lynn with her bare hands, bruising the soft skin of her palms with every strike. Lynn curled into a ball, letting Lucy's anger break against her body. But Lucy's rage was not receding, and soon Lynn's nose was bloodied while Lucy still screamed.

"Carter wanted to live, he wanted babies and a home, he wanted life. He was like me. And you took it from him because all you know is death!" She struck Lynn over and over, but the outpouring of words and tears did nothing to touch the deep pool of grief that had been opened inside of her.

She didn't stop until Nora pulled her off Lynn, her hands and forearms slick with the blood of the woman who had devoted her life to protecting her. "I hate you," she screamed, her hysterical voice breaking on every word. "I hate you and your fucking gun!"

The last thing she saw as Nora dragged her from the room was Lynn curled into a bloody ball on the floor, eyes as blank as they had been when Lucy had left her behind in the desert.

Nora wiped Lynn's blood from Lucy's hands while tears and truth flowed from Lucy in an unbridled wave. She talked about Carter and how his smile was one of her first memories, how years of building tree houses together in the woods had evolved into thoughts of something more permanent for both of them. How broken she had been when Maddy had died, the pain of leaving home knowing Carter was damned, and that she would never see her grandmother or Stebbs again. She talked about Joss left to die on the road and of the mother who had put a gun to her temple. She told Nora that Lynn was not her mother, and now she was glad of it.

Nora drew a warm washcloth across Lucy's face, and the last trails of pink from Lynn's blood were blotted away. "You've exhausted yourself," Nora said, pressing gently on the swollen skin around Lucy's eyes.

Lucy held her hands to her chest to feel the emptiness there, the place where so much love had been.

Nora leaned Lucy back on her own bed and tucked a blanket around her shoulders. "It sounds like Lynn's had a hard life."

Lucy nodded, unable to deny it even in the empty aftershock of her wrath. "She's had to do horrible things to survive."

"I understand," Nora said softly as she wrung the washcloth out over a pan. "But when people have to do things like that, it changes them. I can't say what kind of person she would've been in a different situation, but I can say what she is now. And it's not the kind of person I think you want to be."

Years of emotion tangled up with Lynn revolted in Lucy, and she had the sudden urge to throw the blood-tinged water in Nora's face. But then the thought of Carter's life evaporating from his spilled blood made her shake her head. "No," she agreed. "I don't think I ever could be."

"We don't live like that here, not anymore," Nora said. "We are strong and healthy, with good food and—now you're here—plenty of water in our future."

"And soft pillows," Lucy mumbled, as what remained of her energy slipped away.

Nora smiled and squeezed Lucy's hand. "And soft pillows, as many as you'd like."

Nora wasted no time surrounding Lucy with books, elated to finally have someone with a quick mind who wanted to learn her craft. Bailey was acceptable as an assistant, Nora explained, but her calloused hands and abrupt manner made her a less than desirable caregiver. Nora sat on the floor across from Lucy for days, showing her how to navigate the huge books and pull the streams of information from them. They were piled all around the two of them like a paper fort, the words protecting them from the many-faced specter of illnesses, the pages muffling the sounds of Lander moving Lynn from her room. Lander and Nora had both thought it best if Lucy and Lynn were kept separate for a while. Nothing should strain Lucy's nerves as she searched the desert for water.

As the days crept by, Lucy felt as if her emptiness was growing to fill all her corners, leaving room for nothing else. Worry and fear slipped away, anger and happiness following shortly thereafter. Even Ben's ill attempts at humor could not grate on nerves that didn't exist anymore, and Lucy floated in a cloud of nothing as the cooler breezes of fall played with the short ends of her hair once Lander set her to the witching again.

The big man's patience was stretched. Two of the wells she had marked earlier had run dry only days after being struck, and his hands fell on her shoulders more heavily than when she had first arrived. Lucy tried to ignore the increasing pressure of his fingers on her arm as they walked the flags together and she tried to discern which veins ran deeper than others. She'd been able to make out the wild maelstrom of Lynn's hair in the wind on top of the hotel where her rifle still rang from, and while she could ignore Lynn's presence, she couldn't rid her mind of Lynn's words that had warned of danger.

"So you staying?" Ben asked as they roamed the desert to the east of the city, his arms loaded with flags dirty from reuse after marking failed wells.

"You don't sound too happy about it," Lucy said.

"I don't care either way what you do," Ben said airily, striking a flag into the ground even though she hadn't told him to. "But I know who does."

"I'm not talking to you about Lynn."

"Didn't mean her," Ben said. "It's my dad. Every well you've marked has been as useful as a stream of piss."

"Know a lot about those, do you?"

"Lynn's mowed a path to every unreachable water tank we had. She's earned her way, even if she's not warming up to Dad. You were supposed to save us, but so far all you've done is set us to digging holes with mud at the bottom."

Lucy snapped her stick upward, grabbing it with both hands to keep herself under control. "Oh yeah, and what about you? What do you do that's so special?"

Ben looked at Lucy, imperious even with a bundle of muddy flags clutched to his puffed-up chest. "I'm smart."

"Really?" Lucy slung her stick over her shoulder, finished witching for the day even if there were flags left. "That's your big contribution? You're smart?"

Ben's upper lip curled and his small face contorted into a grimace so fierce that for a moment Lucy forgot she was bigger than him.

"I'll show you. You need to learn exactly where you stand. And where I stand too."

Dormant emotions laced through her and Lucy glared back, grateful to feel something after the weeks of nothing. "You don't know the things I've been through in order to stand at all."

A grim kind of satisfaction rippled across Ben's eyes, and he smiled. "Tomorrow then."

Thirty-Two

"Lucy?"

Lynn's voice crept into her dreams, bringing visions of home and green fields. The present evaporated like the rain that never fell, and Lucy turned toward the voice, reaching her hand out before she was fully awake. The familiar touch of weathered hands brought Lucy to consciousness and she sat up quickly, a streak of fear pulling her forward.

Lynn sat at the foot of Lucy's bed, her face a pale circle in the moonlight, her dark hair lost in the inky blackness of the room. She had one finger to her lips, her eyes cautiously sliding over to Nora's bed.

"How did you get in here?" Lucy hissed, yanking her hand away from Lynn.

"Just be quiet and listen to me," Lynn whispered. "That's all I'm asking."

Lucy pushed herself up against the headboard, knees pulled protectively to her chest. "Talk fast."

"I've been watching, ever since they put me up to shooting the cats. I can see everyone and everything goes on in this town, whether Lander knows it or not."

"I already know all this," Lucy said in a regular voice, and Lynn shushed her.

"They still send out the cars," Lynn said quietly. "Real normal, like, on a schedule. They go out, and they come back with nothing to show for it. Two days ago one of the cars came back way early, with passengers. They picked up three men in the desert."

Lucy shook her head. "I haven't seen anybody new. I know every face around here, and Nora hasn't said anything about having patients."

"I doubt she does," Lynn said. "They looked healthy enough to me. Nothing wrong with 'em but a bit of sunburn and a big thirst, I imagine."

"So where are they?"

"That's the question. I'm asking you to keep your eyes and ears open. And be careful."

"Careful?" Lucy's voice rose. "Who's to say they didn't let them walk out of here on account of them being men? Last thing we need is more mouths to feed."

Lynn raised an eyebrow, an accusatory black line tented in the moonlight. "We?"

"Yes," Lucy spat. "*We*. There's no reason to think any harm was done to them, any more than's been done to us."

"Yeah," Lynn said quietly, the word coming out harsh and ragged. "And what has been done to us?"

Tears sprouted in Lucy's eyes, all the more painful for having been absent for so long. "Get out of here before I wake up Nora," she said. "And don't ask me to look for something to fight in every shadow that crosses the path. I don't want to live like you."

Lynn watched Lucy for a moment before rising, her renewed health evident in the hard lines of her body as she stood. "I didn't want to live like me either, little one," she said. And then she was gone.

Ben was at her door early the next morning, a fresh bundle of flags gripped to his chest.

"Really?" Lucy picked sleep from her eye as she stood in the doorway. "I thought today was the Let's-Show-How-Smart-Ben-Is Day."

"Oh, it is," he said. "But work before pleasure, Dad says. Get dressed, he's picking us up when everything is ready." Lucy dressed quickly, and as the two of them marched out of the city she heard Lynn's bullets flying overhead and wondered if the ghostly conversation from the night before had only been a dream. The sun soon burned away thoughts of anything except water, and Lucy's stick pointed sure and true, as if her own limbs were suddenly clear of confusion.

"You're confident today," Ben said as he placed a flag.

"I feel good," Lucy admitted. "It helps."

"You haven't felt good before?"

"I was . . . unsure."

"What changed?"

Lucy didn't answer for a moment, thinking of Lynn's stealthy conversation in the night, the heavy words weighted with dread. Whether it'd been a dream or not, it had solidified in Lucy that she didn't want to live in fear and suspicion. Lander and Nora would never be Stebbs and Vera. But her affection for them would grow, and she would let it.

"Hello? Water monkey?"

"You, however, I will never like," Lucy said aloud.

Ben shrugged. "Like me, not like me, whatever. After today you'll respect me."

Lucy ignored him, switching her stick over the dry dust in front of her. When the sound of the car engine cut through the air hours later, Lucy realized how lost in her own reverie she had been. Ben's arms were empty, the sterile desert behind them populated by waving blue flags.

"Well done," he said. "I've not seen you that involved before."

The car pulled to a stop in front of them, sending a spray of dust into Lucy's eyes. She shaded her face to see Lander emerging from behind the wheel, his shadow far outreaching either of theirs.

"Lucy." He smiled at her, casting an arm behind them at the expansive waste littered with flags. "You worked hard today."

"I did," she said cautiously, still unsure of his smile.

"How about a break? Ben said you've made a decision to stay, and Nora agrees you're ready to understand the importance of what you do for us here."

"I couldn't ever *not* understand the importance of water," Lucy said as she slid into the backseat. "Whether it's some I've found or not."

"Maybe not," Lander said as he drove, "but Ben thinks you should know exactly what's at stake."

Lucy thought of the endless desert, her tongue so swollen it stuck to the dry roof of her mouth, Lynn falling in her tracks and unable to rise. "I know what's at stake."

"Just enjoy the ride then, and you'll see when we get there," Lander said, his good nature uninhibited by the tartness of her response.

They crossed over the highway, the car bouncing as it made the transition from sand to asphalt and back to sand. Lucy took her backpack off and set it next to her on the seat, rummaging for the bottle of water. It tasted bad as ever, but she forced it down, determined that someday she would forget the cool sweetness of water from her own pond and be thankful for what she had.

A flash caught her eye on the horizon, and Lucy realized they were heading toward the same spot she had noticed weeks before, drawn to her attention by a similar wink of light.

"Where we going?"

"You'll see," Ben said, his tone all the more lofty with his father nearby. Lucy rolled her eyes and took another swig of water, resting her head against the back of the seat.

When the car stopped, Lander came around and opened the door for her, offering his hand. She left the cool of the car for the blast of heat from the desert, and Lander's forearm was suddenly tight around her waist, pulling her back into him and pressing her lungs flat. His other arm snuck around her chest, pining her arms to her side and crushing every inch of her body against his. Lucy gulped hot air into her lungs, feeling as if Lander's body were taking over hers, enveloping her tiny skeleton into his frame and making it his own.

"I'm going to turn you around in a moment," he whispered into her ear, his voice low and thready. "And when I do you'll understand how badly I need those flags to be in the right places. Are you ready?"

She nodded slowly, aware that he was fully capable of snapping her in half. He turned her and she saw what they had dragged her out into the desert for.

A huge plane of glass hung suspended from crudely formed metal beams, their angles awkward and imprecise. The glass was a patchwork mess of different shapes and thicknesses. Lucy spotted tinted car windows, broken pieces of mirror, and even a riot of color where a stained-glass window from a church had been soldered in, all forming an uneven surface that swayed from the unsteady poles. The baking sun's rays bent and refracted through its twisted surface to glisten off the red meat that lay underneath, cooking in the heat of the day. Lucy lay limp against Lander's chest, confused.

Until she saw the finger among the red mess.

She bucked wildly against him and Lander clamped down harder, squeezing the last breath of air from her lungs, the words she would've screamed dying in her throat.

"Listen to him," Lander said. "Ben wants to show you how it works."

Ben nearly pranced in front of her. "I made this," he said proudly. "Well, I drew the plans for it anyway. I can't actually lift things, you know."

Lucy gasped and slid to the ground as her oxygen ran out and Lander went down with her, lessening his grip so she could breathe.

"Tell him it's nice," Lander said. "He wants you to be proud of him."

"What is it?" Lucy managed to ask, and Ben lit up at her interest.

"It's quite simple really. There's another pane of glass underneath that mess. Heat from the sun bounces in between both of the surfaces. Once it's hot enough, the moisture starts to evaporate. And then—check this out, it's the best part. . . ."

He walked to the edge of the suspended pane, his thin arms shaking as he pressed down on the edge. It tilted with a groan of metal that perversely reminded Lucy of a teeter-totter Lynn had shown her in an abandoned park. Accumulated beads of pink water slid to the edge, where they dripped into waiting buckets.

"Moisture?"

"Yeah." Ben grabbed one of the buckets and brought it over to Lucy, grandly depositing it in front of her to look into. "The human body is over eighty percent water. I found a way to get some of it out."

Lucy turned her head to retch, the tepid water she'd drunk frothing over her lips and mixing with the sand only inches from her face. "Oh God," she said, staring at it. "Oh God, that's why it tastes so bad."

Ben crossed his arms, and Lander pulled her back up to face him. "Well, I can't be held responsible for the quality," Ben said. "It's the quantity that's the problem. Nora and I had a long talk about swelling a few years ago, and I figured out that if we broke every bone in their bodies first, there was a much better yield."

Lucy went over into her own mess then, kicking Ben's bucket away from her and spilling the pink water over his pants. Ben wiped at his jeans, looking distastefully at the spreading stains.

Flat on her stomach, Lucy stared at the pile of red that had once been human beings—three men, she guessed—and the tiny amount of water that had come out of the bucket she'd kicked. "What a waste," she cried into the sand, her tears drying on her cheeks before they could cut tracks in the dirt griming her skin.

"I wouldn't say that," Ben said, hands on his hips. "True, we can't cook them long before they start to rot, but everything left over goes right into the garden for the plants."

Lucy dry-heaved, her stomach clenching so tightly she cried out with the pain of it.

"What?" Ben asked. "I thought you liked tomatoes?"

The ride into the city was silent. Lucy sat in the backseat, the blooming hope of a new life here having been plucked and withered within a short time. The emptiness swelled again, making her limbs so heavy Lander had to carry her to the room she shared with Nora. The older woman gave her a smile and tucked her into bed, explaining in her calm and reassuring voice that there was no other way.

"Now do you understand why we need you to witch for us, and to do it well, little one?"

"I can't find water if it's not there," Lucy said. "If the veins dry out, that's not my fault."

"It's not about fault," Nora said. "It's just important you know

343

the situation. We've been adding the water Ben's machine gathers to what we had left of the pool and fountain water."

"Why don't you say what it is?" Lucy asked. "It's not water you've *gathered*. You killed for it pure and simple, and you're drinking . . . I've drunk . . ." Her lungs hitched, spiking her blood pressure and sending black dots across her vision.

"All right, that's enough," Nora said sternly, pushing Lucy back onto her pillow. "I understand you've got your reservations about the process, but you'll understand in time. And remember, if it weren't for our ways we'd have been dead in this city long ago, and you on the road with no one to save you."

Lucy nodded meekly.

"Good then." Nora smiled. "You get some sleep for now. We can talk about it more in the morning."

Nora slid into her own bed, and Lucy listened to her breathing even out and soon hitch with the light snore she'd become accustomed to hearing. Once she knew Nora was deep asleep, she slid from bed, dressed in her threadbare clothes from the road, and dug in her pack for the two Tasers Ben had given her.

"Sorry, Nora," she said, before striking. "I kinda liked you."

Thirty-Three

S he'd never been in the hallway in the middle of the night. The blackness was so deep, Lucy couldn't see her hand in front of her face and had to feel the walls until she reached the stairwell. The walk felt infinite because of her blind, measured steps, and the slow simmer of panic began deep in her gut as Lucy wondered if she'd made a mistake and was on the wrong side of the hall. If Nora was conscious before they were gone, she could only imagine what Lander and Ben would do. She doubted the grisly contraption in the desert was the only machine Ben had created.

The stairwell door wheezed open beneath her hand and she inched forward, toes reaching for the drop-off of the first step, hands flailing for the railing. She found it and latched on, counting each step and sliding her foot forward once she reached the landing, her hands following the curve of the railing as she made the turn to the next set of stairs. The barest smear of gray marked the window in the stairwell door, and Lucy emerged into the lobby to the pulsing light of clouds racing across the face of the moon.

She hit the outside doors at a run now that she could see, the cool desert air threaded through with the smell of rain rolling in. A bank of black clouds lined with the reflected silver of the moon was piling up in the west, and Lucy could smell the electricity in the air. A storm was coming. A homegrown surge of elation at the promise of rain lent new strength to her legs, and Lucy sprinted past the sand-filled fountains into the lobby of the hotel Lynn now shared with Lander and Ben.

Lucy burst into the lobby and came to a sudden halt. She had no idea where Lynn would be. She could assume Lander and Ben would live on the first floor, as the rising heat would make it unbearable to live any higher. They would probably have Lynn nearby to keep an eye on her, but Lucy could hardly go down the hall knocking on doors when she didn't even know which room Lander and Ben used.

"Shit," she said to herself. Lucy peered into a window, teeth sinking into her lip as she thought. A fat drop of rain hit the glass, sliding down to leave a streak in the grime, and inspiration struck. Lucy raced outside, looking for a fluttering curtain. Even though nights were cool, the trapped air inside still baked with the heat of the day long into the night, and Lucy slept with her window open, anxious for the freshness of outside air.

She could only hope Lynn did too.

The face of the hotel stared at her blankly, curtains drawn. A rumble of thunder rolled through the desert, shaking the ground beneath her feet. Lucy's panic grew with it, taking over her body and sending a spasm of fear down her spine. She ran to the back of the hotel, tripping over her own feet in her haste and flying out of control, skidding on her knees and crying out as her jeans gave way and then her skin.

Lightning flickered and she pulled her knees up to her chin, the black threads of blood mixing with the tattered denim. Tears of frustration pooled in her eyes, and Lucy swiped at them viciously as she tried to stand. The thunder boomed again, seconds after the lightning, and this time the vibration was so great Lucy could hear thousands of windows rattling in their panes.

Movement caught her eye and Lucy lunged for the Taser, springing to her feet. Only a few feet away a white hand was pressed against the window, aching to touch the fat spattering of raindrops as they struck the glass.

"Lynn," Lucy breathed, but the other woman hadn't seen her yet, only drawn to the window by the storm. Lucy shuffled toward her, wincing with pain as the newly exposed pink skin on her knees stretched with every movement. The top of her head barely reached the windowsill, and she had to stand on her tiptoes to reach the glass, her own hand spread against it.

Soon she felt the answering warmth of Lynn's hand pressed against hers from the other side.

• • •

There was a guard at Lynn's door, a man whom Lucy had exchanged nods with as she passed him in the city from day to day. He was asleep, and the gray line of light that fell from Lynn's cracked door made his spasms all the more gruesome as Lucy tased him. She hadn't been able to see the grimaces of pain on Nora's face, only hear the bucking as she convulsed in the dark. When he was still, Lucy looked up at Lynn, hating the tears that ran down her face as she did.

"Huh," Lynn said. "I guess those things are useful after all." She was dressed in her clothes from the road, her backpack drawn tight against her shoulder blades.

"We have to be fast," Lucy said as Lynn dragged the unconscious man into her room and shut the door behind them. "I knocked Nora out too. Once they find out, we're dead."

"Probably," Lynn agreed. "But we can't leave without my gun. There's more danger between here and Sand City. We can't face it with two Tasers that'll run out of batteries."

"Shit, Lynn," Lucy said. "We have to go *now*! They're . . ." Her words failed, cut off in her throat by the memory of dark red against white sand. "They're drinking people. *We've* been drinking people."

Lynn took one Taser from Lucy, face grim. "I'm not going to ask what you mean by that until we're out of here. In the meantime, I'm sorry if this hurts much."

"If what hurts?" Lucy asked a second before Lynn zapped her.

Lucy felt a strange vibration coursing through her body, and her wounded knees gave out underneath her as she slid to the floor. "What the hell?" she asked Lynn, curling into the fetal position.

"I set it real low, but you've still got a mark from it. Can you stand?"

"I think so." Lucy pulled herself to her feet using the foot of the bed. "So now what?"

Lynn's mouth set in a grim line as the storm clouds enveloped the moon, leaving the room one shade above black. "Now we go get my gun back."

Lucy sank back against Lynn's strength as they stood before Lander's door, the metal prongs of the Taser biting deep into her neck.

"Knock," Lynn said, and she did, the sound echoing eerily down the empty hall.

Lander answered quickly, already awakened by the storm. If finding Lucy held captive on his doorstep in the middle of the night threw him in any way, he did not show it. Instead he smiled at Lynn over her shoulder.

"I've been hoping you'd come to me in the night sometime, but not quite like this."

"I want my gun, and I want keys to one of the cars," Lynn said. "I know you've got both of them squared away in your room, so let's make it easy and be done with it."

Lander shrugged. "Or what?"

The prongs dug deeper into Lucy's neck, and she felt a trickle of blood slip down her skin. "I'll do her in, Lander, don't think for one second I won't."

The big man's eyes searched Lynn's, then Lucy's, sliding off her face down to the burn mark left on her collarbone from the earlier shock. "You're a cold woman, Lynn."

A white sheet flipped off the second bed in the room, and Ben staggered from the darkness, eyes heavy with sleep. "What's going on?"

The jolt of electricity going into her neck sent Lucy to the ground in an instant, her teeth grinding against one another.

"Holy shit," she heard Ben say. "She actually did it."

Lynn's hand was on her neck and hauling her to her feet before Lucy trusted her own legs, and she buckled slightly against the older woman.

"And I'll keep doing it, 'til she's of no more use and you all die a dry death."

Lander watched the two of them, his mind moving much faster than Lucy's as she struggled to stay on her feet. "I don't know I need her all that much, really. Ben says she was confident about those flags yesterday, wasn't she, son?"

Ben came forward to stand next to his father. "She was," he said enthusiastically. "Although if you think sticking her again might make Dad change his mind, go ahead and do it. I haven't seen a girl dance in a long time."

"Listen," Lynn said, her voice barely masking the beginnings of a quaver. "I don't—"

"LANDER!" Nora's scream ripped down the hall, her robe flapping behind her making her seem like a white specter in the darkness. She ran awkwardly, limbs still deadened by the jolt Lucy had given her. "She's got away from me!"

Lynn turned toward this new threat, and Lucy's legs collapsed without her support. Nora careened to a halt, grabbing the doorway to stop herself and glaring at the huddled form in the darkness of the hall.

Lucy peered up at her, a new kind of electricity surging through her limbs as her body warned her to get up, to get away from Nora, seconds before the older woman fell on her.

"You ungrateful little *bitch!*" Nora screamed, blood trickling from one nostril as she smacked at Lucy's face. Lucy fended off her blows, scooting herself up against the wall. From the corner of her eye she saw Lynn barrel into Lander with all her strength, barely knocking him off his feet. The two of them rolled into Ben together, sending him into the wall. The hard *click* of Ben's teeth slamming together ricocheted around the room, and the moon came back out for another moment, turning the blood that flowed from his mouth a dark purple and starkly illuminating his own fascination with it as he lifted his stained fingers in front of his face.

Lucy pulled her Taser from her belt and slammed it against Nora's torso, forcing the other woman away from her before delivering the shock. Nora jerked and was still, a matching stream of blood now flowing from the other nostril.

Lynn screamed as Lander bent her arm behind her back, forcing her face down into the carpet and digging his knee into her spine. Lucy dove for Lynn's Taser, knocked free during their struggle. Lander let her have it, eyes watching her as she rose.

"I've got all kinds of ways I can hurt this one, little girl," he said, teeth stained with blood from where Lynn had got a good kick in. "You know I will."

Lucy pressed the button and bright-blue electricity jumped from the prongs. "Get off of my mom."

Lander bent Lynn's arm upward. She writhed but refused to cry out, bringing a blood-tinged smile to his face. "She's not your mom."

"The hell she isn't," Lucy said, grabbing Ben from where he lay and digging both Tasers into either side of his neck. "Now you give her back to me or Ben's dead, and not missed by many."

"That's more true than you know," Lander said. "Go on then."

Lucy felt the thunder roll through the room as clearly as the rage that pulsed through Ben as he knelt in front of her, disbelief sagging his shoulders. "Dad?"

"What?" Lander asked. "You really don't think I can make one better than you?" He reached down and touched Lynn's hair with fondness, despite the fact that his other hand was still threatening to crack her arm in half. "This woman here and me combined? Now that's something I want to see."

Ben sprang so quickly that Lucy lost her grip on the Tasers, one of them nearly sliding from her sweaty palm. Ben hit Lander in a ball of fury, his attack so unexpected it sent his father reeling off Lynn, who dragged herself out of the way as the two struggled. There was a loud *crack* and a squeal of pain from Ben, and then Lucy was above both of them, jamming the Tasers into Lander's temples and delivering a jolt that sent electricity flowing from father to son as their entwined limbs danced.

Lucy's arms couldn't keep the connection anymore, and she fell to the ground. The smell of singed flesh and burning hair filled the room, tinged with the tweak of ozone, when another flash of lightning ripped through the night air and the building shook with the rumble of the thunder. Lynn dragged herself to Lucy's side to cradle the girl's head in her lap.

"You okay?"

Lucy nodded, the tender skin of her cheek rubbing against Lynn's jeans. "Did I kill them?"

"Well, Lander's hair is on fire and he's not doing anything about it, so my guess is yeah, you did."

Lucy turned her face into the bend of Lynn's knee, tears dripping onto the denim and the delayed twinges of shock sending her into a rippling mass in Lynn's lap. Lynn's hands moved through her hair, gently pulling the short, damp ends from her sticky face.

"I know it's not easy, little one," she said. "But this is the world we live in, and if we want to keep doing it, sometimes our hands are forced."

"Lucy?" Ben's weak voice floated above the still bodies. Lynn rose to her feet, pulling Lucy with her. Ben's small hands patted out the fires on either side of his father's skull, surprising Lucy in their gentleness until she realized some of Ben's own clothing had begun to smolder, and he'd put those sparks out first.

"Ben?" She hovered over him, leaning down as close as she dared to hear his whisper.

"Lucy, we've got to go," Lynn said as she opened a closet and pulled out her rifle, along with a set of keys. "Others live here too, and the storm will be waking them if that ruckus didn't."

Ben's hand grabbed for hers, and she let him hold it. "I think Dad broke my back."

"Time to go." Lynn's hands were on her shoulders, pulling her back from his weak grip.

"B-Ben," Lucy stuttered, backing away from his pleading eyes and hands still reaching for her. "I'm sorry, I can't."

The plea changed to wrath in a second, and his hands went from penitence to fists as he struck the floor around him. "You *will* take me with you! You can't leave me broken."

"Ben," Lucy said from the doorway, "you were broken long before I got here."

He screamed at them with all the air left inside him, his wordless anger following them down in the lobby, along with the sound of his upper half dragging his useless legs behind him in a futile effort to catch up.

Lucy followed Lynn on wobbly legs to the parking garage. Ben's screams had brought others from their rooms, but no one was willing to face Lynn's gun, and they had the streets to themselves. Lucy slid into the passenger seat with relief, dumping her bag in the back and letting her body go entirely slack.

Lynn drove quickly; Lucy watched her eyes darting back and forth in the rearview mirror, not relaxing until they were well beyond the pale fingers of the dead buildings that reached for the sky. The desert opened up around them again, the emptiness of it all somehow reassuring after the cluttered rot of Las Vegas.

"You know where you're going?" Lucy asked.

Lynn tapped her temple. "It's all been up here for the past two states."

"All right," Lucy said, her head tilting to one side to rest against the cool window. "I trust you."

The three small words swelled in magnitude in the confines of the car, and Lynn tightened her grasp on the steering wheel. "I want you to know there's a lot of things in my life I wish I could take back. If I could only choose one, it'd be Carter."

"I know it," Lucy said, eyes still shut. "But it's done now. It is what it is."

"Maybe so, but I need you to know he asked me for it. Said he couldn't stand the guilt of dead children, bodies of the people he knew burning in a pit, and him being what put 'em there. He didn't want to be alone and . . . he said he couldn't help but hope you'd be happy, but he hated that it wasn't with him."

Tears that she didn't bother to brush away poured down Lucy's face. "But it didn't have to be that way. He didn't have to die."

"I didn't know that, and neither did he. You're the one that holds on to hope, Lucy. The two of us, we'd already accepted that life is unfair. And he died for it, and I can't put together enough words to tell you how sorry I am."

"Neither one of you can be blamed for it," Lucy said eventually. "This is a hard place we live in."

"It is indeed," Lynn answered. The storm finally broke around them, dropping water in great sheets that rolled off the windshield as they headed west.

"But I'm still glad I'm here," Lucy managed to say as her eyelids closed.

The last thing she heard before she drifted into unconsciousness was Lynn heaving a great sigh and saying, "Lord, I wish I had a five-gallon bucket about now."

Part Four

OCEAN

Thirty-Four

L ucy resisted when Lynn tried to get her to drink in the morning.

"That's water from the city," Lucy said. "I don't want to drink it."

Lynn took a swig from her own bottle and swished the water around her mouth. "Knowing what's in it doesn't make it taste better, but it's water all the same." She handed Lucy the bottle and opened her car door. "Hope you're not too spoiled by the driving. We're outta gas."

"I'll survive." Lucy got out, enjoying the feel of the rain-washed air against her skin in the cool morning light. Her lips were dry, and she'd taken a swallow of the water before she had time to think about it.

"How far 'til Sand City?" Lucy asked, looking to the horizon.

"A few hours' walk is my best guess," Lynn said.

Lucy leaned against the car. "What do we do when we get there?"

"That's a good question, and hell if I know," Lynn said. "I never came up with an answer, as I was never entirely sure we'd make it."

"California," Lucy said as she looked to the west. "Kinda seemed impossible, didn't it?"

Lynn shrugged. "You don't have to look in that direction, you know. We're in California right now."

Lucy turned to the north. "California. Kinda seemed impossible, didn't it?"

Lynn snorted and threw a handful of sand at her.

They hit a field of wind turbines hours later, the turning white arms bright beneath the sun.

"What're those?" Lucy asked.

"Kinda like a windmill," Lynn said. "There was a farm back home had one. Stebbs took me out to see it once. They make electricity, though the one in Ohio was all broken down. It didn't work anymore."

"These look like they're working."

"Which means we're close."

"Electricity . . . ," Lucy said, remembering Vera's stories of light after the sun had gone down. "Fletcher said it was here, but I couldn't hardly believe they were that well off."

"Could be it's only used for the desal plants, you know. Something's gotta run them. I doubt they waste energy on things like lightbulbs. Don't get your hopes up."

"I won't," Lucy promised, but she couldn't squash the flutter of excitement in her belly.

They walked through the afternoon, their spirits dropping as unpopulated buildings rose around them. Despite her promise, Lynn clicked the safety off on the rifle, and Lucy didn't mention it. Their footfalls echoed one another as they walked alone, past a residential district with rusted-out cars sitting quietly in the driveways.

A new scent had found Lucy's nose, tickling her nostrils and bringing her senses to a high pitch. "You smell that?"

"I think it's the ocean."

"The ocean," Lucy said, taking a deep breath of the salty tang. "Yeah, I imagine it is."

They moved on, the buildings growing closer together as they went. Lynn became antsy and they went off the highway, picking their way through parking lots with grass growing through ever-widening cracks in the pavement, until they hit the ocean. It rose to meet Lucy, the tide nibbling at her toes as she pulled off her shoes to feel it properly for the first time in her life. The vast blue expanse met the sky, the sun making a new red road on its undulating surface, one that led to the horizon.

"Lucy," Lynn said quietly. "I'm sorry, little one. There's no one here."

Lucy didn't turn. "So far, no, but I don't think Fletcher would've led us wrong."

"Me neither, but maybe something happened to them, maybe . . ."

"We can talk maybes all day long and still not know a thing," Lucy said, toes curling in the wet sand. "I'm heading north. If we get to Oregon, we know something's wrong."

"All right then," Lynn said, adjusting her pack. "Let's go."

"Not yet," Lucy said as the tide swelled over her feet again. "Not just yet."

Lucy walked on, and Lynn followed. They'd been walking along the beach for miles when Lynn's fingers dug into Lucy's arm, nodding up ahead. Lucy pulled her gaze from the ocean to see the figure of a man on the beach. He spotted them seconds later and waved an arm in greeting.

"Well," Lynn said under her breath. "I guess that's how this is done."

They walked toward him, cautiously leaning toward each other, their elbows rubbing with every step. Lynn kept her rifle on her back, and Lucy saw the man's expression change when they were near enough for him to see the barrel rising above her shoulder.

"Hi there," he said as they approached, the sparse gray hair on the crown of his head blowing in the evening breeze. "I thought you were Bridget and Taylor heading home from fishing."

Lucy stood before him, her mouth feeling as if it were sewn shut. Behind her, she heard Lynn sink into the sand, her body giving out on her. The man looked between the two of them. "Well, who are you then?"

Lucy's lips moved, her throat constricted, but no sounds came out. Witching was insignificant next to the ocean, her precious skill useless in this new world. She had nothing to offer in exchange for a life less normal. In the end, she said, "My name is Lucy, and I walked across the country to get here."

"Well done, Lucy," the man said, extending his hand. "I'm Dan."

She shook it. "This is Lynn." She nodded toward the ground, as if Lynn being there were completely normal.

"Hi, Lynn," Dan said, nodding when she didn't reach for his hand. "That's a hell of a gun you've got there."

"Uh-huh," Lynn said.

"We're supposed to tell you Fletcher sent us," Lucy said. "I don't know if that makes a difference or—"

"Fletcher?" Dan smacked his hands together. "How is the old bastard?"

"He's alive," Lucy said. "We met him in Nebraska. He said if we—"

Dan's hands rested lightly on her shoulders, stopping her flow of words. "You prove your worth by your actions, Lucy. You can relax now. You're here." He put his other hand on Lynn's shoulder. "You made it, girls."

The water pulled at Lucy's toes, dragging the sand out from under her feet and making her sink inch by inch into the wet, comforting muck. Weeks after their arrival she still couldn't resist the sea, reveling in it every evening outside the small house she and Lynn had claimed for their own on the edge of town.

Even though there were hundreds of people here, no one was thirsty. The windmills powered the plant, which made the ocean water flowing into their homes drinkable. Solar panels meant electricity. On their first night in their new house, Lucy had found Lynn in the living room with a book in her hand and tears on her cheeks. "I can see," she'd said in explanation. "First time in my life I've ever been able to see after the sun went down. This is how Mother lived once."

Soft footsteps sounded in the sand and Lynn crouched beside Lucy, away from the tide.

"Have a seat," Lucy said, gesturing to the sand.

Lynn shook her head. "I don't feel like I ever get the sand off me, once I do."

Lucy shrugged, watching the moon rise above the ocean to send a white path pointing toward her over the rippling water. "How can you not like it?"

Lynn sighed and sat down anyway, her face contorting with displeasure as her pants got wet. "I learned to hate it young, little one. When I was a kid I found a globe and showed it to Mother, thinking I'd found something that would save us yet, that we didn't have to live the way we did. She told me it was all salt, and no relief in it—'*Water, water everywhere and not a drop to drink.*' I broke the damn thing and swore to never find comfort in anything too good to be true again."

"But it is true, Lynn. And it's different here. It's good," Lucy argued.

"You like it, that's all I need to know to believe it's a good thing."

"Like it? Lynn, it's more than liking it. You should come to the desal plant with me sometime. When Dan showed me how to monitor the salinity, I felt like . . . like I was doing something that mattered. He said they'll teach me how to clean the membranes too, next time I come."

"Which I imagine will be tomorrow," Lynn said slyly.

Lucy went on, barely hearing Lynn. "Dan said he'll have a spot for me to be there all regular like, with real duties and everything after Taylor's baby comes. You should hear the sound the seawater makes when it's pressured through the—"

"I prefer to hear rain fall on my own roof," Lynn interrupted.

"But you can't count on rain," Lucy shot back. "The ocean is always there, and now we can take advantage of it."

Lynn looked out over the undulating waves, her jaw tense. "I know that, but Mother didn't. And I can't help but think maybe if she had, her life would've been longer, and mine much different. That doesn't make me like this damn sea any better."

Lucy nodded, the image of her own dead mother never far from her mind. "I understand."

"So how can you like it so much? " Lynn asked. "After the desert and the mountains and the bigness of everything that frightened you? And now this—you a tiny speck on the edge of the sand, happy to sit by a Goliath?"

Lucy was quiet for a full minute, letting the tide touch her toes and recede while she thought. "You're not the only one who can quote poetry, you know.

I heard or seemed to hear the chiding Sea

Say, Pilgrim, why so late and slow to come?"

"Ralph Waldo Emerson," Lynn said immediately. "I'm impressed."

"Don't be. It's the one poem I read during the last blizzard."

"It stuck with you though. The words meant for us can do that, stick to the crevices inside and come out when we least expect it. Why those words?"

Lucy dug deep to find her own words, new ones that tasted like hope and not the misery of the road. "The desert and the mountains and the plains all felt like they were in my way, stopping me from getting to somewhere I was supposed to be. But this is salvation. Every drop in that ocean can be made to save you or me, and every other soul in this town. I can only wish it were bigger."

"I don't think the ocean's different from those things, little one. What's different is you."

"How do you mean?"

"When we left Ohio, you were scared as a rabbit, jumping at the shadows and hiding in my footsteps. We walked across the country and you changed into a woman who could walk up to a stranger on the beach with nothing more than her own name in her mouth, and you did it."

"You were with me."

"You walked ahead of me," Lynn said. "That whole last stretch of beach you were the one in front. You wanted this place and this ocean, and you've made it your own."

"But you can't, is that what you're going to say?" Lucy asked, a deep hole of fear she'd thought she'd left behind her opening inside her gut again.

"I can't . . ." Lynn trailed off, her eyes on the watery horizon. "Lucy, I can't see around me here, do you understand? To one side there's water and to the other there's buildings. I just . . . I feel like I can't *see* everything like I did back home."

"You never said so on the road."

"I didn't feel this way on the road," Lynn countered. "Then we were always moving. If I didn't like something it didn't matter, 'cause it'd be different the next day."

"What are you saying to me?"

Lynn was quiet, and Lucy counted seven revolutions of the tide before she spoke.

"I'm going home."

Even though she'd been expecting it, Lucy cried out, burying her head into her hands and sinking her fingers into her own hair as if covering her ears could force the words out of her mind. "Don't do that to me, Lynn. I can't do it—I'm not like you!"

"Not like me?" Lynn asked, her hands probing into the mess of Lucy's hair and finding her fingertips, pulling the girl's face up to look into her own. "Now who would want to be that, anyway?"

"Me," Lucy said desperately through her tears, "me, me, me."

Lynn pulled Lucy to her, wrapping her arms around the girl who refused to be a woman. "Don't you see it, little one? You're where you belong now, next to the biggest thing in the world and loving every second of it. The people here are hopeful, with a spark of life about them, just like you. It's not like the city behind us, where they were living off the dead. These people are alive for the love of it."

"And you don't like that? How can you not, Lynn?"

"Oh, I envy them, through and through, don't get me wrong on that point. But I learned hard lessons long ago, and they're so ingrained in me I can't drop 'em now. Like it or not, I've picked up the knack of feeling responsible for others, and you don't need me anymore. There are those back home who still might. Last time I saw Stebbs, his finger was none too steady on the trigger."

"I do need you, I do," Lucy cried, clinging to her. She buried her face into Lynn's neck and made her confession. "I'm like my mother. I need other people, and you most of all."

Lynn pushed Lucy's face back from her own and looked at her in the moonlight. "You're not me, child. You're not me and you're not your mother either. You're Lucy, my little one, and that is no small thing."

And Lucy cried as the tide came in, her salty tears making the ocean bigger.

Epilogue

Lynn waited until spring to go. It was close to a year since they'd left Ohio when Lynn stood on the outskirts of town, holding the reins of a horse that had been given to her by a rancher in thanks for having shot the mountain lion depleting his sheep. Her rifle was strapped to her back, a heavily penciled map in her pack, and enough bottles of fresh water to keep her on the road for a while before she would have to refill.

Lucy stood beside her with clear eyes but dried tear tracks on her face.

"You sure about this?" Lucy asked, even though every line of Lynn's body ached with her need to go home.

"You know I am," Lynn answered, giving Lucy a hug. "And don't be so sad-faced about it. Dan planned a route for me that goes south before east. He said it'll keep me as low as possible, so no worries on the nosebleeds." She swung up into the saddle and cleared her throat. "I don't know what else to say. I'm ready to go, but leaving you is tearing a Lucy-shaped hole in my heart. Don't think anybody else can ever fill it."

"I know it," Lucy said, her hand reaching up for Lynn's. "But I'll be all right here. Stebbs and Vera need to know we made it. You tell . . ." Lucy swallowed hard, having promised herself she was done crying. "You tell my grandma I love her, and that I'm happy."

Lynn sighed. "This caring about people is for the birds. 'Specially when they gotta live so far apart from each other."

Lucy swiped at her eyes. "What do you want me to tell Fletcher, should he show up?"

Lynn shrugged. "He knows where Ohio is."

"The way he was making eyes at you on the road, I wouldn't be surprised if he *accidentally* crosses your path before you get there."

"My luck I'll find his wife instead."

Lucy smiled, shaking her head. "You're a hell of a woman, Lynn."

Lynn reached down to touch the crown of her bright-yellow head. "You're a hell of woman too, Lucy."

She kicked her horse and was gone, a trail of dust marking the beginning of a long path she was willing to travel again, if her pond lay at the end. And the sun rose higher, warming Lucy's face and reflecting off the ocean into a million points of light.

Acknowledgments

I t's much easier to write a novel than acknowledgments because the latter is chiefly comprised of reality and that's not an arena I excel in. However, I shall try.

First, thanks goes to my agent, Adriann Ranta, without whom my literary gunslingers would still live in the slush pile and not in the hearts and minds of readers. In the same vein I heartily thank my editor, Sarah Shumway, for allowing me to be an instinctive writer, as well as not minding when I respond to serious emails with Star Wars gifs.

Thank you also to the HarperCollins family at Katherine Tegen Books, true lovers of books, supporters of writers, and champions of literacy. I must thank my cover designer, Erin Fitzsimmons, whose artwork puts the book in readers' hands, while hopefully my words keep it there. Also I would be remiss not to mention Margot Wood and Aubry Parks-Fried, the "Epic Reads Girls," who tirelessly promote myself and my fellow HarperCollins authors, as well as Ali Lisnow, my publicist, who doesn't mind when I make up fake new names for book fairs.

Also instrumental in the creation of any book I write, my crit partner, R. C. Lewis, who changes all my spelling mishaps from

UK to US and constantly reminds me what time zone I live in, even though she's half a country away and I should know by now. It's a good thing I have a keeper.

Authors need other authors both as sounding boards and friends. My first tour experience was amazing and I can only hope I continue to be surrounded by such amazing women as Rae Carson, Michelle Gagnon, Madeleine Roux, Sherry Thomas, and Amelia Kahaney as my career continues. The Class of 2k13 remains a tight-knit group and I must especially mention my Midwestern cohorts Kelly Barson, Geoffrey Girard, Demitria Lunetta, Jennifer McGowan, and Kate Karyus Quinn for keeping it lively and making me feel like perhaps I'm not crazy, but if I am, I'm in good company.

You can't swing a dead cat in Ohio without hitting a YA author. I especially want to thank Liz Coley for support, encouragement, and good road conversation.

I must thank my boyfriend, who accidentally supplied the catalyst for both *Not a Drop to Drink* and *In a Handful of Dust*. Art is not created in a vacuum, and he has provided more inspiration than he'll ever know.

There are also people in my everyday life who deal with my resistance to phone calls and occasionally answering with, "WHAT?!" Thank you to my family for the support, especially to my mother, who keeps hoping that someday I'll write a happy book about cats. We'll see.